IN PERIL

IN PERIL

A DARING DECISION, A CAPTAIN'S RESOLVE, AND THE SALVAGE THAT MADE HISTORY

SKIP STRONG & TWAIN BRADEN

The Lyons Press
Guilford, Connecticut
An imprint of The Globe Pequot Press

The Lyons Press is an imprint of The Globe Pequot Press

10 9 8 7 6 5 4 3 2 1

Printed in the United States of America

Designed by Maggie Peterson

Endpaper map by Stefanie Ward

ISBN 1-59228-105-2

Library of Congress Cataloging-in-Publication Data is available on file.

To Annie, Emma and Maggie.
Thanks for your patience.—S.S.

To Leah—T.B.

≈

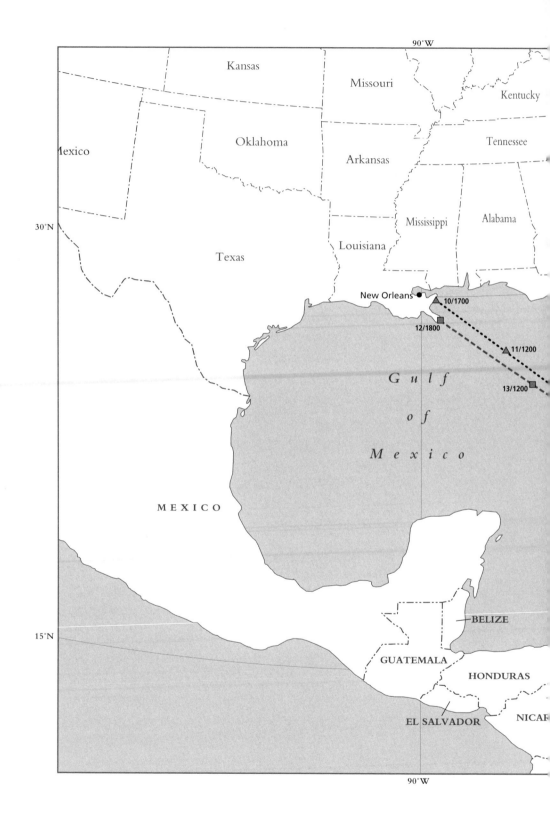

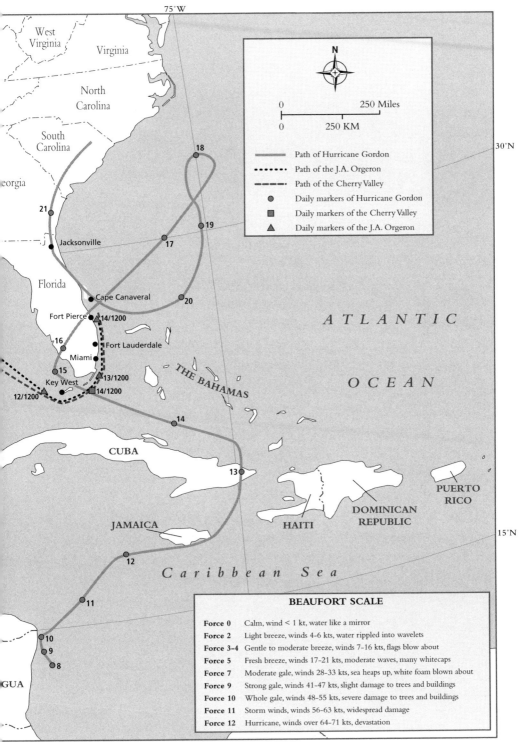

West Virginia
Virginia
North Carolina
South Carolina
Georgia
21
Jacksonville
Florida
Cape Canaveral
Fort Pierce ▲ 14/1200
16
Fort Lauderdale
Miami
15
Key West ▲ 13/1200
12/1200 ▲ ■ 14/1200
18
19
17
20
THE BAHAMAS
14
CUBA
13
JAMAICA
12
11
10
9
8
GUA
HAITI
DOMINICAN REPUBLIC
PUERTO RICO

ATLANTIC

OCEAN

Caribbean Sea

30°N

15°N

N

0 ——————————— 250 Miles
0 ——————————— 250 KM

———— Path of Hurricane Gordon
········ Path of the J.A. Orgeron
- - - - Path of the Cherry Valley
● Daily markers of Hurricane Gordon
■ Daily markers of the Cherry Valley
▲ Daily markers of the J.A. Orgeron

75°W

BEAUFORT SCALE

Force 0	Calm, wind < 1 kt, water like a mirror
Force 2	Light breeze, winds 4-6 kts, water rippled into wavelets
Force 3-4	Gentle to moderate breeze, winds 7-16 kts, flags blow about
Force 5	Fresh breeze, winds 17-21 kts, moderate waves, many whitecaps
Force 7	Moderate gale, winds 28-33 kts, sea heaps up, white foam blown about
Force 9	Strong gale, winds 41-47 kts, slight damage to trees and buildings
Force 10	Whole gale, winds 48-55 kts, severe damage to trees and buildings
Force 11	Storm winds, winds 56-63 kts, widespread damage
Force 12	Hurricane, winds over 64-71 kts, devastation

CONTENTS

Part IV

IN PERIL

ALL OR NOTHING

July 8, 1996

The weather outside is hot and muggy, and I can sense the rain coming. On the short walk from the hotel at the edge of the French Quarter, my brand-new tropic-weight dress shirt has just about soaked through. Once inside the halls of the federal courthouse, whose architecture can be described best as "neo-penal," the heavily air-conditioned air begins to dry out my shirt. The realization, though, that I don't belong here, that I am the captain of an oil tanker and may be about to enter a trial in federal court that focuses heavily on me, starts those sweat glands working overtime.

On their walk to the courthouse, from the Pavillon on Poydras Street and across the outskirts of the Quarter, the men had been pressed by the heat, a mixture of warmth and humidity that only the verdant bayous, percolated like compost by months of summer, can produce. They are now huddled in the fluorescent-lit corridor outside the judge's chambers. The attorneys are the most comfortable, in their tailored clothing and fine shoes; they are in their element, gathered in a courthouse and considering whether to go to trial. They have done their homework: gathered all the evidence, deposed and drawn testimony from numerous witnesses, and now they meet to make a decision.

The ship owner, Don Kurz, president of Keystone Shipping Co., Inc., and Ralph Hill, in-house counsel to Keystone and Kurz's confidant, are dressed well, but they shuffle their feet and divert their eyes, obviously not comfortable with the situation at hand. They speak mostly to each other, only occasionally including the group in their thoughts after they have reached a private understanding.

But the two least at ease, two bulky figures in their early thirties who appear to have been crammed forcibly into neckties and ill-fitting jackets, stand apart from the group, mouths shut, hands thrust—feigned casual— in the pockets of their slacks. Their wide shoulders and large hands, their tanned faces and arms, stand in contrast to the group and to the formal clothes they are wearing. The two men, Captain Skip Strong and Chief Mate Carl Gabrielsson, are eager, fascinated by the proceedings and inter- ested in being part of whatever action might occur, but they are outsiders and will be described later, by the attorneys who command the scene, as re- sembling two kids peering through the glass of a candy store to which they have been denied entry. They look expectantly at the faces of the attorneys.

The men are gathered in a ragged circle, leaning their heads and shoul- ders toward the center, their attention focused on one man. Conversation is hushed and secretive—conspiratorial even—but also excited. The largest of the group, an articulate, barrel-chested attorney in his middle years—in the prime of his lawyering life—is enjoying the full benefits of having a trial to lead in his adopted hometown. Hugh Straub has hosted the group for the past few days at out-of-the-way restaurants, prepared the mariners for trial in a sort of ad hoc torture chamber off his downtown office in which he has set up a video camera for studying his witnesses' testimony, and told countless ribald stories—of the sea, of other courts, of books he'd read—that kept his guests enthralled.

Now, he commands the circle, looking around to each of the others in turn, nodding when a comment is given, reacting quickly and confidently to any questions or reservations anyone may have. His words are sharp, not aggressive exactly, but efficient. He moves the conversation along where it needs to go, not letting it rest unnecessarily. Each has spoken, except Key- stone president Don Kurz, the tallest of the group, whose complexion is paler than that of the others and whose slim physique makes him resem- ble a grave-faced Ichabod Crane. Like the seamen, he, too, stands a bit apart, but for a different reason, and his lips are pressed together, forming a narrow, dark line.

"Mr. Kurz?" Straub prods. Getting no immediate response, he turns to Captain Skip Strong, the man whose actions have brought them to where they are today. "Captain Strong?" he asks. "Three million dollars is a lot of money for a couple of days' work, and you and the crew will get a substantial part of it. We could all walk away right now and be very happy with the outcome. Or we step into the courtroom and take our chances."

> *I look around at the faces in the group and try and decide what it is they want to hear from me. I know that Hugh would like to take this to trial. Mr. Kurz would probably be happiest if we took the settlement. Over the last 12 months I have come to respect and admire the attorneys I have dealt with in this case. I draw strength from their confidence.*

"When we started out on this adventure, we did so because five guys on a tug were having a very bad night in a tropical storm," Captain Strong replies, a little quietly at first. "We didn't do it for money. We did it because we were the only ones around who could render assistance, and we went in to see what we could do. We were very lucky and were able to keep the men safe and save the tug and barge. Hugh, you guys believe strongly in this case, so I think we should go in there, not worry about the money, and see what happens."

Kurz hesitates, and then leans toward the circle, opens his mouth only for a second, allowing a few words to escape: "I'm still uncomfortable with the idea of suing the Federal Government," his words directed to his attorney, Ralph Hill. "We do a substantial amount of business with them each year, managing ships in the Ready Reserve Fleet. I don't like the idea of suing a customer."

The decision has come down to a face-off between these two men, Don Kurz, the reserved company president with the demeanor of an undertaker, and Hugh Straub, the forceful, confident lawyer who has prepared for trial and knows the odds are substantially in his favor. While both are on the same side in the suit against the Government, they are worlds apart right now. Kurz's business is to be cautious, always mindful of the risks that nip at his company. Straub's business is to accept that risk as given, balance it with the law, and seek favorable odds.

Ralph Hill turns to Straub. "We've really got to believe in this. We have an offer; we could settle this right now and not have to sue the Government. They're an important customer for Keystone." Keystone is considering suing NASA. That the two departments of government, NASA and Justice, are not associated, except by name, is immaterial. Kurz knows that government contracts are increasingly lean for U.S. shipping companies. If the government officials who award shipping contracts feel uneasy doing business with Keystone because of an ongoing suit against NASA, the result could be a huge loss of revenue for the Philadelphia-based company. This would have dire consequences for a company already operating at razor-thin margins.

"That's not the point, Ralph," Straub responds instantly. "It's always a gamble going to trial. But you know as well as I do that good fact witnesses win these cases. That figure they threw at us is arbitrary. Our position is strong; it's based in the law, and our witnesses support that. I think the judge will see that."

"What if he doesn't?"

Straub looks Ralph Hill in the eye and then over to Don Kurz, who is still looking away, still clenching his jaw. "There has never been a stronger case," he says slowly. "Never in all my years of lawyering has there been a stronger case."

Ralph Hill turns back to Kurz, his boss, the one man who can make the final decision to proceed with a trial, to bet everything on the fact that the ancient tradition of salvage law, which is now being played out in the courts and discussed in the corridors of this building, will be upheld. Kurz doesn't turn his head as he offers the one word Straub has been waiting to hear: "Okay."

Straub draws a deep breath. He motions toward the door that leads to the chambers: "Shall we?"

PART I

"the ship burns with a furnace heart
steam veins and copper nerves
quivers and slightly twists and always goes—
easy roll of the hull and deep
vibration of the turbine underfoot."

from *Oil* by Gary Snyder

CHAPTER 1

A LIFE AT SEA

March 4, 1991

As the plane banks over the city, I glance out the small window and look down on the port, craning my neck to see over to Staten Island's north shore. The Kill Van Kull, a stretch of water separating the island from Bayonne, New Jersey, is lined with industrial marine facilities and oil terminals. There, on the Bayonne side, is the object of my attention, the 688-foot oil tanker *Cherry Valley*, which I will soon be joining as chief mate, second in command. I have sailed her sister ship, the *Coronado*, for almost three years, spent numerous hours getting the vessel in the condition I want—had the crew scrape the rusted steel bare and apply fresh paint. I nursed the neglected systems back into a state of well-being, overhauling cargo pumps, roller chocks, and hydraulic winches. I had also gotten to know the 25 other crewmembers, many of whom I could call friends. That I have left the *Coronado* for the *Cherry Valley* is somewhat of a disappointment; it means I am leaving a ship and crew I know well to join another with an unfamiliar crew and whose systems, I suspect, will also need lots of work.

Until three years ago, the three vessels in the Coronado class had been under long-term charter to Shell Oil, which meant the vessel didn't have to sell itself on a yearly basis. As a result, the ships' owner and operator, Keystone Shipping Company, had not been interested in spending money on cosmetic maintenance. Now that the ships were available for charter on the open market, and charter representatives visited the vessels frequently to determine their suitability, Keystone was spending money and time to make the vessels look good and operate efficiently. When a vessel is operated continuously, crossing the Atlantic in all seasons, she slips into the first stages of decay, and the process of improving her comes slowly.

The plane lands in Newark and a cab brings me the rest of the way, past Port Newark and Port Elizabeth, the giant container terminals that make New York one of the busiest container ports in the world. We drive through canyons of stacked steel boxes, packed with goods from across the globe. An efficient container port features numerous cranes that can whisk the boxes from the ships, which can carry as many as 3,000 containers, onto trains or trucks. The boxes will fan out by rail and interstate to their final destinations.

New York is also one of the largest oil ports for the East Coast, its refineries and pumping terminals lining the waterways around Staten Island and New Jersey. As we approach the pier, I see the *Cherry Valley*'s dark rust-streaked hull sitting low in the water. I step from the cab onto the pier, the raw March wind taking my breath, and look up at the white superstructure, some five stories high, and feel a mix of emotion. There is plenty of work ahead, but I will be joining my old friend and mentor Bill Peterson, now sailing as the *Cherry Valley*'s captain.

I sailed with Bill when he was chief mate of the *Coronado* on my first trip with Keystone. I was a newly minted third mate, fresh out of Maine Maritime Academy, and my only real experience had been as a mate on an awful tugboat, towing a barge full of coal up the East Coast in January 1985. The tug *Capt. Bill* was small, dirty, and not suitable for working in the unforgiving Northeast winter. The 400-foot barge was a converted T-2 tanker that had been built during World War II. Its oil tanks had been converted into bulk cargo holds with large hatches to speed loading and unloading. The coal had frozen around the edges of the holds, which meant that when we arrived in Portsmouth, New Hampshire, we had to break it apart with pickaxes so that it could be sucked out with a big screw pump. On the return trip to Norfolk we were hit by a storm; the gyrocompass broke; and we ended up spending three days chasing the barge around the North Atlantic after we parted our tow wire. The enormous captain—he easily weighed 400 pounds—had nearly killed me when he had us drop anchor as we approached Norfolk, Virginia. He had asked me to go forward with one of the deckhands, a completely inexperienced kid whose last job had been flipping burgers, and release the port anchor—an act that would release the three-and-a-half-ton anchor and send it and the links of chain to which it was attached through the hawsepipe and shooting to the ocean bottom 80 feet below—a process normally controlled by using the brake on the windlass. As the anchor dropped, its chain came screaming out of its locker, and I quickly and frighteningly realized there was no functioning brake on the windlass. "Throw down that riding pawl!" the captain screamed at me. "Throw down that riding pawl!"

If I dropped the riding pawl—a large steel tooth on a hinge above the chain that in normal circumstances served as backup to the windlass brake after the chain was stopped and the barge safely anchored—with the chain running that fast, it would drop between the links, shatter, and produce a lethal cloud of shrapnel. I did not want to be anywhere near the pawl if it came down on the chain that was speeding out of the locker and flying through the hawsehole in a blur. Seeing my hesitation, the captain came charging up the deck toward the fo'c's'le, the raised area of the bow, as only a 400-pound man can, bellowing all the way for us to "get the fuck" out of his way. I grabbed the deckhand by his shirt collar and dove for cover behind the starboard windlass just as the captain reached the port windlass and dropped the pawl. There was an explosion of steel and a horrendous noise as the chain slowed and then caught up on the bitter end. Incredibly, no one was injured. I caught the next boat ashore and swore off sailing tugs.

My next job was as third mate on the *Coronado*, which I joined in Brunsbuttel, a pretty little North Sea port city on the west end of Germany's Kiel Canal, and I was greeted by Bill, the tall, boyish-faced chief mate. He had a mischievous sparkle in his eyes, which peered out from beneath a shock of brown hair cut page-boy style. He shook my hand and showed me around the ship. I would come to think of him as a friend, admiring his ability to maintain a ship in good order, run a crew of men, and yet maintain the playful manner of an oversized seven-year-old.

I confessed to him and the captain, Tim O'Connor, another man I would grow to admire, that I hadn't the slightest idea what I was doing in my role as third mate on an oil tanker. When I was hired by Keystone, over the phone, the personnel director asked if I had any tanker experience. Anxious for the possibility of a good job sailing "deep sea," I replied that I had just worked on a converted T-2 tanker. I was not forthcoming with the fact that it had been "converted" into a coal barge. After I had come clean with Tim and Bill, they were both more than fair in helping me acclimate to the ship's operations. In the coming months, as I grew to understand the ship and respond to my new life at sea, we would sail the *Coronado* from Europe across the Atlantic with oil for the East Coast and then down to the Caribbean to load in Venezuela. We then headed back for Northern Europe and repeated the process. As the mate, Bill's responsibility was cargo and maintenance as well as standing a navigation watch, and he instilled in me a sense of how to run the ship efficiently. His style was to ask me and others in the crew if we knew how to do a given task, line up the cargo systems or repair a piece of equipment. If I confessed I didn't, he would show me exactly how he wanted the task done. If I responded that I knew how to perform a task, he would let me alone, giving me the leeway to do the job. We learned that he demanded perfection, but also was fair and willing to help us with difficult tasks. He also managed to get along with everyone, not an easy task as the mate.

After graduating from Massachusetts Maritime in the early 1970s, Bill had served as an AB, or able-bodied seaman, an unlicensed position that many academy graduates are loath to accept since it is not a position of great responsibility. Most people want to go straight to work as a third mate, the license an academy graduate earns, but Bill had been content to bide his time, learning from the bottom up how the deck of a ship was run. As a result, he had firsthand knowledge of how all the deck systems, including winches, pipes, valves, and cargo pumps, worked and had a full appreciation for what it was like to sail as a deckhand. This knowledge served him well when he went on to become a mate, rising through the ranks to become chief mate, and eventually, serving as captain.

≈

On this bitter March day, the rust-streaked hull of the *Cherry Valley* is not the most welcome sight as I climb the gangway and step on the deck: the gray expanse of deck and piping is brown with rust, and it looks like she has been through a hard winter at sea. Heavy accumulations of salt—patches of grayish-white crystals—give the deck a dirty, mottled appearance where the water has dried. Rust is everywhere, but fortunately most of it looks cosmetic, nothing a good scraping, priming, and painting can't cure. The ship underneath the rust looks good and strong; she just needs some TLC, and for the next four months I am the person to provide it. Bill and I have worked this routine together in the past and have developed an ability to accomplish such maintenance, despite the fact that when sailing transatlantic you have to squeeze out brief periods of maintenance from an already hectic schedule between storms, cargo operations, and the regular operation of the ship.

One of the benefits of working on a black-oil tanker, particularly one like the *Cherry Valley* carrying the heavy, viscous No. 6 fuel oil—a product burned in power plants that is just one step up the refining process from being asphalt—is that the oil is maintained by heating coils in the ship's tanks at a temperature between 120 and 130 degrees. This allows the oil to be pumped from the ship to shore facilities and means that the decks remain warm in winter. A nice side benefit is that no ice builds up and our feet don't freeze as we go about cargo operations.

"What's the rate, Mate?" Bill greets me with a smile and reaches out a large calloused hand. "When will we be finished? When will we be ready to sail?" I have scarcely been given the rundown of the discharge plan by the mate I'm relieving when Bill is already firing good-natured questions at me. As chief mate, it is my responsibility to manage loading and discharging cargo. In port the mate is typically the one getting the least time ashore, making sure that the cargo operations go smoothly.

While the *Cherry Valley* and the *Coronado* are sister ships, identical in size and construction, it will take time to get used to the quirks of both my new ship and her crew. I'm looking forward to working with Bill again and hope to learn more from him about running the ship. I've had my master's license for about a year and want to learn as much as I can so if I get the call to sail as captain, I'll be prepared.

We'd sail the *Cherry Valley* together for the next two months, crossing the Atlantic twice, logging nearly 12,000 miles and trying to get the ship back in good condition. Bill worked hard, but he played hard too. He would frequently disappear in the Mediterranean ports we visited, telling me before he slipped down the gangway that he was going out to have fun for me—since I was stuck onboard doing cargo operations.

CHAPTER 2

THREE YEARS LATER

November 9, 1994

The weather is beautiful on this early November night in the Gulf of Mexico as we make our way on the *Cherry Valley* to the GATX terminal in Good Hope, Louisiana, to pick up a load of oil. We are making an easy 15 knots on our approach to Southwest Pass, the main entrance to the Mississippi River. Even at 2200 hours the temperature is warm enough to wear shorts on the bridge. The light northeast breeze brings the rich scents of the delta down to us on our approach. The bridge wing doors are open, the breeze flowing pleasantly across the bridge, as I watch our progress toward the pilot station at Southwest Pass. Chris Sotirelis, the third mate and the youngest person aboard, has the watch and is conning the vessel up to the arrival point. He's responsible for the safe navigation of the vessel, making course and speed changes as necessary, within the limits laid out by the captain in advance. Tommy Prevost, one of the ABs, is at the helm following Chris's orders. Roberto Rodriguez, the other AB on the 8-to-12 watch, is on the bridge wing acting as lookout.

It has been 11 months since the call came from Keystone's personnel director, Karen Watson. I had been serving as chief mate on the *Coronado* when she called the ship, via satellite phone, and told me that Keystone had a captain's job for me aboard the *Cherry Valley*. In today's merchant marine it's not uncommon to move to various ships within the same company. At 32 years old, I was thrilled to be so entrusted. Karen told me to report to the company's headquarters in downtown Philadelphia, meet the department heads, and receive a crash course in managing my own ship. The actual skills of running the ship—handling the vessel in port, managing a crew, navigating across oceans—were all familiar to me after 10 years and some 400,000 miles at sea. I had benefited from my experience as chief mate and the exposure to the numerous captains I had sailed with, but there were other things to learn. The captain is responsible for payroll, stores, safety, and piles of paperwork—the running joke is that when you take command of a ship, you really take command of a desk and all the attendant paperwork. The days of the independent, freedom-from-ties-ashore world of the shipmaster have been long gone since the invention of the radio—you're now in constant contact with the home office via satellite phone and telex.

Arriving at Southwest Pass is always a challenge. Hundreds of stationary oil rigs dot the Gulf; scores of crewboats that serve the rigs, shrimpers, jack-up rigs, and ships that are approaching or departing the busy Mississippi River add to the mix. While I know the ships will be piloted responsibly, the same can't be said for all the other vessels. Remove the clarity of daylight and navigating an oil tanker in this area becomes even more interesting, since you have to rely on the lights of other vessels and the ship's radar. There have been some spectacular collisions right in this area. Since I am just starting my second trip as captain aboard the *Cherry Valley* I want to make sure that all the little blips on my radar screen stay away from the one big blip in the center, the *Cherry Valley*, so that I do not become one of those notable incidents. The ship, with a deadweight of 44,000 tons, is more than two football fields long and requires time and anticipation to maneuver. The *Cherry Valley* has the shapeliness of a city block. Maneuvering a ship of this size is like driving on ice; you always need to prepare long in advance for what might be happening ahead of you. When the ship is fully loaded it takes us eight-and-a-half minutes and almost a mile to go from full ahead to dead in the water. In ballast, like we are today, it would only take us five minutes and just over half a mile to stop from full ahead. Despite her awesome size and ungainly characteristics, the *Cherry Valley* is known affectionately as a "she" by her crew.

Oil tankers serve one purpose: to move large quantities of oil from one port to another and do it safely, efficiently, and profitably. The *Cherry Valley*'s hull was designed around 14 cavernous cargo tanks, each about 76 feet

long, 30 feet wide, and 47 feet deep. The tanks, each of which has more volume than an Olympic-size swimming pool, are located in the forward five-
sixths of the hull. As cargo is loaded at a dock, the ship settles in the water.
For each 123 tons of oil loaded, the ship settles one inch. When empty, the
Cherry Valley has a 12-foot draft at the bow and, because of the weight of
the engines and accommodations housed in a large steel superstructure, a
22-foot draft at the stern. When fully loaded, the weight of the oil balances
the stern and the ship settles to an even 35 feet. Once alongside at GATX it
will take us about nine hours to load the first part of our cargo, 85,000 barrels, before shifting downriver to load the balance of the cargo, 152,000
barrels, at IMTT in Gretna. After finishing at Gretna we will sail for Jacksonville, Florida, to discharge the cargo.

When a receiver, like Florida Power and Light, needs a load of fuel for
a power plant, they place an order with a "trader," such as Enjet. FP&L says,
for example, that they need 235,000 barrels of No. 6 oil with an API gravity, a figure achieved by blending certain oil products together, of, say, 10.5.
Enjet, a company that leases storage tank space at many of the terminals
along the Mississippi River and Houston Ship Channel and buys oil in
bulk, fills the order. Enjet may or may not have a vessel available to move
the oil from the supplier to the receiver, and if they do not they will charter a vessel on the "open market" to move a particular load.

This is where Keystone and the *Cherry Valley* come into play. The char-
tering department at Keystone contacts with the trader to see what needs
to be moved. Keystone will offer the *Cherry Valley* starting on a given date
and will have a window called "lay days" to arrive at the loading port to
pick up the cargo. Most of the time Enjet will have to take oil from more
than one facility to make the correct blend the receiver wants. This is why
we often stop at two berths to load cargo.

The *Cherry Valley,* built in 1974, has a single hull, which means that oil
in the cargo tanks is separated from the water outside the hull by only three-
quarters of an inch of steel plate, just as the *Exxon Valdez* was. More recent
ships are "double-hulled," fitted with a void between the cargo tanks and the
outer hull. Ballast tanks, of which there are four on the *Cherry Valley,* are

pumped full of water when the ship is "light," without cargo, as on our early-morning approach to Good Hope. This process lowers the vessel in the water, making her easier to maneuver than when she is completely empty. When she's fully laden, maneuvering in close quarters is a lesson in patience and appreciation for the laws of physics. Especially the one stipulating that a body in motion tends to stay in motion.

An hour before midnight I order the engine speed reduced to seven knots to pick up a pilot. We are just south of the sea buoy, which marks the beginning of the river's navigable channel. The pilot boat, *Federal 1,* comes roaring out of the dark pass as only a crew boat can and comes along our port side to put Captain Tommy Bauer aboard. The deck crew has already put the pilot ladder in place, and within seconds he is scrambling up the ladder to the ship's deck, 30 feet above the waves. I see his dark figure reach the top, where he is greeted by the mate, and makes his way aft. Tommy reaches the bridge— up the boarding ladder and five flights of stairs—without being winded.

Federal and state laws require that each ship entering or departing port have a pilot aboard. Pilots are not only expert ship handlers—they're typically former ship or tug captains—but must also have perfect recall of the port. Pilots are hired for their local knowledge, for their ability to guide a ship into port in all weather without referring to a chart. Applicants for pilot positions are given blank sheets of paper on which they are required to draw from memory all the minute details of the port: the shoals, hundreds of navigational buoys and their lighting characteristics, and features of the current. The usually flippant Mark Twain, who was trained as a Mississippi River pilot before turning to storytelling for a profession, had this to say about the pilot's job: "A pilot must have a memory of substance; but there are two higher qualities which he must also have. He must have good and quick judgment and decision, and a cool, calm courage that no peril can shake." I have recently completed my exams and been approved to serve as a pilot in my home state of Maine. If the plan comes to fruition, I will eventually become a Penobscot Bay and River pilot, a post that will include as a side benefit the chance to have a stable home life—the forbidden fruit of every mariner's life.

"It's good to see you again, Tommy," I say, reaching for his hand. "I'll tell you what we have tonight while you're getting your night vision back." Even though I have some ship handling experience, it is always comforting to get a pilot you know and trust. I will be handing over the conn of the ship to Tommy—all the helm commands and engine speeds will be his— but this is the pilot's role, and I know he's capable.

"Right now we are at slow ahead and steering 000 degrees. We're making about seven knots. The ship has a 12,000-hp steam turbine, right-hand-turning wheel. She goes ahead great, but she backs like shit." Steam vessels are notorious for having just 50 percent of the power in astern propulsion.

As the pilot, Tommy needs to know all the particular handling characteristics of the *Cherry Valley* as he conns the ship through the myriad twists and turns as the river snakes through the Lower Mississippi Delta of southern Louisiana. Any errors on his part will result in the ship plowing into the muddy banks of the river. I want him to have all the information he needs to do his job well. I continue describing the finer points of maneuvering the ship. "On 'maneuvering full' we will do about 12 knots; we can go up to 'sea speed,' and we will do about 15.5 knots, but we need to give the engineers about five minutes' notice to get back to 'maneuvering.' Our draft is 12 feet forward and 22 feet aft."

I close my opening monologue by informing him that we're bound for the GATX oil terminal in Good Hope.

Once finished with the master-pilot conference, we fall into the easy chatter of talking shop. Unlike most pilot groups that spend a good deal of their time maneuvering foreign ships, the Federal Pilots handle only U.S.-flag coastwise traffic. I get a chance to catch up on what is happening on other vessels and with friends. Last I saw Tommy, I was sailing as chief mate on the *Coronado*. He congratulates me on my promotion to captain.

Once his eyes have adjusted to the dark bridge, he sets the radar up the way he wants it, dropping the range to a lower setting to see the finer points of the approaching coastline. He checks on the progress of outbound traffic, which we will meet as we enter the river. "We have a nice window to get in the pass," Tommy says. "So if you don't mind, I'd like to bring it up to sea speed and get ourselves in there."

"Sounds good to me," I say with more assurance than I feel. Of all the ports I know, of all the ones that I have approached at night, approaching Southwest Pass under these circumstances, coming around the light at 15 knots, at night, has got to be the scariest. It takes a 45-degree turn to starboard to get into the pass, a turn that brings us within 150 feet of a rock jetty. We then will quickly steady up on a set of range lights before following the 600-foot wide channel up to the head of the passes. The lighthouse at the end of the pass seems to be about a billion candlepower and it sweeps right through the bridge every 10 seconds. If you don't close your eyes as the sweep approaches, you'll be blinded for a few seconds and lose your night vision instantly. And to top it all off there is usually some unsuspecting fisherman trying to catch his dinner in the middle of the channel. That he would be worse off than I if we were in a collision is immaterial; a collision with anyone, even someone stupid enough to be hanging around the shipping channel of one of the country's busiest ports in the middle of the night, will ruin our night.

Waiting for our command, Chris stands by the engine order tele-graph—essentially our throttle—which will communicate our desired rpm setting to the engineers. "Full ahead," I say, relaying the pilot's order. "Chris, after you ring it up, call down to the engineroom and tell them to bring it up to 78 rpm, and we will give them five minutes' notice to maneuver. And the pilot has the conn."

The tightest stretch is from the mouth of the river to the Head of Passes, about 20 miles. It always makes me the most nervous: the channel is narrow, the current can be fast, and there is usually a lot of traffic. Once above the Head of Passes, the river opens up into a wide, meandering wa-terway, and I relax a little bit. Heading upriver, into the current, is also a blessing, making our maneuvering easier. The tugs will not be coming alongside for docking until about 0930, so I head to the settee in the after part of the wheelhouse for a little sleep.

The pilot may be conning the ship, but the captain still has the ultimate responsibility for the safety of the vessel. The captain–pilot relationship is complex: I am obliged to turn the conn over to him, but I'm the one holding the bag if anything goes wrong. So I try to not leave the bridge unless absolutely necessary. Nonetheless, I'll attempt a few hours of rest. It isn't real "sleep" that I'm getting, not a full-night's rest anyway. It's more like dozing, a practice that helps recharge the batteries without slipping heavily into dreamland. It is enough to keep me going on a long run such as this.

As the sun rises over the levee I'm fully awake. I duck below to my stateroom and grab a quick shower before the pilot change in New Orleans.

As we approach Good Hope, we round 26 Mile Point. Ahead in the river, sitting low in the water, two tugs are standing out in the stream just below the berth, awaiting our arrival. They will assist us in our docking maneuvers. The nice thing about docking in the river is that you are always stemming the current. It helps you slow down and makes steering the ship at slow speeds easier because water is flowing past the rudder. Going against the current effectively increases the speed of water going past the rudder, giving you more control. When you're moving a ship downstream you face the opposite problem. To keep water flowing past the rudder, you have to be moving faster than the current. We could probably do the job without tugs on a ship in ballast, but the tugs make it a whole lot easier—and they lessen the liability.

The deck crew splits into two groups for docking. Carl Gabrielsson, the chief mate, is in charge of the group on the bow and Jim Kuijper, the second mate, is in charge on the stern. The two groups are standing by on deck to catch the heaving lines from the tugs. The heaving lines, small-diameter lines thrown up to our deck by a deckhand on the tug, are tied to heavy mooring wires that will keep the tugs attached to the ship for maneuvers. With all of us still moving at about seven knots there are a lot of forces at play, and it would be easy for someone to get hurt if something goes wrong. Wires under tension can snap like string and have deadly recoil. I've heard of deck crew getting their legs cut off and have seen 1,000-pound steel chocks torn from the deck and fly through the air like toys.

Tugs can capsize if they are caught against the side of the ship, instantly drowning the crew. Docking ships is slow and tense.

The forward crew on the raised fo'c's'le deck are also standing by to let the anchors go in case of an emergency. Mounted on each side of the bow are the anchors, each weighing 14,000 pounds—about as much as a couple of Humvees. They are each shackled to just over 1,000 feet of chain, with individual links that each weigh 100 pounds. The ship's windlasses, winches fitted with high-powered engines, heave up the anchors at a rate of about a "shot," 90-foot sections every three minutes. The crew have the anchors ready to let go at a moment's notice from the bridge if the ship loses power and needs to stop before running aground.

The tug *Louise* is made fast to the *Cherry Valley*'s port bow, and the *James Smith* to the port quarter. These are good, capable tugs built for ship assist work. They may not be the prettiest boats on the water, but they are good at what they do, using their horsepower and weight to nudge us gently into the berth. The pilot uses the current of the river and gentle angles of the rudder to slow the ship and steer us close to the dock. As we near the position where our manifold—the connection through which we load and discharge cargo—lines up with the shore connections, the pilot radios the tugs to help push us the last 20 feet to the berth. With the river low and slow, the tugs are able to work out almost perpendicular to the ship; they make short work of getting us positioned snugly alongside.

Less than 20 minutes after taking the tugs alongside we have our first line out to the dock, and in another 40 minutes we are all secured, the tugs and pilot released to go on to their next jobs. For us the real job starts now.

CHAPTER 3

THE *POSEIDON* AND ET-70

November 7, 1994

The Martin Marietta facility dominates the Gulf Intracoastal Waterway several miles east of New Orleans in Michoud, Louisiana. A mile and a half long and a mile wide, the sprawling complex is a hive of high-tech aerospace fabrication. The largest of its buildings, an ugly metal structure that resembles a huge airplane hangar, covers 45 acres of the property with its expansive roof. It was built in the 1940s by Andrew Higgins, the inventor of the Higgins Boat, a small landing craft that was instrumental in landing troops in France on D-Day. (Because of these boats, Higgins was referred to by Dwight Eisenhower as "the man who won the war for us.")

Inside, teams of scientists and technicians fabricate enormous aluminum fuel tanks for NASA's space shuttle missions, anywhere from eight to 12 per year. The actual construction process of a single tank can take as long as four years. Once complete, the tanks will stand more than 150 feet in height.

Each space shuttle will ride piggyback on its phallus-like tank, which will feed the shuttle's engines with a mixture of liquid hydrogen and oxygen at a rate of 3,500 gallons per second during liftoff and ascent. The "umbilical" lines from each of the interior tanks are 17 inches in diameter, which blast the fuel into the engines like oversized fire hoses. The shuttle's engines—each of which are only the size of a Chevy V-8 yet produce 78,000 horsepower—will burn through the tank's 305,000 gallons of liquid hydrogen and 143,000 gallons of liquid oxygen in just eight minutes, feeding off this gigantic tank until the shuttle is safely clear of the atmosphere.

The liquid hydrogen and oxygen are fed into the engines at their storage temperature of minus 200 degrees Fahrenheit. In the space of a quarter inch, the fuel reaches a temperature of 1,700 degrees Fahrenheit. After serving its brief but essential purpose, the tank is jettisoned from the base of the shuttle and continues to orbit, one-and-a-half times around the Earth, before it reenters the atmosphere and breaks up over the Pacific Ocean. Unlike the solid rocket boosters, the external fuel tank, which costs an estimated $50 million to construct, is not recovered. It is used for a total of eight minutes.

The external tanks are constructed in stages from raw panels of nearly sterile aluminum. The employees at Martin Marietta move about the expansive building on bicycles, tools tossed in baskets on the handle-bars. There are hundreds of the cruiser-style, industrial bikes, provided by the century-old Brooklyn-based company Worksman Bicycles, in the complex, each fitted with a license plate under the seat. Technicians navigate carefully along roads painted on the building's glistening floor. Working from one end of the building to the other, workers shape the tank's three sections: the nose, which is the oxygen tank; the main body of the hydrogen tank; and the Intertank, a coupling that connects the two tanks together. By the time four years have passed, the tank's components have been assembled and stacked one atop the other in the north end of the building and given a coat of orange insulating foam paint.

When beckoned by Cape Canaveral, crews gently ease the tank onto its side and tow it aboard a specifically built trailer called a transporter to the dock on the Intracoastal Waterway and load it onto a barge for delivery to Cape Canaveral.

To make the tow from Michoud, Louisiana, to Cape Canaveral, the tank is loaded on the deck of a specially built barge. Towed by an oceangoing tugboat, they proceed down the Mississippi Gulf Outlet, southeast through the Gulf of Mexico, around the Florida peninsula and into Port Canaveral on Florida's northeast coast. The tanks are simply too large to be transported by truck, train, or airplane.

≈

On a balmy November morning in 1994, tank ET-70 was ready for the trip to the Cape. It was November 7, two days before it was to depart for Cape Canaveral, and the hangar's sliding doors had been thrown open. The aluminum tank was already lying flat on the transporter as it was towed into the morning sunshine for the first time. ET-70 would be used a few months later to launch the shuttle *Atlantis* into space on NASA's 100th manned space mission. *Atlantis* would be docking for the first time at the Russian space station *Mir*—the first step toward establishing an international space station.

In preparation for the tow, the tank had been "inerted," pumped full of nitrogen to keep out all moisture and unwanted gases, for the delivery to Florida. The tank-handling team, eight workers wearing hard hats and steel-toed boots, were arranged systematically around the transporter. From opposite ends of the trailer, two men steered the vehicle's four enormous wheels; one drove the Brute, the squat, heavy tractor that pulled the transporter. The Brute resembled the block-like trucks that nudge airplanes in and around their gates—except this one was several tons heavier, designed by NASA engineers expressly for this purpose, and capable of producing enormous torque at low speeds. Walkers, one stationed forward and the other behind the slow parade, served as extra sets of eyes to the Steerers; and the supervisor, in touch by two-way radio with each person, remained out of the way but aware of every movement from his vehicle at the front of the slow procession. A safety worker watched for possible dangers to the ground crew. It took 20 minutes for the tank to be rolled from the hangar.

There was no rain expected, a critical stipulation, and the crew needed to be sure that lightning remained no less than five miles distant as the transporter progressed the mile and a quarter to the pier. The wind was calm. A security escort had closed the road to other NASA traffic for the event, orange lights silently revolving on the roofs of the trucks. The tank was towed at walking pace through the complex. NASA's Michoud facility is so long and flat that a few years earlier a commercial jet suffering mechanical problems with its engines on its approach to New Orleans's Louis

Armstrong International Airport was able to put down in the field adjacent to the river. The jet's landing gear was undamaged and no people were hurt. Following repairs to the engine—its seats stripped out for weight savings—the jet took off from the half-mile-long stretch of road along which ET-70 was towed.

By 0930, nearly two hours after the start of the workday, ET-70 pulled alongside the barge, where Bill Knodle, Martin Marietta's fastidious harbormaster, had been pacing, consulting his wristwatch every few minutes. He was somewhat surprised there had been no delays. The *Poseidon*, the barge in his care, had already been prepared to receive its precious cargo.

No ordinary harbormaster, Knodle was a graduate of the Naval Academy with two advanced degrees in oceanography and military budgeting. Following his four years at Annapolis, the lanky Texan went on to fulfill an entire career in the Navy, sailing battleships, destroyers, minesweepers, and ammunition supply ships. Although he rose steadily to earn the rank of commander and serve as executive officer of several ships, Knodle was not one to call attention to himself, choosing instead to work hard, keep his head down, and focus on his duty.

Knodle was a meticulous man, not prone to exaggeration or hyperbole. He managed the waterfront at Martin Marietta with precision, his Texas drawl unembellished with fancy language. When frustrated by delays, which were common in departments other than his, Knodle had been known to utter an emphatic "Confound it!" He might even admonish others to "Get a move on." But he considered himself a team player and a hands-on kind of person, not prone to complain even though he usually considered himself short-handed for the amount and nature of his work.

The *Poseidon* had been carefully prepared for sea. An old World War II Navy barge built to transport cargo into the shallows of Pacific atolls, the *Poseidon* was converted by NASA to deliver the tanks on the end of a tugboat's wire. The barge had a large, rounded canopy running the length of the deck, making the barge resemble a Quonset hut or a covered wagon for giants. Open at one end, the canopy fully enclosed the fuel tank, protecting it from the corrosive effects of the salt and sea during the 1,000-mile tow to Cape Canaveral.

The *Poseidon* had been ballasted, its numerous tanks filled with water to preserve its stability and to lower it in the water so the transporter could be rolled into place on deck. In preparation for loading a barge, the ballast level must be carefully adjusted to trim the barge a foot and a half by the stern. Once a vessel begins to move through the water, its bow tends to go down by the head, especially if it is being towed. Without this trim, the barge would yaw wildly on the end of its wire, its stern flailing out of control behind the buried bow. Knodle drafted a plan that was consistent with each of the other ballast plans he had drafted for other deliveries of the external fuel tanks.

Meticulous to the final detail, Knodle never used a ballast plan from a previous voyage, even though he easily could have since the deliveries of the tanks are all nearly identical.

"Nice and easy," he said to himself as the Brute rolled onto the barge, the tank-handling crew making final adjustments to the transporter's angle as it approached its loading position on the barge's deck.

During the loading process the barge was "hard-docked," resting on a lip protruding over the river, to keep the barge at the same level so that its stern would not settle lower in the water as the transporter's tires rolled onto the deck. Once loaded, the barge would be de-ballasted to float it free of the lip before recovering its trim.

Knodle directed his men to position the four jacks to suspend the transporter—one end at a time—to allow the crew to insert steel pedestals between the deck and transporter. These were locked with steel pins; large chains were shackled to padeyes on deck to prevent the tank from swaying side-to-side. The chains were then tightened with "steamboat ratchets," long, steel turnbuckles with one-inch-diameter screws used to secure cargo on the decks of ships. The pedestals would take the load of the tank off the rubber tires of the transporter, which would remain suspended above the barge deck through the delivery, so that the tank and the barge would be locked together as one unit. Without the pedestals, pressure from the bouncing, air-filled tires at sea could potentially damage the tank during the tow. After testing the tightness of each ratchet, Knodle checked the accelerometers on each of the jacks and chains. These devices would measure and record the forces imposed on the tank during delivery, which would be across a stretch of ocean that included the tumultuous waters of the Gulf Stream. Knodle reflected on the warnings from NASA's marine supervisor that the tank could not be allowed to endure forces greater than one G in the vertical and half a G in a lateral motion.

Once the jacks were removed and the barrels of the steamboat ratchets tightened to the point that the chains were nearly bar-tight, the tank and its fittings were considered safe to handle the forces imposed by the sea rolling the barge up to 30 degrees. If more than one G were registered on the gauges upon arrival at the sea buoy off Port Canaveral, the tank would be returned to Michoud for an extensive inspection, which would determine whether the tank was serviceable—or a total loss.

By the end of the day Knodle and his crew effectively locked in place a very expensive Easter egg—the size of a jumbo jet.

Removing the tank from the hangar, towing it to the barge, and jacking the tank into position on the barge's deck engaged the Martin Marietta crew for the better part of a day—the day before the tug was slated to arrive at Michoud. On the morning that the tug arrived, Knodle was at his office by 0600, going over notes and checking the weather. He placed a call to his tank-handling manager to see that they were still on schedule for the tow. He called the towing contractor, Yowell International, to learn of the tug's progress. All set, came the response, the tug was on its way and the weather looked good. He reminded the contractor that he would need to speak directly to the tug via VHF radio when they were within range to advise them of their final approach to the barge dock.

CHAPTER 4

PREPARING FOR THE TOW

November 10, 1994

As the *Cherry Valley* was docking at the GATX terminal, just a few miles away downriver and along a narrow waterway known locally as the Navigation Channel, an oceangoing tugboat was preparing to get underway, its air-powered, dual-engine controls hissing as they were engaged. The tug's trim 40-year-old captain, Lanny Wiles, a native of the river towns of Tennessee and a veteran Gulf tug and crew boat captain, was maneuvering the boat from a set of remote controls mounted overlooking the stern. Wiles was respected by his employer, Lee Orgeron of Montco, as one of the most seasoned and skilled Oil Patch captains, having had command of sensitive operations in the past. Wiles was reserved and, like most of the Cajuns he worked with, stoic to the point of stubborn. In a previous post with Montco, Wiles had commanded a rig tug, a powerful vessel that tows an oil rig to its platform, a job that involves maneuvers that are considered to be among the most difficult in the marine industry. Installing an oil rig, a floating structure worth upwards of $100 million, above a stationary platform is accomplished by maneuvering the rig with three tugs, backing the assembly into place with a tolerance of 18 inches. Now Wiles was captain of one of Montco's oceangoing tugs, the 114-foot, 3,500-horsepower *J. A. Orgeron*, a job just as sensitive but arguably requiring less in terms of ship handling skill.

Just miles apart, the *Cherry Valley* and the *Orgeron* were engaged in two of the many disparate maritime businesses that crowd the industrial facilities along the Lower Mississippi River. In the coming days, after the *Orgeron* and the *Cherry Valley* departed the river, crossed the Gulf of Mexico, and approached their destinations on the east coast of Florida, the vessels would get much closer, and the crews would learn each other's names. For now, they remained two distinct cultures—a tugboat with a crew of five towing a barge, and an oil tanker with a crew of 25 delivering oil between the world's refineries and numerous storage and distribution facilities.

Tugboats are a cheaper way than ships to move products. Most tugboats are uninspected, not subject to the extensive rules and regulations that apply to ships. Only the tug's captain and mate need to have a license; the only cooks aboard tugs are the crewmembers themselves who rotate through the position. Even the tug's captain will take a turn slinging hash in the cramped galley. Aboard ship, there are at least eight licensed crewmembers, and meals are prepared by a steward. Tugs can be made to tow or push anything, oil or grain barges, or perform ship-assist maneuvers. Ships are designed and built with a single purpose in mind: to move specific products from point A to point B.

One of the primary differences between ships and tugs is that ships can usually sail in any weather. They cross the Pacific and Atlantic with the regularity of a long-haul truck, regardless of storms. Ship crews watch the weather, to be sure, and they can adjust the ship's course to lessen the effects of large ocean storms, but they are built to withstand the worst the ocean can deliver. Tug crews, on the other hand, must watch weather reports with grave concern. Tugs lack the speed to outrun fast-moving storms, and their crews will often head for port when storm warnings are issued for an area. With their short-handed crew, lack of size, and vulnerable cargo barges, tugs must avoid storms.

Later that morning Bill Knodle and the NASA transportation director, Ernie Graham, a cautious man himself, stood shoulder-to-shoulder on the dock as the tug *J. A. Orgeron* pulled around the bend of the Navigation Channel, its low black hull pushing aside a wide bow wave.

One of the radios in the tug's pilothouse crackled: "Can you see me on the dock here? I'm waving my arm." The tug captain saw two figures standing on the dock, one with his arm in the air.

Without lifting the mike from its mounts, Captain Wiles pushed the transmitter button and responded in a low voice, "Yep, I'll bring her right alongside."

Air hissed from the dual throttle controls as Captain Lanny Wiles slowed the vessel to a stop at the pier. Knodle and Graham waited for the deckhands to secure the tug's lines on the pier's steel bollards before climbing down the ladder to the tug's after deck. Knodle greeted the *Orgeron's* trim captain with a quick handshake.

"Captain," Knodle acknowledged with a nod of his head, preferring to use his title over the man's given name. Wiles, shorter than Knodle by nearly a head but just as lean, had spent nearly half of his 40 years at sea, serving tugboats and offshore oil-drill supply boats in the Gulf of Mexico.

Wiles greeted Knodle similarly, a firm handshake accompanied by a mumbled courtesy. He had served the previous night's watch from 1800 to midnight, but he had been awake for the early-morning hours as well, supporting his co-captain, Bob Reahard, in their final approach up the Mississippi River. At mid-morning, it was once again his watch.

Both Wiles and Reahard knew the river well, but this was their first time doing business with NASA. They had wanted to be sure to arrive on time and without incident. Despite his lack of sleep, Wiles was attentive, having mustered the necessary reserve. He would need his full attention to absorb the minute details that this unusual job would require. He would listen carefully, offer input only if it were asked, and he would comply with every request that NASA or Martin Marietta would make. First they would inspect the tug itself, Knodle and Graham explained to Wiles.

"We'll start with the tow wire," Knodle said. "Let's pull out the first few hundred feet or so, just run it right down the dock. I want to see its condition." If a wire had been used beyond its time, Knodle knew that the first part would be the area to show most of its wear. This is the part that is constantly used, chafing over the tug's stern and connected to a barge's bridle; it will exhibit numerous meathooks where the wire is beginning to come apart. Replacing a wire is costly, and many tug companies try to "get one more trip" out of the towing gear before replacing it.

Wiles ordered the deckhands and engineer to unwind the spool, work-ing the wire onto the pier. The wire was in good shape, Knodle found, and the rest of the inspection, including the ship's papers, safety gear, and crew certificates, were all similarly up to date and in good order. One thing Kn-odle noticed was that the tug was not required to have a licensed engineer, a dedicated person trained in diesel mechanics whose shipboard responsi-bilities were solely dedicated to maintaining the systems. This is one pro-found difference between tugs and ships, which are required to carry one chief engineer and three assistants who stand a rotating watch in the en-gineroom 24 hours a day. The assistants are each accompanied by a QMED, a qualified member of the engine department, who fills the en-gineroom equivalent of the able-bodied seaman role.

Knodle knew they were not required to have a licensed engineer. It was something that bothered him, perhaps because of his naval training in which redundancy was a matter of course. But, strictly speaking, it was not his job to approve or disapprove of this tug and crew. He was responsible for the barge; if he'd had serious concerns about the safety of the tug, if he'd had doubts about the abilities of the crew, he would have taken them to NASA and made them known. The lack of an engineer, after all, was an industry standard.

Knodle had slept in his office the night before departure and had got-ten up at 0500. He walked down to the barge and checked it one last time before anyone else arrived and found that the *Orgeron*'s crew was also up. Invited aboard, Knodle took a seat at the galley table and was given a cup of coffee. "It was a sailor-to-sailor thing," Knodle said later, "a chance to talk about the coming voyage, to get a feel for the weather and to share notes." After a quick breakfast prepared by the tug crew, Knodle was back in his of-fice checking the latest weather reports. Later Knodle discussed "a little thing way down in the Caribbean" with Ernie Graham, the transportation director. The pair agreed that the small storm was not much of a threat, at least as it appeared at the time. The tow could proceed, they concurred.

Only one external fuel tank had ever been caught in a storm during the tow from Louisiana to Florida. In November 1985, Hurricane Juan worked its way through the Gulf and into Louisiana, coming ashore west of New Orleans. Once the storm went ashore, the decision to go ahead with the tow was made. By the time the tug and barge reached the Gulf, however, the storm reversed direction, heading back into the Gulf, leaving the tug with nowhere to hide. Knodle was woken from a sound sleep at 0200 by his phone ringing: "In the middle of the night I found myself talking with the tug captain about the situation," Knodle said. "We discussed his dilemma in detail and talked about options. In the end the captain decided to heave-to—head into the wind and ride out the storm. I think he felt better for having been able to talk it out. After Juan passed east of him and went ashore for the last time, he made course for the Straits of Florida and on to Port Canaveral." The transit time to Port Canaveral on this voyage was eight days instead of the normal four and a half, but the tank was not damaged.

In years past, when the barge carried a crew, Knodle would have made this particular trip aboard the barge to Cape Canaveral. On the morning that the *Poseidon* was to carry the ET-70 for delivery the barge had just come out of the shipyard for normal repair and maintenance, and it was his custom to make the first trip to ensure that all repairs and improvements worked. Since there was no longer a crew aboard the barge, he would do the next best thing and meet the barge when it arrived in Canaveral.

Wiles stood in the tug's aft wheelhouse, an enclosed remote station that looks down on the tug's stern. His neck was craned slightly forward to see his crew as they tended the tow wire below him. The tug *Angus Cooper*, which had been contracted to assist the *J. A. Orgeron* in getting the *Poseidon* safely away from the dock and down the Gulf Outlet to sea, pressed its bow into the *Poseidon*'s side, keeping it securely alongside as the tow wire was made up to the bridle.

Unlike the assist tugs that were bringing the *Cherry Valley* alongside the GATX terminal, the *J. A. Orgeron* was rigged for towing barges on long passages. A large spool of two-and-a-half-inch steel towing wire was mounted on the stern, the end of which snaked aft along the worn deck.

The bow of the *Poseidon* loomed above; its chain bridle was secured to the end of the towing wire with a steel shackle the thickness of a man's arm. The shackle rested on the tug's deck, having been secured by the towing crew under the watchful eyes of Ernie Graham and Bill Knodle. Each man had a checklist that needed to be worked through carefully with the tug's crew. They each witnessed, for example, the insertion of a steel cotter pin in the shackle's base that would keep the shackle from working loose during the 1,000-mile tow. "We could not have them put in a welding rod or some other soft metal," Knodle said. "This had to be the real thing."

The *Orgeron* was operated by Montco, a marine transportation company based in an industrial bayou hamlet south of New Orleans called Golden Meadow near a shallow patch of water called Bayou Lafourche. The narrow bayou river, snaking south from the Mississippi River and wending its way through Golden Meadow, is lined with shrimp boats, oil-rig supply boats, crewboats, and tugs, all moored at the shipyard facilities that employ the area's residents. Along Highway 1, which follows the bayou from the Mississippi to the waters of the Gulf at Grand Isle, hand-painted signs advertise the availability of fresh frog legs and gator meat. Aside from sugarcane farming, there is little other industry; serving the needs of the Oil Patch has been a way of life since the late 1940s when oil was discovered beneath the seafloor of the Gulf of Mexico.

Montco's founder, Juan Orgeron, was one of the first Cajuns to see opportunity in the oil service when he started Montco Offshore in 1948 with a single battered tugboat. Montco's current president was Lee Orgeron, Juan's grandson, an affable Cajun with a French-twanged accent who ran the business with a brutish charm. Orgeron conducted most business from a steel house-barge, built in a shipyard the family operates, moored in a shallow bayou on his 4,000-acre hunting compound just north of Golden Meadow in Valentine, Louisiana. The barge, decorated inside like a trailer home with its shag carpet and faux-wood paneling, featured a full kitchen, in which any number of family members or colleagues could be found roasting or deep-frying game, and a living room with over-stuffed sofa and easy chairs arranged around a large-screen television.

Orgeron stood six-and-a-half feet tall and, while well fed, wore his mass high on his body so that he filled a room with his bulk. He ducked his head and turned his shoulders sideways to pass through doors. He had served in the Gulf aboard his grandfather's and father's boats as a young man and knew his business from the bottom up. The people who worked for him were sons and grandsons, nephews, nieces, and other assorted relations of the people who had worked for his father and grandfather, families with last names of Gisclair, Danos, and Hebert. When talking about ships and tugs in storms, Orgeron waved his arms wildly and with his deep blue eyes looked intently in the faces of his audience when making the point of his story. The Montco fleet was all named for family members. The *J. A. Orgeron* was named for Joseph Anthony, Lee's younger brother.

The agreement between Montco and NASA was representative of the many joint ventures between the Federal Government and private businesses, arrangements that may appear to make financial sense but often lack accountability. Montco had been hired by a subcontractor that didn't have a vessel available when it was announced that ET-70, one of the space shuttle program's external fuel tanks, was ready for delivery to Kennedy Space Center in Cape Canaveral. This subcontractor had been hired by Yowell International, a transportation company that had bid for and was awarded this job by NASA. Montco's tug the *Orgeron,* then, was the subcontracted vessel representing a subcontractor's subcontractor—the lowest bidder for delivery of a device that had taken several hundred workers four years to complete and was estimated to be worth some $50 million.

Wiles jockeyed the *Orgeron's* twin-engine controls, expertly "walking" the tug away from the pier and at the same time maintaining tension on the wire. At Wiles's command, the assist tug *Angus Cooper* backed gently on its engines to draw the barge away from the pier. "*Orgeron,* Harbormaster, all clear," said Knodle, his twang coming over the radio. "Stern's all clear, Cap, ready to depart. She's all yours."

"Harbormaster, *Orgeron,* roger," Wiles responded.

On the stern deck, deckhands Chris Gisclair and Terry Perez watched the tension on the tow wire carefully. With tension on the wire and the

Angus Cooper backing, the barge slowly peeled from the pier and edged ahead, and Wiles pressed gently up on the engines' rpm. Brown water roiled from beneath the two tugs, whose propellers, at nine-and-a-half feet in diameter, churned the rich mud from the river bottom.

"*Angus,* take in your line and prepare to make up astern," Wiles ordered. With Wiles's command, the assist tug backed away and the barge began to slip away from the dock and head toward the center of the channel.

The *Angus Cooper* backed away from the barge and turned toward its stern. It would be made off astern of the *Poseidon,* serving as a rudder and brake for the tow, providing an added measure of control. Since the tow would be moving down-current, making for the Gulf, Wiles needed to keep the tow moving faster than the current to maintain steerageway. He did not want to move so fast, though, that he risked overshooting the turns. So, once the *Angus Cooper* was made up on the stern of the *Poseidon,* Wiles navigated the *Orgeron* at about half throttle, finding the optimal speed that would allow the most control. He occasionally called for the *Angus Cooper's* captain to back the tug down to keep the tow from swinging out in the current and zigzagging down the river.

All eyes were on the tow as it slipped down the river toward the first bend in the channel. Knodle, Ernie Graham, and the rest of the NASA crew watched from the dock, all sharing a single thought: A couple of dents and a little salt water, and ET-70 would be reduced to nothing more than $15,000 of scrap aluminum. As the *Poseidon's* stern slipped from view, Knodle looked at his watch—right on time—and turned back to call his boss.

CHAPTER 5

LOADING CARGO

November 10, 1994

After the ship is all fast at GATX and the gangway put out to let the shore personnel come aboard, Carl Gabrielsson, the *Cherry Valley*'s mate, assumes responsibility for loading cargo, 85,000 barrels of No. 6 oil. Carl is a capable mariner, two years my senior, who graduated from SUNY Maritime College at Fort Schuyler, New York, a school whose campus is in the shadow of the Throgs Neck Bridge and fronts the swirling waters of New York's Hell Gate. Fort Schuyler, as the school is known in the industry, stands in contrast to the U.S. Merchant Marine Academy at Kings Point, the other New York maritime academy just up Long Island Sound. Fort Schuyler turns out well-trained officers, but with none of the pomp of Kings Point, whose groomed campus resembles an Ivy League university and whose lush lawns roll gently down to the Sound. Fort Schuyler, while a good school, is grittier, more "New York" than North Shore Long Island. In the words of one of Fort Shuyler's alumni who is also a faculty member: "At Fort Schuyler, even though you get the same degree and license as at Kings Point, you get a chance to be a mug. You get dirty hands."

Carl reflects this. From a small town on the St. Lawrence Seaway, he stands more than six feet tall and is powerfully built, with broad shoulders and large hands. I rely on Carl to run the deck during docking and undocking, execute the cargo operations efficiently, and maintain the deck and all its attendant equipment in excellent condition. Carl is also responsible for managing the deck crew, including the second and third mates and the six ABs and bosun. He has a good rapport with the crew, and he is known for his steady manner. He has worked for Keystone for more than seven years and in the last year has been promoted to full-time chief mate. Carl and I have not worked together for long, only one other trip, but I respect his quiet manner and dry sense of humor.

The *Cherry Valley*'s deck officers are all graduates of maritime academies and, like me, fairly young compared with others in an industry known for an aging population that clings to the few jobs left in the dwindling American fleet. Keystone has made a point to hire young officers for its small fleet of tankers, and the plan has worked well in terms of operations and morale.

Carl accompanies the surveyor on a check of the level of cargo in the ship's 14 tanks; this is called the ROB check, an acronym that stands for "remaining on board." The surveyor works for an independent company to measure how much cargo from the previous voyage, if any, remains aboard the ship. Once loading is complete Carl and the surveyor will repeat the process. The difference between the two figures is the amount of cargo we have loaded.

As they are finishing the calculations for the ROB, the two chicksans, shoreside loading arms used for oil transfer, are lowered from the dock and connected to the ship's manifold. The oil will flow through the manifold and down the cargo "drops" to the pipelines in the bottom of the ship and be distributed evenly to all 14 tanks. Our ship is often used as a blender to take several different grades of oil and blend them into a final product—specified by the customer.

While the oil is loading, the mate on watch keeps track of the rate and follows the chief mate's loading plan. The ABs tend the mooring lines, open and close valves at the mate's direction, and make sure there are no leaks or spills on deck.

Chris Sotirelis, the brand-new third mate, has the deck watch this morning. Just 24 years old, Chris graduated from Texas A&M's maritime program the spring before and has sailed on his license since August. As is customary, Chris stands the 8-to-12 watch, a time when the captain can likely be awake to keep an eye on him.

Breaking in a new mate is time consuming. The newly minted mate has plenty of book knowledge about how a ship is run, but his practical experience is limited to brief cruises aboard the academy's training ship—not real-world training. When he stepped aboard as a glorified cadet just two months ago, he had a license, sure, but no one would trust him—yet. We had hoped that Chris was smart, would keep his eyes open and his mouth shut, except to ask questions. While there is no such thing as a stupid question, the same question asked repeatedly sends out warning signals. The new third mate must learn the layout of the ship, where the firefighting equipment is stored, how the lifeboats operate, and where his emergency station is located. He also needs to learn the piping diagram to know which valves, among the dozens scattered about in the maze of piping on deck, perform which function. He has to learn how to fill out the log without making mistakes. The most important thing he can do to gain the confidence of his shipmates is to ask questions if he is unsure of something. We've come to appreciate that Chris is a pretty quiet guy, willing and interested in working hard.

The captain's time during port is particularly busy, especially during these short turnarounds. There isn't much incentive to go ashore, either. These small, riverfront towns are mostly just industrial marine terminals, proper towns being some miles away. Occasionally a crewmember will take a bicycle ashore for some exercise. We keep a few ships' bicycles for these occasions in a storage locker on deck. But unless we're alongside in New Orleans or Baton Rouge, I choose to stay aboard, especially since there is so much paperwork to do: crewmembers may need to be signed on or off, trips to the doctor or dentist coordinated, repairs approved or arranged, stores brought aboard, and meetings held with the charterer's representatives or vessel inspectors like the Coast Guard or USDA. I don't get much rest, which, combined with the fact that I only had a few brief naps in the previous 24 hours, means that I can't wait to get back to sea.

Ten hours after the oil starts flowing we have finished loading the first 85,000 barrels and are getting ready to shift downriver to the IMTT terminal in Gretna to load another 150,000 barrels. Gretna will be our last stop before departing for sea. Ships will often load several times in a single port, the amount of cargo carefully measured by the surveyor and the chief mate.

I call the pilot and tug companies just before finishing loading and inform them that we will be ready to sail at 0100, three hours from now. Getting the ship ready to sail is an all-hands operation. The entire deck department, three mates and six deckhands, are up to take the tugs alongside. Each tug will pass up a bow line, which will allow them to push or pull as requested by the pilot on the ship's bridge. Then the mooring lines will be brought aboard and made ready for the next dock. Down in the engineroom the first assistant engineer, Paul Donnelly, whose role during these operations is answering "bells" from the bridge and managing the rpm at the engine console, has been called to get ready for maneuvering.

On the bridge, I have views of the ship's deck reaching out ahead; I can see many miles; I can see the sky. I can go out on the bridge wing for better views. Seven stories below, the engineers have no sense of the world around them. They rely on my orders to give them a picture of what is happening. There is no daylight in the engineroom; in fact, the operating area—the console room—is located a few feet below the waterline of the ship. Not only are they shielded from views, they are about as low in the ship as it is possible to go.

The engine department has a similar hierarchy as the deck department. There is a chief engineer, called "the chief," responsible for the safe operation and maintenance of the engineroom and all its systems. He answers to the captain. The *Cherry Valley*'s chief is Tim Croke, who is sailing with Keystone for the first time. The chief is not to be confused with the chief mate, called "the mate." The chief, like the captain, does not stand a watch. There are three other engineering officers: the first assistant engineer, who is called "the first"; the second assistant engineer, called "the second"; and the third assistant engineer, "the third." Each of the assistant engineers stands a four-hours-on, eight-hours-off rotating watch.

The *Cherry Valley* is powered by a steam plant. Two steam turbines, one high pressure and one low pressure, are the centerpieces of the engineroom and create power to turn a 90,000-pound, 22½-foot-diameter bronze propeller. The turbines receive their steam from a pair of three-story-high boilers that are more than 20 feet long and are located aft of the turbines.

In the forward end of each boiler are the two burners, long nozzles that re-semble slender—albeit very heavy—shotguns, which the engineers change depending on the volume of steam power needed. For open-throttle speed, when the ship is steaming across the ocean at "sea speed," the largest burner tips are used. For maneuvering, when slower speed and finer levels of control are desired by the pilot or captain, combinations of burner tips are used. When it's time to change the burners, an engineer, usually a QMED, which is the unlicensed rating in the engineroom, dons a pair of asbestos gloves that cover his entire arms. He pulls a burner, its tip im-mersed in a chemical solvent, from its rack next to the boilers, and climbs the platform to the boiler. Peering over the turbines, he catches the eye of the engineer in the console area some 30 feet away and waits for his nod. Once the nod comes, indicating that fuel to the burner has been shut off, the QMED releases the burner from its locked position, pulls it out and sets it aside, and then slides in the new burner. He locks it in place and then nods to the engineer at the console, who will then fire it off.

While there are a few steam-powered ships still in operation, steam propulsion is being phased out in favor of electronically controlled diesel plants. While a well-maintained steam plant can last indefinitely, diesel engines have a shorter life expectancy, about 10 years. The trend is reflec-tive of the industry as a whole, which favors short-term benefit in ex-change for lower operational costs. Ships with diesel engines are cheaper and easier to run but are not built to last. Engineers running diesel plants spend the majority of their time on maintenance; engineers who run steam plants spend the majority of their time actually operating the ma-chinery, which requires little maintenance but constant operational atten-tion. With a diesel plant, an engineer simply presses up the throttle to gain more speed. Steam plant engineers scurry like rats in a catacomb: chang-ing burners in the boilers; circulating steam throughout the system and constantly monitoring pressure; and generally remaining one step ahead of not only what *is* happening but what might happen if pressure is lost in any part of the chain. In the old days, before automation, a steam plant was far busier—at any given time a team of some eight engineers would be scrambling through their maze of pipes opening and closing valves to increase or decrease steam. The *Cherry Valley*'s automation system, considered the most sensitive equipment in the engineroom, links some 40 systems between the control lever in the engineroom and the propeller at the end of the shaft. Automation in the *Cherry Valley*'s steam plant measures steam flow, pressure, water level in the boiler drums, the amount of fuel being burned to create new steam, and numerous other tasks that used to be performed by humans. What this means, then, is that while we have fewer men in the engineroom than in the past, the stress of the job is left for a single person: the first assistant engineer, in our case Paul Donnelly, whose role is to answer the bells from the bridge immediately and with complete confidence.

The relationship between the bridge and the engineroom is complex. When an order is sent from the bridge for an increase or decrease in revolutions from the propeller, there is not a direct mechanical connection from the controls on the bridge to the machinery. There is a human connection. The third mate posted at the engine order telegraph on the bridge console responds to my orders, or the pilot's as in the case of docking or undocking. When I say, "dead slow ahead," for example, the mate turns the telegraph to Dead Slow Ahead and this order is repeated, accompanied by a loud bell, at the console in the engineroom, which jangles loudly until the first assistant engineer responds to the order. Engine orders are given in increments in the following manner: Stop, Dead Slow Ahead, Slow Ahead, Half Ahead, and Full Ahead; and the same for astern. Seeing the command, an engineer standing at the console in the engineroom—70 feet below the bridge deck—will slap at the response bell to let us on the bridge know that he's heard us and then increase or decrease steam pressure to achieve the desired rpm at the propeller to match the ordered speed. All the while he is keeping a careful eye on steam pressure to be sure he doesn't overstress the system and cause a "flame-out" in the boilers, which will cause the ship to lose power for several minutes—not an option when we are maneuvering in congested areas like the Mississippi River, or any other harbor in the world.

One advantage to a steam plant is that I can specify the exact rpm I want, whether it means a little more than the standard full ahead or any number of rpm between stop and full, 0 to 78 rpm.

The worst order I can give to the engineroom is to stop the engine immediately after I have had them providing full power. For full power I have asked them to give me everything, which brings the pressure to its maximum of 600 pounds and a temperature of 900 degrees. If I order "stop" after full ahead or full astern, all this steam has nowhere to go and must be vented. If the venting isn't done, we begin to blow seals and destroy valves. Engineers explain that maneuvers such as these are "why we hate you deck guys." Although I'm not the one standing in the 120-degree engineroom worrying about whether the plant can handle the sort of demands being asked of it, I still must appreciate the limits of the system and know that the engineers need fair warning for certain maneuvers. After all, their problems will quickly become mine.

With the tugs alongside holding us in, the deck crew begins to let go the lines. The long head lines and stern lines, the ones that lead forward or aft from the ship's ends, are the first to be taken in, followed immediately by the breast lines, which lead straight across to the dock. When moored alongside in the river, we keep the spring lines attached until the last moment, since they keep us from slipping back in the current. With all of these lines aboard, the spring lines are let go from the each end of the main deck. After the lines have been pulled clear of the water by the mooring winches, the pilot orders the tugs to "back easy" to pull us away from the berth.

As we move out from the dock and into the stream, the force of the current helps to push the bow around and help us on our way down the river to Gretna, two hours' steaming time away. The deck crew is sent below for a little rest before doing it all over again.

As we approach the dock in Gretna we are met by a different set of tugs. This time they are made up on the starboard side since we will be docking port-side-to in Gretna. The pilot backs the ship to slow our headway so we are moving at the same speed as the river. While he is backing the ship, the transverse thrust of the propeller helps to walk the *Cherry Valley's* stern to port and with help from the tugs gets us turned 180 degrees so we are pointed upriver just off the dock. Once securely alongside, the deck crew repeats the gauging and loading process.

Relaxing in my stateroom after a long day, I turn on the television to watch the evening news. A tropical depression, an area of disturbance identified by its low barometric pressure and distinctive coil-like shape when viewed from above, is taking shape in the Caribbean. A depression is not dangerous on its own; according to the World Meteorological Organization, a tropical depression is considered to be a disturbance with winds less than 34 knots—mildly unpleasant conditions for us. But it is the potential of these systems that concerns meteorologists, and mariners—that they can blow up, in a space of just 24 hours, into a full-blown gale or cyclonic storm, generating winds anywhere from 40 to 200 miles per hour. The depression is predicted to move northeast into the Atlantic, skirting south of Cuba. It shouldn't cause us any trouble on our trip around Florida. But it is worth keeping an eye on.

The following morning Steve Worden, the radio operator, has copied the latest marine weather forecast from WLO, a radio station in Mobile, Alabama, and has hung a copy on my door. As I head down for breakfast I read the overview of the weather for the Gulf, Caribbean, and southwest Atlantic. The depression has been upgraded to tropical storm status and is moving northeast toward Jamaica. After breakfast I climb the four flights of stairs to the bridge, grab the latest weather off the NAVTEX receiver, and read through a repeat of what Steve had given me. In theory, the storm should not pose a threat to us.

During a class on ship stability at Maine Maritime, I remember the instructor, Captain Louis "Hap" Hathaway, telling us, "Many are the children who have been lost at sea due to the excessively high freeboard of beach balls." On this particular day it was a sunny spring morning in Castine, the colonial seaside village on Penobscot Bay that is home to Maine Maritime, and my mind was not as focused as it could have been. Seamanship is the catchall course that covers all the general knowledge we will need once we graduate and, to the mind of a 20-year-old cadet, have little to do with the adventures of going to sea in ships. What he meant by his dry comment was that a ship unladen, or light, rides the waves like a beach ball. It is unstable, difficult to maneuver, and even dangerous in moderate sea conditions. It was his way of explaining the importance of learning how to freeboard affects the handling of a ship at sea—especially in heavy weather.

We weren't taught much about dealing with heavy weather in school. We had courses in meteorology, ship construction, ship handling, and navigation, but not much about the specifics of running a ship in a storm. After all, we were graduating as third mates, not masters. We would have time to learn all of that in the years it would take as we rose through the ranks. The difference between feeling safe on a ship in a storm and being terrified as the ship ploughs along, its decks repeatedly swept by tumbling waves, is to have experience on many ships in all kinds of weather. You learn what a ship can handle and what it can't. Most of my knowledge came through on-the-job training and getting the shit scared out of me. I also had the advantage of learning from the mistakes of others.

I had one of my first big lessons in heavy weather on my first trip, sailing with Captain Tim O'Connor, making his first trip as captain. We sailed in ballast (without cargo) from St. John, New Brunswick, headed to the Caribbean for our next load. It was March, and a late-season northeaster blew through as we were approaching the Gulf Stream. The high winds working against the Stream made for horrific seas, and we took a real pounding that night. The bow would rise off the backs of 30-foot seas and come slamming down into the next ones. The whole ship would shudder, starting in the bow and working its way aft to the house. With the deck lights on you could see the shudder visibly work its way back through the ship, and when it hit the house it felt like you were driving at high speed down a late-winter road full of potholes. When we hit the really big ones, the crew needed to hang on to keep their footing. Fortunately, the worst lasted only about 12 hours until we got through the Gulf Stream, and then we had a pleasant trip to Aruba. Of course when we got there it took a shipyard crew seven days to weld up all the new cracks to the structural frames and longitudinals.

On a trip a year or so later, I was a third mate under Captain Bill Peterson on a voyage from Europe to the States. The weather-routing service had decided to send us on the great circle route, starting at the top of Scotland and going to New York. In February. The great circle route is the shortest distance between two points on a sphere, but the great circle route in the North Atlantic carries you through some of the most tumultuous waters on the globe at that time of year. Bill questioned the people at the service—you don't deliberately sail the great circle route in the North Atlantic in February unless you want to get your head handed to you—but they assured him we would miss the "big" storms. To suggest that we sail through this area in February either meant that they had knowledge of other, more dangerous storms elsewhere or they didn't know what they were doing. Bill chose to follow their advice. After the third storm finished beating us up I heard Bill mutter under his breath, "If it's the last thing I do I'm going to get me a motherfucking weatherman!" After that trip every time we crossed the Pond we would leave the Channel and head south until we reached 40 degrees north latitude, then run due west to the East Coast. It added some time to the trip, but we knew we would get there without beating up the boat.

By 0930 the tugs have arrived alongside and the pilot is aboard. We are loaded to our marks with 235,000 barrels, the engine is warmed up, and we are ready to go. I have Chris, the third mate, ring up SBE, standby engine, on the telegraph and have Jim and Carl start letting the lines go. The tugs back us away from the berth and turn us to point down the river and start our voyage to Jacksonville. Just after 1000 the tugs are let go and as we bring the ship to full ahead we pass under the GNO Bridge, sliding noiselessly by the New Orleans waterfront.

After passing Algiers Point I tell Carl he can knock off and just keep an AB on the bow as lookout with a radio to contact the bridge.

"What do you want to do with the lines?" Carl asks over the radio as he is walking down the deck.

I am looking at the weather report as he asks, and I have a little debate with myself. Stowing all the deck gear and lines takes about four hours, and then the same to get everything back out again before entering the next port. The weather, other than this tropical depression in the Caribbean, doesn't look too bad, and we could probably keep everything on deck and be all right. But then again...

"Have Junior stow all the gear and lines."

CHAPTER 6

CROSSING THE GULF

November 10, 1994

After departing the Mississippi River Gulf Outlet at 1730 on November 10, Bob Reahard, the tug's alternate captain, adjusted the autopilot for the rhumb line course, roughly south-southeast, that would take them across the Gulf and around Dry Tortugas, a patch of sandy shoals and islets about 75 miles west of Key West that mark the turning point for all shipping that runs between the Gulf Coast and Florida and into the Straits of Florida. The sun was just setting as the crew stretched out the wire some 1,500 feet, its full length for offshore towing—more than a quarter of a mile, or, as the crew would say, "about six layers." Easing the tow this far astern allowed the giant towline to sag between the tug's stern and bow of the barge, creating enough catenary to act as a shock absorber if the tug encountered big seas. For each layer played out between the barge and the tug, the wire could drop as much as 10 feet. The barge was only drawing nine-plus feet and the tug about 14, but the wire could hang as much as 60 feet deep. Where the wire passed over the stern rail, a length of slotted pipe was bolted to the wire to act as chafing gear.

As the tug's bow punched through the two- to four-foot chop of the Gulf, the waves hit the bluff hull and forced their way upward between the tire fenders and chains, producing a rhythmic clank. The tires would lift free from the hull until the chains came up taut, then the bow would clear the wave and the chains and tires rattle back against the hull. The noise was not unpleasant to the *Orgeron*'s crew; it could even be soothing if the seas were not too confused.

Once out of the Gulf and into the Florida Straits they passed closely to Fort Jefferson, a brick, octagonal fort set on a shovelful of sand in the Dry

Tortugas. Fort Jefferson, now a national park featuring an old iron light-house, served as a Union stronghold—and prison—during the Civil War, enabling the North to intercept ships attempting to run supplies between the Mississippi delta and the Florida peninsula, the same route that the *Orgeron* was now taking. It is here where the narrow channel between Florida and Cuba, the Florida Straits, begins to squeeze the Gulf Stream into producing its full force, flowing along at three or four knots as 80 million cubic feet per minute pass through the Straits. Eastbound traffic, such as the *J. A. Orgeron* once it completed the crossing of the Gulf, can get a free ride, but because the prevailing winds tend to blow directly opposite the Stream, the Straits are known for their steep breaking seas. South-bound vessels tend to hug the shore near the Keys to avoid the strongest effects of the current.

The night and following day, November 11, passed uneventfully, the typical routine of life aboard a tug proceeding at its appropriately gentle pace—sharing the preparation of meals while off watch, cleaning the tug, servicing the engines and monitoring the flow of fuel, and keeping watch in the pilothouse. Wiles and the Reahard brothers split the watch in three parts, each standing four hours and then taking eight hours off: Wiles serving the 8-to-12, Bob Reahard the 4-to-8, and Pete Reahard, Bob's younger brother, the 12-to-4. Chris Gisclair, the son of one of Montco's longtime shore-side employees, Rodney Gisclair, was sailing as the tug's unlicensed engineer, splitting the engineroom watch in six-hour shifts with Terry Perez, the only designated deckhand.

On watch, Wiles and Bob and Pete Reahard sat in the captain's chair, staring blankly from their pilothouse perch at the horizon. With the helm on autopilot there was no need to steer manually. They could relax with a cup of coffee or cigarette—their feet up on the console—standing every hour or so to plot a position on the chart using the GPS receiver and make notations in the log of their speed, position, and the weather conditions. They routinely checked the high-seas and coastal forecasts on the VHF and single-sideband, keeping track of the storm that was working its way across the Caribbean. At that point, they were confident the storm would pass well ahead of them when they approached Florida—if the storm even lived that long and if it ever swung close to Florida at all. The two radars, one port and one starboard, were visible from the chair, and they could lean to either side to switch the range settings, change the variable range rings and bearing lines to determine the CPA—closest point of approach—of other vessels. One radar was set on long range, six to twelve miles, looking for other traffic; the other was set at a short range, three miles or less, to be sure the tow remained in its relative position. When near shore, the radar could also be used to navigate by using ranges and bearings from land masses, to double-check the GPS for fixes. But offshore, especially at night, the radar was used to avoid close-quarters situations with other ships. With the tow trailing 1,500 feet astern, they would want to keep a mile off from other vessels, altering course or reaching for the VHF mike to contact the target if a close-quarters situation seemed to be developing. Wiles used the single-sideband to place a ship-to-shore call to his boss, Lee Orgeron, to let him know of the progress that had achieved in the previous 24 hours. With the main engines making turns for 9.5 knots, they were managing just over 230 miles every day—good speed for a tug because of the fairly light tow.

In the engineroom, Gisclair transferred fuel from the main tanks to the day tank, monitored the rate of consumption of the fuel oil, and changed filters. The other critical check was cylinder head temperatures. The operating rpm for the engines was between 800 and 825 without a load; when towing a barge or when laboring in heavy seas, the rpm were adjusted to keep the temperatures in the cylinders below 800 degrees Fahrenheit. If the temperatures were allowed to rise above that, the excessive heat could warp the valves or the head could crack. Since there was no readout in the pilothouse for this, Gisclair monitored the cylinder temperatures from a dial on each valve and told the person on watch to adjust the rpm accordingly. The *J. A. Orgeron*'s eight-cylinder main engines, a pair of Polar Nohab diesels, were each capable of 1,750 horsepower, and burned fuel at the rate of about 2,500 gallons per day. To maintain electrical power for the tug's navigation instruments, galley appliances, house lights, and the television, Gisclair kept one of the tug's two

Detroit 671 diesel generators running, switching between the port and starboard generators every 24 hours.

"It was normal, boring, at-sea routine," Bob Reahard recalled in his guttural drawl of the first days of the trip. "Lanny makes an excellent squash casserole, but other than cooking and eating and sleeping, not a lot goes on. We'd worked together, Lanny and me, for a number of years. We had a good rhythm, didn't talk much."

But the routine didn't last. At a few minutes before midnight on November 11 as Wiles was about to go off watch, the tug lurched through a wave and suddenly sheered off to starboard. The rudders had gone hard to starboard, forcing the tug to circle back on its course, heading toward the barge. Wiles pulled back on the throttles to slow the tug just as Pete Reahard reached the pilothouse for the change of the watch. Wiles made sure the barge, which was still moving ahead at more than nine knots, was not in danger of running them down before handing the conn over to Pete Reahard.

"Feels like the rudders jammed," Wiles said. "Keep her at clutch speed while I go check."

Once they slowed, Reahard could keep the tug clear of the barge with just a little power, idling in position. The water was so deep that they didn't have to worry about the wire fouling on the bottom, but they did need to maintain power to the propellers to prevent the weight of the wire from pulling the tug and barge together. Wiles moved quickly down the companionway and out a watertight door to the tug's stern deck. He pulled back the hatch in the deck that led to the cramped rudder room housing the mechanical equipment for the steering system. On a twin-screw tug like the *Orgeron,* there are two rudders, mounted just aft of each of the nine-and-a-half-foot-diameter propellers. Each rudderpost, which emerges from the hull straight into the rudder room, is fitted with a short tiller. A jockey arm, a length of steel bolted to each tiller, allows the hydraulic rams of the steering gear to move both rudders together. Using a flashlight, Wiles inspected all the gear, section by section, quickly discovering that the linkage controlling the autopilot signal from the pilothouse to the rams on the rudders had come off. The linkage, which is like a ball joint on a car, had come off the joint because the nut that held the linkage together had worked loose. Wiles climbed back out of the hatch to retrieve a wrench and in a few minutes had the linkage back together, tightening the nut and wiring it closed to prevent it from happening again. One of the benefits of having mechanical problems at sea is that there's nothing around to run into, no shoals to hit, and no confined channels. Had this incident occurred in confined waters it could have been a disaster. It was almost 0100 before Wiles climbed back to the pilothouse.

Before heading off watch for some sleep, Wiles entered a terse note in the log: "Lost steering. Jockey bar came off rudder arm."

November 12 saw the return of the quiet routine that all mariners look forward to. Life at sea is months of boredom interspersed with moments of sheer terror. With their steering gear mishap behind them, they were looking forward to an uneventful rest of the trip.

The following morning, November 13, as the *Orgeron* was passing south of Key West, Wiles noted that the ragged depression that he had been following had been upgraded to Tropical Storm Gordon by Dr. Richard Pasch, the forecaster on duty at the National Hurricane Center. A late-season storm, Gordon had appeared on satellite images November 6 off Nicaragua unobtrusively—anonymous, a mild disturbance. Only in the last 48 hours had it built in strength, fed by the tropical sea's heat and moisture as it crossed the Caribbean. The storm was not a hurricane. In fact, it was displaying characteristics that were opposite a typical hurricane. Where hurricanes begin life in Africa, stomping their way across the Atlantic and then hitting the balmy bathwater of the Caribbean—building heat and moisture and strength in the process—late-season storms tend to be scattered, lacking a tightly formed center, or eye. These storms can be just as dangerous as hurricanes. Hurricanes tend to be more predictable, with the strongest winds concentrated near the eye, the trackline tending to take a parabolic curve that can be avoided. Avoid the center, and you avoid the worst part of the storm.

Late-season storms are still powered by heat and moisture, but the relatively cooler water makes the storms shiftier. If there is such a thing as a perfect storm, Gordon, and other later-season storms, could be said to be the imperfect storms. They are ragged, follow uncertain paths, and are therefore harder to avoid than hurricanes if you're in a ship at sea attempting to anticipate their track. Yet they can pack winds and rain that are just as devastating as hurricanes. Dr. Pasch would note that Gordon was acting more like a subtropical storm, whose tracklines are affected by the fast-moving winter weather systems in North America, the winter westerlies. Such late-season tropical storms often see the greatest wind speeds on the outer edges of the storm, as opposed to the center. Pasch was concerned that his "gale warnings," which had been broadcast repeatedly for the past two days, were not being taken seriously enough. By upgrading his warnings to "storm" status he had hoped the warnings would be taken more seriously.

The storm was still moving slowly, creeping northeast after glancing off the coast of Nicaragua and heading toward Jamaica. With winds blowing a maximum of 40 knots, it was not terribly fierce, not even close to being considered hurricane force. But its sodden clouds were dropping torrents of rain over Central America and the islands in the Western Caribbean, according to the broadcast reports that Wiles heard in the *Orgeron*'s pilothouse. The storm center, now located about 400 miles to the south of the *Orgeron*, was forecast to move northeast, out into the Atlantic.

While skirting the Central American shores, the storm lived in stasis, neither building in force nor dying out altogether. Hurricane Hunter aircraft, attempting to define its exact center, found that it was lumbering along as a minor tropical depression, producing some rain but not clocking winds much over 25 knots. Hours later, when the storm encountered an upper-air trough that sent it careening to the northeast toward Jamaica, it suddenly strengthened, as if sensing a break, gathering power from the warm, late-autumn surface waters of the Caribbean. Hurricane Hunter aircraft plunged into the storm center several times, which they would continue to do over the next several days in an attempt to monitor a storm that could go anywhere at any time.

The rain was not welcome. Jamaica, Hispaniola, and Cuba were already sodden with moisture from the long wet season. Though it was still considered a small storm, it presaged two dangers: flooding and landslides. Forecasters predicted the storm would continue northeast through the Windward Passage, the eye crossing the southern tip of Cuba and the western fringes of the island of Hispaniola. The following day, as the storm slowly passed over Haiti, more than a foot of rain was released by the heavy clouds, setting off a string of floods and landslides that would claim the lives of more than 1,100 people in 24 hours and earn Gordon a place in the National Hurricane Center's archives as one of the deadliest storms. As the storm crossed Cuba's southern peninsula, it took an unexpected sheer northward, and then quickly northwest, as if drawing a bead on the tug.

But none of this was known to Wiles, and even if it was, rain is no danger to a tug at sea.

At this point the cloud cover associated with Tropical Storm Gordon was spread over much of the northern Caribbean Sea, Bahamas, and the Straits of Florida, its strongest winds swirling more than 200 miles to the northwest. As night fell over the tug and tow, the storm's center was in the Old Bahama Channel between Cuba and the Bahamas. Gray clouds began to appear on the southeastern horizon, and a strong northeast wind was beginning to blow spray over the *Orgeron*'s blunt bow as it plunged through the waves off the lower Keys. The rattle of the tire fenders and chains was now a cacophony of deafening metallic crashes that, to unseasoned ears, made it sound as though the vessel itself was rattling apart. Combined with the roar of the wind and the spattering waves and spray, the noise inside the pilothouse strained conversation. As each wave broke over the bow of the tug, streams of water several feet deep ran down the tug's sloping decks before rushing through the scuppers. Any crew venturing outside would be drenched, either from the seas sweeping the decks or the spray blasting the tug every few seconds. While the storm was nothing serious for the crew of the Orgeron—they had each experienced far worse—life was getting uncomfortable; simple movements, like moving through passageways or up and down stairways, required the use of both hands. Every motion required twice as much energy; sleep was more elusive. In the pilothouse, the pitching was more pronounced, forcing Wiles and the Reahards to brace themselves in the chair to keep from landing in a heap on the deck.

By noon of November 13, after the *J. A. Orgeron* had rounded Key Largo at the tip of Florida for the northward leg, the homestretch, the wind and seas conspired to slow the tug's progress. Bill Knodle at NASA had requested that Wiles start logging a description of the weather if conditions deteriorated. "Wind and seas increasing," Wiles wrote. The speed was entered as 8.6 knots, a full knot slower than the tug's previous speed. However, with the Gulf Stream providing some 2 to 3 knots of speed, the tug's speed through the water was more like 5.5 knots—a combined speed that should put the tug in Port Canaveral at noon on the 14th.

By evening of November 13 the forecast for Tropical Storm Gordon began to change dramatically for the area the *J. A. Orgeron* was transiting. The storm was building power and approaching the U.S. shipping lanes, delivering ferocious winds of more than 60 knots out of the northeast—opposing the flow of the Stream. At the leading edge of the storm, winds swirled into the center from the northeast, the same direction that the *Orgeron* crew continually noted in their log. This section of any cyclonic storm, the right-hand side when viewed from above, is considered by mariners to be the "dangerous semicircle." Wind speeds, because of the storm's forward motion, are typically stronger than in other parts of the cyclone. To make matters worse, as the storm advances, the winds tend to draw ships on this side into its center, prolonging the time that the effects will be felt. As Gordon progressed northwestward, its cloud cover now blanketing much of South Florida, Cuba, and the Bahamas, Hurricane Hunter aircraft repeatedly plunged into the eye of the storm to track its progress. Only after it crossed into the territorial airspace of Cuba, into the no-fly zone, did the airplane crew lose track of the center. At this point, however, the storm developed the distinctive comma shape, cyclogenesis, making it easier to track by satellite.

At 1800 forecasters essentially doubled their previous estimates of wind speed and wave height. Northeast winds were now expected to blow from 40 to 55 knots, with seas as high as 30 feet. Wiles realized that his tug was caught in the convergence zone between the low-pressure system of Storm Gordon to his south and a stationary high-pressure system located over the Carolinas, to his north. Northeast winds in the sea lanes off South Florida were feeding both systems. He couldn't be in a worse place. Wiles wasn't immediately concerned for the safety of his tug and the barge. He had been through worse. Life aboard the tug was about to get more uncomfortable. But he remembered the warnings that Bill Knodle and Ernie Graham had made shortly before departing Michoud—that the accelerometers on the securing chains could tolerate only one G of force. Wiles had never towed a cargo with such a stipulation.

The *J. A. Orgeron* was just north of Miami, and it would be possible to turn back and duck into port to escape the storm conditions. Yet Wiles knew that the narrow approach into Miami, Government Cut, was likely to be a maelstrom of big seas and strong tailwinds that could snatch the barge and dash it onto the rock jetties. Wiles had been in and out Miami many times and knew the approach well. But his light barge, even with an assist tug, would challenge even his expert ship-handling skills. With no gauges in the pilothouse monitoring forces on the fuel tank, and no experience with this sensitive a cargo, Wiles reached for the radio to talk things over with his boss, Montco's Lee Orgeron.

The call was quickly established through the marine operator, and Wiles related the events, the tug's slow progress, the worsening conditions, and the threatening forecast. Would Orgeron check with NASA, Wiles asked, to see if he could stop in Miami to wait out the storm? Wiles then cleared with Orgeron, who said he would call back when he had an answer. Meanwhile, Wiles should continue to make progress to the north.

In the 45 minutes that he waited for Orgeron to call back, Wiles played over in his mind an approach through the 500-foot opening to Miami, envisioning the direction of the seas and wind in relation to the cut. Because of the barge's significant sail area—the tall canopy serving as a broad sail—

he would have to keep the barge on an especially short wire to prevent it from being blown out of the channel. When towing on a short wire in following seas there is a greater risk of parting the wire as the tug surges down the backs of the seas. If the wire parted as they were entering the channel, there would be no chance to save the barge. It would also be extremely difficult, if not impossible, for an assist tug to make up outside of the entrance. The marine operator's voice, sounding the name of the tug three times in slow succession, came as a welcome reprieve from his thoughts. "Continue on," Orgeron relayed. "They want you to keep going."

As captain, the decision to continue or pull into Miami was his alone to make. Yet the difficult entrance to Miami was not necessarily a way out of the situation; it could make matters far worse if the approach went wrong. And Port Canaveral was only 142 miles away, just 17 hours' steaming time.

It would probably be a sleepless night, but with any luck the crew of the *J. A. Orgeron* would be sleeping soundly alongside the dock at Port Canaveral the following evening.

The *Orgeron* was not the only vessel experiencing the ill effects of the storm, the center of which, by the evening of November 13, was fast approaching Guantanamo, Cuba. One hundred fifty miles southeast of the tug was a small Belizean-flag freighter, the *Jeano Express,* one of the hundreds of such ships that ply between Miami and the countless island communities in the Caribbean and Bahama Islands—delivering groceries, vehicles, construction equipment, and building materials. These are old ships, their steel plates worn thin by rust, their engines and machinery held together with what little money the island crews can manage. Their ingenuity keeps the tired ships going as long as possible, but every Caribbean freighter likely ends up in this way sooner or later—used long past the time that it should be sold for scrap by a company that can ill afford sufficient maintenance and repair—the sea claiming what it will.

The 180-foot ship had been bound from the Bahamas through the Old Bahama Channel to Miami, laboring in ballast as the storm caught her. As

she entered the Gulf Stream she began to roll and pitch heavily. During the
dark night part of the hatch cover let go and allowed water into the single
cargo hold. The effect of this water roiling around in the big empty hold
was to cause the little vessel to roll 40 to 50 degrees and put enormous
stress on the aging ship. In the early hours of the 14th something let go in
the engineroom and water began flooding in, slowly at first. But the captain knew what fate awaited his ship, and before losing all power issued a
Mayday call on the radio and switched on the ELT, hoping someone would
respond before it was too late. She had taken on so much water that she
was now suffering a 40-degree list to starboard with four feet of water in
the single cargo hold. After failing to stem the flow of water, the crew, nine
men from the Dominican Republic and Haiti and the ship's dog, were huddled in the wheelhouse in life jackets, wedged against bulkheads to keep
from sliding down the dangerously sloping deck. The ship was dead, without power for propulsion or electricity, the engine compartment having
flooded. At this point they could do little besides await help. To abandon
ship in the rotting hulk that was their lifeboat would be suicidal. The torrential rains alone would swamp the boat in minutes, the seas then smashing it to pulp. They were drifting with the northeast winds at a rate of 2.5
knots toward Tennessee Reef near Marathon, Florida. If they didn't sink
first, the ship would be aground on one of the numerous reefs that formed
part of Florida's Marine Sanctuaries, in less than 12 hours.

PART II

"The sounds of the ship were all around me . . . . I felt
as if I were a part of her, as if we formed one body, of which
I was the center of awareness; all nerves and tendons and
veins and viscera, reaching into the remotest corners, were
concentrated in me . . . . I could interpret every sound, trace
every tremor to its origin. It was a healthy body, full of
strength."

—Captain Martinus Harinxma (*The Captain,* by Jan de Hartog)

CHAPTER 7

STORM CLOUDS BUILDING

November 12, 1994

After departing Southwest Pass at 1830 on the 12th the *Cherry Valley* crew settles into the normal routine of being at sea. Everyone aboard feels a measure of reprieve when the land drops below the horizon—the ship's motion, easy in the swell, bringing the sense that life will return to the orderliness that is otherwise absent when we're alongside in port. At sea, everyone has a job, knows his duties. Every crewmember has his own space, every object a place. In port there is the hectic pace of loading and discharging oil. Stores are arriving, guests and agents need accommodating, and, afterward of course, there are reams of paperwork to process.

We're sailing coastwise on this voyage, never more than a day or two from our next port. On a foreign trip we might not see land for a week or two and would really have a chance to set up a routine. But our trip from New Orleans to Jacksonville, a distance of some 1,000 nautical miles, will take us just under three days at 15 knots and is a calm period that everyone enjoys. As the ship's captain, I have a feeling of control, however illusory. Yet the problems that I may have at sea are my own, not the result of outside forces. In port I might worry about the crew going ashore, getting drunk, and finding trouble, which means that I will need to bail them out. There are doctor and dentist appointments; a tug and barge can slip out of the channel and ram the ship. At sea, there is peace.

As the sun sets over the blue waters of the Gulf and the pilot departs, I am on the bridge, sitting in the captain's chair, which affords broad views of the darkening sea and sky. Carl, the mate, has the watch and we fall into the easy chat of master and mate, talking about the coming days and the maintenance we can accomplish on the trip to Jacksonville. Carl had gotten a fair amount of sleep during the day—after he had spoken with the bosun after sailing, he had a shower and a long nap as we transited the 104 miles down the Mississippi—and is refreshed for his watch this evening. Even I have had a relatively easy day, since everything happened during "normal" working hours, but I'm looking forward to the relative peace of being at sea.

The only thing a ship does on its own is rust—the saying goes—while everything else takes work. There's always chipping and painting to do on a steel ship, the result of corrosive effects of the salt, water, and wind.

We agree that there is enough work to "break watches" for the ABs. We will have one on watch, on the bridge, and the other doing maintenance on deck. This arrangement makes it possible to have the three ABs who were not on watch working an 8-to-5 day—which is called day work. Breaking watches greatly increases our ability to stay ahead of the efforts of salt and time to destroy the ship and still run it safely. If the mate on watch needs an additional AB for lookout, or any other task on the bridge, he can call the other AB.

In the morning Carl will turn the ABs to chipping and painting in an area clear of spray, aft on the deck near the superstructure. Carl and I are serious about maintaining the deck in fine condition. If a surface shows signs of rust and time allows, we have it blasted back to bare, shiny metal. The deck crew will then coat it with a two-part epoxy primer and then paint. If sandblasting isn't feasible the crew will chip away the heavy rust and apply Coroseal, a metal primer that converts rust into magnetite, or iron oxide, to create a dull, black sheen of metal that, when coated, is impervious to rust. Over the years we have refined our methods of painting as well, feathering the paint edges so the finish won't crack and allow water to get in and rust the steel. The ship may be 25 years old, but it is our home, and, especially when you're in the business of transporting black oil, it doesn't take long for small messes to get out of control. The maze-like piping on deck is complex yet trim in appearance, a grid of brightly colored piping and assorted equipment: red for fire lines, yellow for foam equipment (used to extinguish oil fires), gloss black for winches and chocks, and bluish-gray piping for oil cargo.

As I rise from the captain's chair, Carl has the word passed below that at midnight we will go to one-man watches until midnight prior to arrival.

After turning in to the southeast traffic lane I leave the bridge to Carl and go down to my office to send the departure messages, information on everything that transpired in port, since someone is always paying for our time, accounting for every minute. I type them up on my computer in my stateroom office and then give them, on disk, to Steve Worden, the radio electronics officer, or REO, to send out over the satellite communications system. Keystone's office personnel in Philadelphia receive my transmissions and relay our ETA to the agent in Jacksonville.

After handing off the paperwork, I return to my stateroom and flop down on the couch to watch the news from coastal stations in Louisiana and Alabama. I can feel the gentle motion of the ship as we meet the chop of the Gulf. The moderate east-northeast wind is crossing the deck just forward of the beam on our course of 127 degrees—on our way to the Straits of Florida. The seas are building slightly, yet the *Cherry Valley* has a nice, easy roll. I can hear the occasional shower of spray coming over the port bow as we shoulder into the oncoming waves. On the television screen, the Republicans, led by Newt Gingrich, gloat over their recent victory in the mid-term election this past week, ending decades of Democratic rule. A young doctor from Tennessee has routed a three-term Democrat for a senate seat; New York governor Mario Cuomo has lost his 12-year tenure to a man named Pataki, whom analysts, searching for a way to measure the new governor, are simply calling "plain."

I flip off the television—hearing nothing that will affect my life one way or the other—leave my stateroom, and take the 12 steps to the bridge to check on the weather a final time and to make sure Chris is settled down on watch. "Call me if you need me, Chris," I say as I leave the darkened bridge and head below, "but try not to need me." I drop onto my bed and escape into Clive Cussler's *Inca Gold,* a rollicking tale of high-seas adventure that details the exploits of legendary—albeit fictional—hero Dirk Pitt, who in this book is pursuing a 16th-century Spanish treasure. Tall, power-fully built, and with a razor wit even in the face of unimaginable danger, Pitt travels the world as a sort of *übermariner*, foiling evil plans to destroy the world and at the same time recovering valuable underwater treasure. Dirk Pitt is the James Bond of the sea.

Monday morning dawns clear and bright, a beautiful mid-November day on the Gulf of Mexico. As I swing my legs out of bed, I cross to the port-hole that faces forward and squint out at the lightening sky. It is just after 0630 as I shower and shave before heading to the bridge to check on our progress and find out what Carl has planned for the day. I scan the weather report that Steve Worden has posted on my door and notice that the trop-ical depression we had been watching has now developed into a tropical storm. Not great news to start the day, but at least it is predicted to head out into the North Atlantic, well away from us.

"Morning, Carl," I say as I cross the bridge for a cup of coffee, which Carl always has brewed by this time. On previous passages, sailing foreign across the Caribbean or South America, we would have stocked the bridge with some of the world's best coffee, straight from Colombia and Jamaica. Having sailed foreign for most of my seagoing career, I have built up a list of delicacies: fresh pasta and cannolis from Italy; fresh swordfish from Hon-duras and Venezuela; sole and halibut, and excellent port, from Portugal; and even barbecued dog in China. I would stock up on red table wine in Spain, the unlabeled bottles from a vintner outside Gibraltar; in the Caribbean I developed a taste for 25-year-old rum; in Russia it was chilled vodka. But here on the *Cherry Valley*, sailing coastwise, we are subject to the same supermarket inventory as other Americans, although I've secreted away a stash of Venezuelan coffee just for the bridge; nothing but Maxwell House in the galley. I drop in some cream and sugar, take a sip through the steam, and head for the chart table. Carl's 0700 position has us just short of halfway across the Gulf about 240 miles northwest of Dry Tortugas. I settle into the chair, cocking my head to one side to avoid the direct rays of the sun, and remember an old joke about the blessedness of this chair.

A ship's chief mate and second mate, both native New Englanders, are on the bridge of a ship at sea, discussing the various merits of insulation material for winter jackets. Each insists that he knows best.

"I'm partial to goose down," the chief mate says. "It's fluffy; it's warm . . . it feels good."

"No way," the second mate responds, shaking his head. "These new modern fibers, these spun plastics, they're much warmer than anything a goose can produce."

The ship's captain, a big, fat Southerner, a man of few words who rarely mingles with his crew, is sitting in the captain's chair staring through the bridge windows. "You boys don't know shit," he drawls. "Naugahyde. That's the warmest material there is."

There's a pause as the mates look at each other, not daring to challenge the captain and point out their natural, native advantage to knowing more than he about the cold. Finally, the chief mate speaks: "Naugahyde, captain?"

"Yep," he says. "When I haul my ass out of this chair at night it's nice and warm. When I get up here again in the morning it ain't cooled a bit."

"So what's new in the wide, wide world of shipping, Carl?" I ask after another sip of coffee.

"All quiet, Captain," Carl answers, saying the word "captain" in full instead of clipping it to "Cap" or "Cap'n." If we were alone, he'd call me Skip, yet on the bridge, we maintain formalities. Carl and I fall into the easy talk of the ship and what will happen for the day. We look out over the deck and absorb the beauty of a sunrise at sea.

I leave the bridge before the change of the watch at 0745 with another cup of coffee and head back to my office to start getting the never-ending paperwork ready for the next port. I must prepare a draw list for the crew in case anyone wants a cash advance; I need to telex the stores list. I can hear the door to the bridge open and close several times, and I can hear Steve start to move around in the radio shack, so I know it's getting close to 0800. Time to head down for breakfast.

I take the three flights of stairs down to the main deck quickly, knowing just how much force each of the heavy fire doors requires to open so I don't slam the door on the bulkhead. It might be approaching 0800 and the beginning of the day, but with a rotating watch schedule someone is almost always asleep on either the officers' or crew deck. Exiting the stairwell on the main deck I see the bosun standing outside the crew mess giving the day workers and the off-watch ABs who want to work overtime their morning assignments.

"Morning, Junior," I call to the bosun as I head past them to the officers' mess. As I swing the door open and step over the threshold and into the mess, I see Jim Kuijper, the second mate, and Ron Spencer, the second engineer, sitting at one table, quietly finishing their breakfasts before heading out to start their overtime work for the day. For the extra cash, just about everyone works twelve hours a day onboard—eight hours of watch and four hours of overtime.

"Hi, Cap!" Paul Donnelly, the bear-like first assistant engineer, bellows between forkfuls of bacon and eggs from where he sits at the table. Carl, collecting himself a whopping plate of eggs, bacon, and potatoes at the galley counter, moves to join Paul and Tim Croke, the chief, at the table. After you've been aboard ships for long enough you can tell the day of the week just by looking at the menu. I look over the menu and can see by the selections it is Sunday: beef and vegetable soup (leftover steak from Saturday) and roast turkey for dinner.

I order up a plate of breakfast and move to join the others at the captain's table. As usual when Paul is at the table, the conversation is about sports, the latest ball game in particular. Paul, a Boston native and former professional weightlifter, is a dedicated sports fanatic who follows all teams. His beloved Patriots are suffering shamefully in last place, but he is undaunted.

He asks if we will be by the Keys later—close enough to receive a signal from shore to watch today's afternoon game, the Patriots taking on the first-place Minnesota Vikings.

"I don't think we'll be in range yet," I reply. "We won't make the turn around Tortugas until about 2100. You might get lucky though, or, better yet, you could crank her up to warp speed, and we'll definitely get there in time to see the game."

The conversation moves from sports to home to ship and work—and back again before breakfast is finished and we're all spilling out of the mess area, the engineers going below to the engineroom and Carl and me going out on deck for a survey of how work is progressing. Since welding work cannot be performed on an oil tanker in port, the engineers are anxious to start on a welding project in the engineroom. Jim and Ron head to the engineroom to check the area for vapors and combustible materials before I give permission to start the hot work. Both the captain and chief need to review and sign a release before any hot work can begin; numerous engineers have been blown to bits for a lack of a sniff test that checks a confined space for explosive vapors.

Each evening, weather permitting, I try and walk a couple miles around the deck of the *Cherry Valley*, up one side to the bow and then down the other to the stern, six laps to the mile. I like this ritual because it is a chance to inspect the condition of the ship while I get a little exercise. I check on progress of work being done and make sure that gear has been put away and the ship is secure for the night. I also look out at the water and up at the sky; it's a chance to breathe fresh air and experience firsthand the weather conditions that are affecting the ship.

This evening, as I emerge from the watertight door on the starboard side of the superstructure, I don't plan to reach the bow because of deteriorating conditions on deck. Steve Worden, the radio officer, has just handed me a weather report indicating that the small unnamed storm I'd been keeping an eye on is now called Tropical Storm Gordon—and it is heading our way, having taken a hard left off the eastern tip of Cuba and started barreling northwest down the Old Bahama Channel. The barometer has dropped from about 1018 millibars in the afternoon to 1014 just before dinnertime. The wind is blowing at Force 5 now—a near gale—and the seas are building. I walk to the midship deckhouse, glance forward at the spray-covered deck, and decide I don't need a full dunking. The deck crew stowed the maintenance equipment a few hours earlier as the spray started sweeping the deck, and I make a final check to see that everything is well secured.

Even before I get out of bed to look out the porthole the next morning, I know we're closing on the storm. I can feel the ship heave in the heavy seas, and on the bridge the ABs are having to clear the windows of salt spray every 15 minutes. The surface of the sea is streaked with white foam from the waves that are starting to break. For the 0700 entry in the log, Carl has noted the conditions as Force 7, just under a gale, and that the barometer is down to 1009.4. We have made the turn around Dry Tortugas and are 20 miles south of Key West, getting a boost from the Gulf Stream but starting to slam seas that are opposing the wind. The course of the ship through the waves is punctuated by explosions of white spray that envelop the bow and reach well over 100 feet in the air.

"Pretty ugly this morning, eh, Carl?"

"Yeah, it's gotten worse since we made the turn at five," Carl answers.

"Make sure the main deck doors are secured and it is posted that no one goes out on deck," I say. I ask Carl to adjust our course to port keep us inside the main axis of the Gulf Stream to avoid the biggest seas. Our forecast is calling for 15- to 25-foot seas with higher waves in the center of the Gulf Stream, an area I'd just as soon avoid.

Below, in the officer's mess, Paul Donnelly is already seated and vigorously tucking into a mountain of food. "Crushed those bastards yesterday, Cap!" He is grinning at me from across the breakfast table, clutching his fork like a weapon and describing in detail how his beloved Patriots inexplicably routed the Vikings, 26 to 20. "Bledsoe, man, he tossed a sweet one to Turner in overtime." From his description I can tell he must have been listening intently to sports radio early this morning.

"We might get a beating ourselves before too long, Paul, if this weather keeps up," I answer, making for the galley to order up some breakfast.

"As long as we get a signal tonight, that's all that matters," Paul responds, turning back to his plate. Monday Night Football will be featuring a showdown between Pittsburgh and the Buffalo Bills, a team Paul loathes.

After breakfast I head back for the bridge and open the door in time to hear the last of a Coast Guard Pan-Pan broadcast on the VHF radio, describing the position of a ship in distress. A small Belizean freighter is taking on water and the Coast Guard is already planning an airlift evacuation of the crew. Chris has plotted the position on the chart, some 45 miles ahead of us and not far from our trackline. He tells me that another ship, the *Star Florida,* is already on scene to assist the crew if the airlift fails or another form of evacuation is necessary. For everyone's sake, including the crew of the *Star Florida* who would have to launch a lifeboat in these seas if a helo can't do the job, I hope the Coast Guard air crew can manage a swift rescue.

CHAPTER 8

SMALL VESSELS IN
A BIG OCEAN

November 14, 1994

By 0900 on November 14, a Coast Guard HH-65 helicopter was circling over the listing *Jeano Express,* its side door open, a rescue swimmer perched in the doorway. Twenty-four-year-old Brian Farmer was clipped into the winch, waiting while the crew, shouting into their headsets, discussed the two choices that confronted them. Should Farmer be lowered onto the steeply angled deck that was awash in breaking seas? Or should he be dropped into the water and swim to the ship? Each had its risks. If he were lowered to the deck, he risked being slammed against the steel deck or superstructure while dangling from the wire; if he dropped into the sea, he would be forced to swim through breaking seas to the hull and climb his way to the wheelhouse as thousands of tons of water pounded him against the wreck.

Farmer opted to be lowered to the ship, despite the fact that the helo would need to hover in the 50- to 60-knot winds as the dead ship heaved in the 25-foot seas, its masts swinging wildly with every roll. He double-checked his clips as the pilot nosed the helo closer to the deck, avoiding the masts as they swung through the air like the blades of a windmill, waiting for Farmer's thumbs-up. With the aircraft in position, some 40 feet above the waves and just 100 feet to the side of the ship, Farmer swung out and, the winch whirring as cable spun off the spool, was swiftly lowered to the slanting deck, awash in seas and spray made all the worse by the wash from the helo's rotors. Once his feet hit the steel, he was blinded by the rain and spray from the seas, blowing horizontally in the tumultuous winds.

Working his way aft, hand-over-hand past the tattered hatch covers to the watertight door on the ship's port side, Farmer found the crew of nine in the wheelhouse, wedged into various corners on the bridge; a dog, a small, nondescript mutt of the kind that seem to live in the streets of every Caribbean city, was cowering at the feet of the ship's master.

"Okay!" he yelled, his voice barely audible above the shriek of the wind, the spatter of the spray against the windows, the smashing of the waves against the hull and the roar of the helicopter's rotors. "We're going to go for it—one at a time. We're going to jump into the water and swim to the basket. I will help each of you in, and then you'll be lifted to the helo."

Farmer was met by blank, frightened faces. No one moved. After several minutes of bullying and cajoling, pantomiming of some of the more technical explanations for the crew whose English skills were limited, he succeeded in convincing the first six of the crew to go. Farmer jumped into the waves with each, opened the basket hatch, and clipped them in before giving his thumbs up to the hoist operator peering out from the doorway above. The dog went in the lap of the sixth person, its legs splayed crazily in all directions. At this point the helo, running low on fuel and having reached its payload capacity, headed back to the Air Station at Marathon Key. Farmer, exhausted and battered from repeated boarding and reboarding of the wreck, was left behind with the three remaining crewmembers, including the captain. As the helo retracted its wire and careered north, he swam back to the ship and crawled aboard, and once again worked his way into the wheelhouse to catch his breath. To the questioning eyes of his new shipmates, Farmer formed an okay sign with his fingers. "They'll be back," he said. "They'll be back soon."

But after landing at Marathon the Coast Guard ground crew noticed a problem with the aircraft's engine. The helo could not return. Because of a prudent watch officer's interest in redundancy, the crew of a Navy helo, K709, on the ground at Naval Air Station Key West, had been asked to stand by in the event that they were needed. Within minutes the Navy helo was in flight, covering the 30-odd miles to the drifting hulk in less than half an hour. Hovering over the listing wreck, still swaying in the beam seas and being battered by the waves, the helo crew lowered their basket. Farmer was ready, calling for the final three crew to prepare to be lifted. With the last of his strength, Farmer assisted the men one at a time until only he remained on deck, clinging to the rail of the doomed ship. Without a backward glance, Farmer scrambled into the basket as it dropped and was lifted to safety, the ship left adrift.

"I was all alone in those unbelievable conditions. My gear was all ripped up and my body was bruised and battered. All I wanted was to get out. I was totally shot. There was nothing left," Farmer said later.

Commercial salvors, professionals skilled in the art of rescuing vessels in distress and in these days minimizing the risk of pollution, didn't bother with the wreck; it was not valuable enough. To a commercial salvor, the ship was essentially worthless, certainly not attractive enough to risk the lives of a crew of highly skilled salvors in the middle of a tropical storm. The owner's representative and agent in Miami, Jean Joseph, had made several gratuitous calls to local salvors in an attempt to save the ship, reporting back to the Coast Guard that no one would respond until after the storm had passed, another day or two, maybe more. They knew as well as anyone that the abandoned vessel would long since have sunk or be aground, its bottom torn open on the jagged coral reefs of the Keys.

That evening, lacking further recourse, Joseph signed a boilerplate government form, signing over the rights to the ship to the Coast Guard. It read in part, "Jean Joseph, owner's rep. on behalf of owner is apprised of condition and location of M/V *Jeano Express,* and gives permission for the U.S. Coast Guard to intervene on the high seas and dispose of vsl. prior to entering U.S. terrtorial [sic] seas."

Jeano Express was 22 miles from Tennessee Reef, drifting to the northwest at 2.5 knots. The crew of a Coast Guard aircraft would keep track of *Jeano Express* to be sure it sank before threatening the reefs of the Florida Marine Sanctuary.

"I can't believe they told us to keep going!" Terry Perez shouted to no one in particular. "Those people don't know what the *hell* is going on out here. All cozy and safe in their houses." Aboard the tug *J. A. Orgeron,* Perez was the only one who was articulating the difficulty of their circumstances. The four other crewmembers were gathered in the tug's pilothouse, wedged in corners or gripping the overhead handrail to keep from being pitched to the deck. As the *Orgeron* heaved, crashing into troughs and rolling with a snapping motion, they all wedged themselves deeper into their corners or tightened their grips. But none of the others spoke, preferring to endure their discomfort in grim silence. A few minutes before, at 0800, the tug's engineer, Chris Gisclair had been on watch in the engineroom when he heard what he described to Wiles as a "loud grinding" that seemed to be coming from the port clutch. He called Wiles in the wheelhouse as he was shutting down the engine. They had had problems with this clutch in the past, and Gisclair didn't want to risk stripping the gears, leaving the port engine useless. After consulting with Wiles, checking the gears through the inspection plate and not finding a problem, Gisclair decided to restart the port engine. No sooner was the engine firing, however, than the No. 1 cylinder began making a hellacious banging and rattling. He lunged for the kill switch—but not before something blew a hole in the exhaust flex coupling, a length of thin steel duct that takes the exhaust gases from the engine and runs it to the turbo to increase the horsepower of the engine. Smoky exhaust began leaking into the engineroom.

Gisclair quickly realized that the mechanical difficulties developing aboard the *Orgeron* were surpassing his ability to handle the current conditions. Monitoring temperatures and changing filters and even injectors was one thing, but the problems developing in the innards of the port engine were fast becoming complicated. Gisclair reported to Wiles that he suspected the engine had a dropped valve in the No. 1 cylinder, and the two men agreed to place a call to Jerry Danos, Montco's port engineer, who managed the mechanical needs of the fleet. Gisclair spent the morning troubleshooting the engine's problems, following Danos's suggestions as carefully as possible.

The starboard engine, although running a little hot because of the heavy seas and therefore being operated at slightly reduced rpm, was still functioning normally. The tug's speed, however, had suffered. Under only one engine and attempting to push through seas that ranged from 18 to 22 feet high and against winds that were now blowing at more than 40 knots, the tug's forward progress was slowed to about 1.5 knots. They were just north of St. Lucie Inlet, with Port Canaveral only 70 miles away, less than 10 hours in normal circumstances. But they could not hope to reach port in this weather and in this condition. The closest port, Fort Pierce, just 15 miles away to the west, was not a viable refuge, at least not in this weather and not if they were to avoid grounding the barge on the approach through the narrow inlet. The crew was now taking a few minutes to regroup and strategize about how best to cope with the storm and their mounting problems.

Just let me get through this, Perez thought, and I won't go to sea anymore. The last time Perez rode out a storm—a hurricane that sacked the Gulf of Mexico and caught much of the oil industry vessels by surprise—the supply vessel he was aboard was overtaken by the storm while serving a rig more than 100 miles offshore. Meanwhile, fearing for her son's life, Perez's mother stomped into the dispatch office in a Louisiana bayou town and cornered the dispatcher, making violent threats on his life if the company did not return her son safely to shore.

"Where is he?" she had screamed. "When is he getting back?" She had browbeaten the poor dispatcher until he finally admitted that he had no idea whether the crew of the ship were safe or not since they were no longer in communication. The dispatcher would later be relieved to learn, if only for his own protection against the wrath of this commanding elderly woman, that the vessel had had its antenna shorn from the pilothouse in the storm, and was unable to communicate as it slowly made progress back to port, where it arrived safely the next day.

"We'll be all right," Wiles finally said. "Chris, why don't you and Bob see about isolating that cylinder and getting her going again. Terry, you've been up all night. Why don't you try and get some sleep." At his command, Reahard and Gisclair disappeared down the main companionway, while Perez, quiet for the moment, looked away—at the gray waves rushing the tug's bow.

Wiles slipped out of the chair and, glancing at the numbers on the GPS and picking up a pair of dividers, worked out a quick fix on the chart. He was tense and tired, the creases on his face exaggerated due to a lack of sleep. Back in the captain's chair he gripped both armrests and braced his legs stiffly against the dash of the console. It had been a long night with little sleep, far worse than he had expected when he hung up the radio's mike following his conversation with Lee Orgeron the night before about pulling into Miami to avoid the storm. Now, the storm was upon them, thrashing the tug repeatedly with mountainous waves. Although they had continued to make good time during the night, their speed had progressively slowed in the worsening conditions until the port engine had failed.

A dropped valve in the engine could mean any number of mechanical failures within the particular cylinder. The injector might be clogged with debris and the cylinder starved of fuel. Or the valve stuck open, flooding the cylinder with raw unburned fuel, in which case the fuel would be pumped into the cylinder unburned and out into the exhaust manifold—and cause a fire in the stack. On the eight-cylinder engine there were still seven cylinders thrumming away in the block prior to Gisclair shutting it down, but running an already-hot engine with one cylinder down would only contribute to the problem later on, likely causing more cylinder failures. Within minutes, Gisclair and Reahard had begun troubleshooting the fuel system, beginning at the bunker tank and working their way through to the day tank and the numerous filters and fuel lines that led to the injector pump and the injector at the cylinder in question. By the time they reached the cylinder, they hoped, they would have found a clue to the failure.

Fuel aboard the *Orgeron* was stored in several main tanks throughout the hull. Twice a day fuel would be transferred to the day tank for use by the main engines and the generators. As fuel was transferred to the day tank it passed through a sock filter to catch large pieces of debris or sludge. From the day tank the fuel passed through a set of dual Racors, cylindrical filters about the size of a two-liter bottle of soda, and a secondary filter, to catch any debris or water before getting to the engines. Nothing can stop an engine quicker than dirty fuel, which is why checking the filters is one of the most important duties of the engineer on watch, especially in rough weather. When Gisclair checked the sock filter it looked about normal, but when he bled off the day tank the fuel, instead of being a translucent honey-brown, was black and sludgy. The Racor filters are equipped with gauges that measure the difference between the inlet and outlet pressure to indicate if they are clean or dirty, and these both pegged in the red—dirty—very quickly. When the gauge indicated that a filter needed to be changed, a valve was swung closed to isolate one filter, allowing the engine to continue running, so the dirty filter could be changed. Under normal circumstances, filters generally last a day and a half or two days, and Gisclair had already changed them twice during the day. The Racors appeared to be doing their job because the secondary filters were staying clean.

Each time a filter is changed, though, there is a chance that air will get into the fuel lines, which could shut down any number of cylinders. Gisclair and Reahard were as careful as they could be, considering the circumstances, to maintain the fuel level in the filter reservoirs to prevent an airlock. But in the engineroom of a pitching and rolling tug, its floor slippery with diesel fuel, each badly fatigued man, able to work with only one hand—the other dedicated to keeping themselves from flying across the engine space—could be excused for such an error.

If sediment in the bottom of the tanks had been stirred up—a likely scenario given the nature of the seas—Gisclair and Reahard could only hope to maintain a clean flow of fuel through to the 16 main engine injectors by constantly changing filters—all the while hoping not to introduce air into the system. They could isolate a cylinder and replace a clogged injector, a slender nozzle, weighing about five pounds, that delivers atomized fuel to the cylinder in precise amounts. To change one requires the use of a few basic hand tools and about 30 minutes, but if the cylinders were failing as a result of sediment running through the fuel lines, choking the filters, of which their supply was limited, and clogging the injectors and injector pumps, their race to stay ahead of the problem would already be doomed if they couldn't keep the fuel clean.

Throughout the day Gisclair and Reahard continued to change the fuel filters and pull and clean all eight injectors on the port engine. Wiles visited the engineroom only once, to see about the feasibility of changing the head on the No. 1 cylinder. The head, or the top of the cylinder, weighs about 400 pounds and has to be lifted off using a set of chain falls, which can be rigged above the engine—a relatively easy job for a skilled engineer when the tug is alongside the dock. But it is next to impossible to expect anyone to perform such a task in the middle of a storm at sea, and Wiles quickly decided the risk to his crew was too great. Wiles returned to the pilothouse, carefully noting in the log the hourly position. He kept the *Orgeron* limping along on one engine, providing a small measure of resistance, headway even, against the rushing seas—waiting for the weather to break.

CHAPTER 9

HEAVY WEATHER

November 14, 1994

As the *Cherry Valley* approaches the scene of the *Jeano Express* rescue, we listen intently to the radio for updates on the *Express*'s condition and the evacuation. Partly, we can be accused of being radio voyeurs—it's a good story, after all—but we also listen to hear if they'll need our assistance. The *Cherry Valley* is not yet in the vicinity, still some 30 miles away, but we learn that the rest of the crew has just been taken off by the Navy helo, and a ship called the *Star Florida* has been asked to stand by a bit longer until the Coast Guard can drop a marker on the ship to track it. The *Star Florida* is soon released to continue her voyage, wherever that may lead. I'd been thinking that had we been a few hours farther along, it might have been us assisting in the rescue. I'm glad they are safe, and it has been interesting to hear the saga unfold to a happy ending. Even the dog is safe.

The Coast Guard continues to put out radio advisories to mariners, Pan-Pan announcements to watch out for the abandoned vessel. At 0910 I ask Chris to have the engineers reduce the rpm from 72 to 65 to help the ship ride easier. Contrary to popular perception that ships have only one speed, full ahead—it's not at all like the movie command "full speed ahead" as the cinematic ship clears the harbor and heads to sea—we would often adjust our speed to keep the vessel from pounding in big seas.

On my morning tour of the ship I am limited to a walk through the accommodation spaces, the engineroom, and the upper decks of the house. Below, in the engineroom, I climb down two stories to the console area and speak briefly with Tom Campbell, the third engineer, asking what projects are in the works. I like to stay in personal contact with the engineers and the engineroom itself—it is, after all, the driving force of the ship—to see and hear about ongoing tasks. If a cargo pump or a feed pump is being overhauled, for example, I won't be surprised with a request by the engineers for a certain part when we reach port. Recently the engineers had completed a modification to the engineroom's catwalk system that gave the crew access to the steering gear without going on deck. They had cut through a bulkhead and installed a watertight door through which we could now pass for an inspection of the steering gear. I pass through the shaft alley and climb the catwalk that allows me to stand directly over the rotating shaft, and then climb over the boilers to the inert gas house. From there I can emerge through a watertight door on the stern and climb a ladder to the stack deck and return to the bridge after having a look around the deck in the lee of the superstructure.

At 1200 we are passing Tennessee Reef and are only about four miles north of the *Jeano Express*'s last reported position, but we can't locate the stricken ship, visually or by radar, probably because the vessel, its gray hull already lying low in the water, is camouflaged by the large waves. There is also a good chance that it has already gone down, but I haven't heard this confirmed. On the radar I can see some dense squalls passing, some with torrential rain that reduces our visibility as they move over the ship. And then, just as quickly, there are flashes of brilliant sunshine that light up the glistening deck for a few minutes. The ship is still pounding. My unofficial policy is that if we slam into a sea once it is okay, the result of an isolated wave, but if we get pounded two or three times in quick succession it is time to drop the rpm. As I am standing on the bridge before lunch, the ship punches through a set of waves that sends a series of shockwaves back to the superstructure. I can see the bow slam, watch the spray burst, then see a quiver work its way aft until a split second later the whole house lurches, forcing me to brace myself at the bridge windows. A ship is meant to flex, to bend and twist in the seas, but at a certain point the dynamic energy of repeated slamming can start to crack the longitudinals and stringers, structural members that help form the backbone of the ship. I have Jim take another 5 rpm off just after noon.

Our speed is down to around 10 knots, and in the noon message I type to Keystone, Enjet, the charterers for the voyage, and the agent in Jacksonville, I change our ETA at the pilot station at the mouth of the St. John's River from 1200 tomorrow to 1800. I figure we will be slowed down for a while but as we move away from the storm we will likely be able to pick up our speed again. I hadn't counted on the big high-pressure system over the Carolinas to interact with Gordon and build the wind and seas, but the National Hurricane Center was obviously right—we are in the storm's outer edge and getting slammed by both systems. We will still be in Jax tomorrow—and at a relatively decent hour of the day.

With the rpm reduced, the ride isn't too bad as I duck below for lunch. It could get really uncomfortable if the storm moves rapidly north from Key West, giving us easterly winds that will deliver the seas right on the beam. The *Cherry Valley* is long and narrow and likes to roll. Even with bilge keels, 30- to 35-degree rolls are not uncommon in a big beam sea. On a tanker with all the weight down low it can be a very fast roll, almost a snapping motion, and it's hard to hang on at times. Everything on a ship has a place to be stowed, and most objects like chairs and tables and lamps are tied or bolted in place to prevent them from coming adrift. Any loose files or papers tend to seek the lowest spot in a storm, and it is not uncommon to see a mass of paper moving eerily back and forth across the deck with the roll of the ship, as though reminding me of their need to be processed. I once saw a 30-pound IBM Selectric typewriter launch off a desk during a particularly bad roll, fly 10 feet, and crash into the opposite bulkhead. Other than a bent carriage return, it survived. A rolling ship can make simple tasks like eating a meal a challenge as well. If you want soup, you'll manage about four tablespoons in a bowl so it won't slop out over the edge. Everything else wants to side across the plate and roll onto the table. Fiddle bars are set up on the tables to try and prevent things from hitting the deck, and tablecloths are moistened to provide traction for the bottoms of dishes.

A life at sea doesn't come with immunity to the ill effects of seasickness. A good number of the crew tend to wear the tell-tale greenish look when the weather kicks up. I feel especially bad for the engineroom crew, whose hot and humid workplace, with no view of the horizon, lends itself to seasickness. Although the roll of the ship tends to be lessened in the engineroom because it's so low in the ship, I don't enjoy the smells of hot fuel or other chemicals during rough weather.

Sleeping is another basic need that is fleeting in rough weather, especially when the ship is in the grips of a beam sea. The bunks on the ship are all arranged fore-and-aft, so a beam sea will try to roll you out of bed. As a countermeasure most people will jam a survival suit, which is stored in each cabin in a duffel bag, under the outside edge of the mattress to make a kind of hot dog bun. Not very comfortable, but it keeps you from rolling onto the deck. Some will go as far as rigging hammocks to get a decent night's sleep.

I grab a nap in the afternoon, anticipating a lack of sleep during the coming night, especially if we have the seas on the beam as we parallel the Florida coast. On TV the evening news programs show scenes of the wind-blown, sodden streets of South Florida, including satellite graphics that illustrate the patches of circular cloud hovering over the Keys. It is almost stationary over Key West, not changing in form. We are definitely seeing more wind and seas on the outer edge of the storm, as predicted, than they are getting at Key West, near the center.

After dinner I catch up with Dirk Pitt's adventures off Central America, then climb to the bridge to watch the lights on the coast of Florida about nine miles away. The cloud deck is low, and the lights reflect off the base of the clouds like a well-lit ceiling. There is no rain, so the visibility around the ship is good.

I leave night orders for the mates, telling them to "stay on the line" until we are abeam of Jupiter Inlet and then to come left to stay inside the Stream, which is about seven miles offshore, if we start rolling too heavily. I instruct the mates to adjust our speed to ensure arrival at Jacksonville on time. I ask for Carl to call me at 0600 with our speed and ETA, and I sign my name at the bottom and head for the rack.

CHAPTER 10

SWISS CHEESE

November 14, 1994

If conditions aboard the *J. A. Orgeron* could be said to have been deteriorating slowly since the vessel first encountered Tropical Storm Gordon, several days later the bad news began accelerating. By 2000 on Monday evening, November 14, the crew's troubles began to mount swiftly, building on themselves in a way that must have felt to the crew as though this bad luck had been premeditated by an unseen force. It had not taken long for Gisclair and Wiles to agree that morning that they could not reasonably change the head on the failed cylinder of the port engine. They had shut the port engine down and had been running the starboard engine alone, hoping that the storm would blow itself out. Darkness had fallen, and the weather reports were unchanged; the storm would continue to drop heavy rain and draw air into its center from hundreds of miles away, generating winds in excess of 40 knots.

During the course of the day, Gisclair continued to monitor the day tank, every hour bleeding off fuel from the tank's bottom to remove some of the sludge. Since the feed for the engines was through a valve a foot above the bottom of the tank, he hoped he could drain out enough of the silted fuel to get clean fuel to the engines.

At 2000 Gisclair reported to Wiles that the starboard engine's No. 5 and 6 cylinders were no longer firing. Wiles immediately slowed the engine to clutch speed as Gisclair and Perez returned to the stifling heat of the engineroom, which was another 30 degrees warmer and even stuffier than normal because several vents had been secured against the crashing waves. After double-checking the fuel filters and bleeding off a little more sludge, he restarted the port engine. Instead of one cylinder banging, he now heard that distinct sound coming from two cylinders. With no options left they kept the engine running, praying it would hold out while they worked on the starboard engine. Out of 16 cylinders, between the two engines they were down to 11, and no one could figure out why. They repeated their troubleshooting efforts, this time on the starboard engine, locating the damaged cylinders and changing the injectors in hopes of recovering some lost power. None of this seemed to have an effect.

Back in the wheelhouse Wiles quickly called Montco by SSB through station WLO in New Orleans and kept an open line with Lee Orgeron, who was camped out in his office in Golden Meadow, Louisiana.

With both engines at idle, firing on a combined 11 cylinders, the *Orgeron* was able to maintain its position. As long as nothing else went wrong they would just ride out the storm and continue to attempt repairs.

If Gisclair had changed the filters and changed the injector and fuel was still restricted, what was preventing the engine from running at full power? The *J. A. Orgeron*'s fuel injector pumps—devices that are the most complex mechanical contraptions at work on ships today, more finely manufactured and tuned than a Rolex watch—were overdue for an overhaul. Coupled with the fuel sediment problem, events soon unfolded into what marine accident investigators refer to as the contributing factors to ultimate failure.

Investigators working for government agencies like the Coast Guard and, in serious accidents, the National Transportation Safety Board, as well as private ship classification societies, are fond of discussing an event's contributing factors. Taken singly, these factors are innocuous, but as they combine with other like events they arrange themselves in a manner that leads to a major failure. A ship loses power and drifts toward a reef; a loose connection on an electrical panel causes a fire. These events are likened to holes in slices of Swiss cheese. Holes in the cheese are contributing factors, representing weaknesses in the safety system. Most of the time they don't line up. A pilot anticipated a potential loss of power and had asked that the anchor be ready to drop in case of engine failure and then ordered the anchor dropped in time to avoid grounding; a vigilant engineer making his safety rounds noticed the loose screw. Generally speaking, no one hole passes entirely through the block of cheese from one end to another. But when the holes are lined up in just the right (or wrong) way, accidents will happen; the error chain will connect. The drifting ship goes aground and spills its cargo; the fire overwhelms the engineroom and kills an engineer.

For the crew of the tug *J. A. Orgeron,* the holes in the Swiss cheese were beginning to line up.

After Gisclair and Perez left the wheelhouse, Wiles, left alone, swung out of the chair and turned aft to the chart table. Placing a pair of dividers at a point indicated by the GPS, he stepped off the distance to Cape Canaveral. "Only 63 miles to go," he thought to himself. "We'll make it when this weather lays down a bit. Maybe we can limp our way through the storm long enough and reach port when the seas settle down." He picked up a pen and hunched over the weather log: "11–14–94, 20:00, Seas increasing—barge OK. Lost two cylinders on starboard main—restarted port—two cylinders down on it. [Winds]: NE 45–55, Higher gusts; [Seas] 18' to 25'; [Speed]: 1.2 knots." And in the "remarks" column, "Holding position." Being prudent and aware of how quickly things can go wrong, Wiles reached for the VHF, set to Channel 16, and hailed the Coast Guard, reporting the size of his vessel and what he was towing, the number of crew on board, and the situation he was faced with. He wasn't asking for help, just seeking assurance that someone else was out there if something else happened.

Between 2030 and 2300 the tug held position at idle speed, barely making headway.

Bill Knodle, NASA's Michoud facility harbormaster, arrived at Cape Canaveral on the afternoon of November 13, setting up in a nearby hotel, ready to ride the barge up the Indian River to Kennedy Space Center. He would check the lashings and accelerometers to be sure there had been no damage during the trip. And he'd make sure that the fuel tank would be ready for immediate removal when the barge docked. Knodle knew the weather had been slowing the tug but still expected them to arrive on the morning of the 15th, and then make the trip upriver that day or the next, depending on the sea conditions at the river bar. After taking a post-dinner walk, Knodle returned to his hotel room shortly after 2200 Monday evening to find several messages waiting for him. It was a good thing he had taken a walk to settle his stomach, he would say later, because what he heard made him clamp his jaw and utter his most profane oath, "Confound it!"

The first call was from Richard Babcock, a retired NASA employee living in Florida whose job it had been to deal with the transportation of the fuel cell. Babcock had been called by an acquaintance at the Coast Guard at Fort Pierce after they heard that the *Orgeron* was towing the *Poseidon*. The Coast Guard knew he had been involved with the barge but didn't know he had retired. Babcock, no doubt relieved that he was now retired, relayed the problems that the tug was having in his message to Knodle. Knodle's second message was from Bill Cantillon of Yowell International, the prime contractor for towing the barges, alerting him of the *Orgeron*'s problems. "We're having some trouble with this storm," Cantillon added. Cantillon was already trying to find another tug to go out and assist the *Orgeron* but had not gotten any replies yet.

Wiles had been to sea on tugboats and offshore supply vessels in the Gulf of Mexico for years and had weathered hurricanes before. On this evening he no doubt recalled in vivid detail the time he had been straining his offshore supply vessel against the wind and seas—in 1985 during Hurricane Juan, when 75- to 80-knot winds had ripped the tops off waves and turned the surface of the Gulf into a froth of driving spray—to rescue the trapped crew of an oil rig. He had skillfully maneuvered the vessel close to the rig only to realize that no matter how close and how carefully he brought the ship to the rig, buffeted as it was by the pounding seas, no man could survive the dash to the heaving deck of the makeshift rescue vessel without being swept into the sea, possibly being crushed in the process. Finally, under repeated orders from the company, he had turned back, and the crew was left to wait out the storm on the shaking rig. A seaman like Wiles had a near religious respect for one of the sea's accepted codes: a quid pro quo that obligated the offering of aid, if at all possible. It is a brotherhood of people at sea. To admit that there was nothing more to be done, for a seaman like Wiles, was to admit a measure of defeat, that conditions had become so extreme that no amount of skill could solve the problem at hand. During that storm Wiles had not had engine problems to contend with.

Wiles was concerned, but, as was his manner, not overly so. It had been unpleasant for the last two days, what with the weather-induced sleeplessness and the engine problems, to say nothing of meals consisting of cold cuts and coffee. So far, the crew had remained civil to each other. They had the professional and easygoing manner of a crew that has worked together for a long time. They had, indeed, for the most part worked this vessel together on and off for the past year, running between Miami and Ponce, Puerto Rico, towing a container barge.

The tug, to a certain point, could likely handle the weather—at least stay afloat if the situation didn't worsen. But what about the cargo on the barge? Wiles was accustomed to hauling containers. He had never towed something as complex and sensitive as an external fuel tank for NASA's space shuttle, and therefore lacked the experience to know what the cargo's limits might be. The way they were riding that night Wiles likely wondered how close they were getting to that one-G limit stipulated by Bill Knodle and Ernie Graham back at the Michoud facility. They hadn't told him what the fuel cell was worth, but you don't put accelerometers on cheap cargoes.

A few minutes later Chris Gisclair and Terry Perez returned from the engineroom and wedged themselves back into positions of relative comfort, the settee and a corner of the cabin next to the chart table.

"We changed out the filters and injectors on the starboard cylinders, the No. 5 and 6. It might work for a while, but if we keep pumping that dirty fuel in there, I don't know how long she'll last," Gisclair reported to Wiles. "We'll keep changing the filters, keep bleeding the day tank, though."

Calls to port engineer Jerry Danos had proved fruitless. There was no magic solution to the myriad mechanical problems of the engines. The five men, their unshaven jaws and pale faces grim in the dull glow from the tug's instruments, had gathered in the pilothouse to regroup, strategize about their condition. The air in the small pilothouse was close, rank from the lack of fresh air and unwashed bodies.

"We'd better get life jackets on," Wiles finally said. "We don't know what's going to happen here."

Each man dropped below to their cabins to retrieve their life jackets, the bulky, Type 1 horse-collar variety that made their arms stand away from their sides. A few minutes later the men were all back in the pilothouse—fingering the straps on their life jackets. Each man realized the potential seriousness that the life jackets represented. But it was nearly 2300, so they were making it through the night, Wiles thought, even though they were not making much way against the storm.

A few minutes later the port tachometer dove—the gauge dropping to just 100 rpm. Gisclair leapt from the settee and scrambled down the three sets of stairs in one fluid motion, tumbling into the engineroom, where, once inside, a shrieking of metal chewing against metal greeted his ears, an ominous grinding racket that seemed to be coming from the port reduction gear. As he killed the engine, the grinding slowly subsided, leaving only the muted rumble of the starboard engine and the pounding of the water against the hull. He picked up a receiver mounted on a bulkhead, which rang Wiles in the pilothouse.

"We just lost reduction gear," he reported to Wiles. "There was this awful noise, a terrible grinding. So I shut her down."

Wiles hung up the phone, and turned to look at the GPS over the chart table: 0 knots. He scrawled a note in the log about the speed and engine situation and slumped back in his chair. On the bright side though, we are not going backwards, he thought, at least not yet. Backwards in these winds and seas meant drifting with the wind and waves, helpless, toward the beaches of Florida. Time to call the office again.

"If we start losing ground we can always drop the barge," Wiles said. "And we will be able to keep the tug off the beach." A quiet settled over the cramped wheelhouse as the crew thought about what might lie in store over the next few hours. The radio, its country music from a shore station sounding tinny and cheerless in the background, was barely heard above the howl of the wind outside and the groaning of the tug as it bucked through the waves.

"Fire! Fire in the engineroom!" came the voice of Gisclair from the bottom of the companionway stairs.

"What the fuck is going on?" Wiles yelled back, losing a bit of the cool that he was known and respected for. No need to hustle out the crew; they all were tumbling down the stairs as soon as the shout was heard.

Thick black smoke was belching out of the starboard stack and being sucked back in the aft door of the engineroom and a few of the remaining vents that had been left open. As the crew raced past the galley and through the watertight door into the upper level of the engineroom, they were choked by the billowing smoke. But through the acrid haze they could see that the exhaust for the starboard engine was glowing cherry red as it passed through the fidley (upper level of the engineroom) on its way to the stack.

"Kill the engine, Chris!" Wiles yelled from the fidley, knowing that it would leave them without power. As the engine died, quiet descended over the engineroom, just the quiet humming of the generator giving a small sign of life in the tug. There is nothing quite as unnatural as a quiet engineroom at sea. At least the generator was still running, Wiles thought.

After determining that the fire was limited to the exhaust stack, Wiles returned to the wheelhouse and glanced at the GPS and saw that he was now making more speed, only the direction was west—backwards. The tug and its tow were now adrift in the roiling seas not far from a lee shore. Captain Lanny Wiles then did what every mariner is loath to do: he reached for the radio mike from its bracket over his head and, speaking slowly and clearly, called for help: "United States Coast Guard, United States Coast Guard, the tug *J. A. Orgeron* on Channel 16."

The *J. A. Orgeron* and barge *Poseidon* were now drifting downwind at a rate of 1.5 knots and were six miles to windward of Bethel Shoal, a spur of shallow water jutting from the shore near Fort Pierce, Florida—an area of breaking seas they would likely glimpse, through the windows of the pilothouse, in the gray, pre-dawn light of the coming day. For Wiles and the crew of the *Orgeron* the holes in the Swiss cheese had just lined up.

CHAPTER 11

A CALL FOR HELP

November 15, 1994

Two short rings from the phone next to my bed wake me instantly. Looking at the clock I see it's a few minutes after one o'clock in the morning. "Captain," I say softly into the receiver.

"Captain? It's Jim on the bridge."

"Yeah, what's up?"

"Listen, I just got a distress call on the VHF from the Coast Guard station at Fort Pierce." He pauses briefly to let it register. "It's about a tug and barge with engine trouble, 40 miles north of us by Bethel Shoal. They asked us to render any assistance we can. And I told them where we were and when we could be up there."

"Okay. Where are we now?"

"Off Jupiter Inlet."

"Hang on; I'll be right up." I drop the receiver back in place and swing my legs out of my bunk. Like most people in the business of running ships, I have never had a hard time waking at odd hours and jumping into work. The ship operates 24 hours a day and has little regard for the setting sun. I turn on the reading light and stand up, steadying myself against the 15-degree roll. But the swell that should have decreased, actually feels larger than it was when I had fallen asleep just an hour before. Obviously the wind is still up, funneling into the big low-pressure system behind us and generating these big waves.

I look out the porthole. It's still a miserable night: wind, spray, and a big sea are rolling in from the northeast, slamming into the ship's starboard side. I can't see much. The glass is streaked with spray, but several decks down I can see waves coming over the rail, tumbling wildly across the deck in a clean sweep of solid green water and foam that rises in the wind and flies off into the darkness. Although I can't see it, I know the bow is plowing deep into the waves and sending streams of white water high into the air. I can feel the ship shudder each time it drives into a wave, the rhythm of any storm at sea. A tug with engine trouble, I think to myself as I turn from the window.

I don't envy them, that's for sure. I try to picture the crew attempting repairs to their engines while the tug is bouncing all over the place. If we are rolling and pitching like this, what would it be like on a tug? Not pleasant, I'm sure.

I pull on a pair of shorts, a T-shirt, and my Tevas and leave the darkness of my stateroom, squinting in the brightness of the hallway as I cross to the stairs. I take the 12 steps up to the next deck two at a time and enter the darkened bridge where my eyes adjust. Jim, the second mate, is standing over the radar on the port side, his face lit by the screen's green glow. I walk by Frank Dover, one of two able-bodied seamen, who is standing at the helm controls, his dark face barely visible in the dim red light of the gyro compass that shows our course is due north. Bracing himself on the console against the motion of the ship, looking forward through the bridge windows, he doesn't turn as I pass.

I hear the rush of wind and roar of the waves through the open door that leads to the port bridge wing. Outside, Alex Rivera, the other AB, is standing in the darkness in the lee of the bridge. As the designated lookout, he is assigned the role of looking for other ships, which he would report to Jim, who, one would hope, would already have tracked the vessel on radar and planned and, if needed, executed a way to avoid a close-quarters situation. On a dark night such as this the lookout is barely able to see the bow—let alone a ship ahead in the storm-tossed darkness. The bridge windows are speckled in salt spray; our only glimpse into the dark night is where the wipers have cleared the glass. The spaces are clear, dark holes through an otherwise milky set of windows.

I join Jim at the radar, gripping the sides of the console with both hands. The green outline of the coast is seven miles off our port side and with it starting to curve away from us I know that we have just passed Jupiter Inlet. Jim sways with the roll of the ship and starts filling me in on his conversation with the Coast Guard. He repeats the location of the tug, a few miles to the east of Bethel Shoal. I can picture ahead of us the spur of shallow water that juts into the Gulf Stream. It's a marked shoal, as shallow as 28 feet in parts. Our draft, the distance from our waterline to the lowest part of the keel, is 35 feet. That is, if we were afloat in a glassy sea. On this particular night, in 15- to 20-foot seas, it means that our keel might drop as much as 55 feet below the surface. Bethel Shoal is an area we want to stay well clear of. Not only is the water shallow here, but the waves are likely to be steep and breaking as they pile in from deep water. In other words, on a night like this Bethel Shoal is to be avoided by just about anybody—but especially by us, a fully loaded oil tanker.

"I told them we were a 688-foot tanker, and that we were northbound off Jupiter Inlet," Jim tells me. Despite our condition—the fact that we are a heavily laden oil tanker laboring along with our decks being swept repeatedly by breaking waves—he had not hesitated to respond to the call. Jim tells me that he had been listening to the chatter on the radio, the tense exchange of information between a crew in distress and a faceless, nameless Coast Guardsman somewhere in a fluorescent-lit, air-conditioned office in the city of Fort Pierce. Jim and the ABs had been scanning the radio, listening for anything, curious to hear if there were others out on that dark night. He was not, of course, expecting to overhear an exchange that would draw him in. There had been references to loss of power in the engines, maybe even an engine fire, Jim says, but he can't be sure since the tug crew was barely audible because of the range. And the Coast Guard had asked the tug crew about the barge, which apparently is carrying something for NASA. That's all he knows.

When he heard the call, Jim was not about to ignore someone in peril, at the mercy of the driving seas, even someone he did not know. He responded to the Coast Guard not with promises to save the day but to let them know that we were out here and headed in that direction and might be able to help.

But he had not presumed to command the fate of the *Cherry Valley* and had not hesitated to call me up to the bridge. We are still several hours away—and who knows what might happen between now and then—but if we do try and help and something goes wrong, the *Cherry Valley* could go aground and tear its bottom out on Bethel Shoal. Rescue or not, 10 million gallons of oil released a few miles upwind of some of Florida's busiest beaches will be a one-way ticket into the annals of maritime hell—in the best tradition of banished and shunned Exxon captain Joe Hazelwood.

Despite being the favorite whipping boy of environmentalists and self-righteous politicians, Captain Hazelwood is acknowledged by most people I know in this industry as one of the most skilled captains Exxon had at the time the *Valdez* went aground just five years earlier in Alaska. While the captain has the ultimate responsibility for his ship, Hazelwood was hung by Exxon, allowed to be perceived as a careless drunk who was an exception to Exxon's otherwise faultless operation of running supertankers.

Yet there were circumstances at work beyond Hazelwood's control aboard the *Exxon Valdez* that night. His third mate, the mate on watch during the grounding, was overworked and fatigued, an investigation found. And Exxon failed to react quickly and decisively following news of the spill. Is Hazelwood entirely responsible for all this? For spilling every gallon of oil and killing every animal?

In the years that followed, Hazelwood's life fell apart. His career ruined, his name is now perpetually linked with infamy and shame. Last I heard, Hazelwood was picking up trash on Alaska's beaches as part of his community service and earning his living as a teacher at a maritime academy.

As captains, we have the public trust to transport enormous volumes of oil safely from one port to another. Whether the treatment of Hazelwood following the spill was right or wrong, spilling oil is something every mariner dreads. And I am no exception, even if I am simply trying to reach out to a crew in danger in a drifting tugboat. I need to know my limits, especially since after the *Valdez* spill the Oil Pollution Act of 1990 has criminalized acts considered negligent by the Coast Guard, and prosecuted by the Justice Department.

We stare silently at the radar for a few moments before I speak up.

"You told them that we were fully loaded."

"Yeah, and that we were drawing 35 feet. But they just asked us to try and intercept the tug and render any assistance possible."

I don't say anything for a minute and think about those nebulous words. The Coast Guard is often making these announcements, which could refer to various events, people who have fallen overboard or vessels that are overdue, aground, or adrift, as in this case. The phrase "any assistance possible" is one that any mariner is familiar with; implicit in the Coast Guard's request is the understanding that mariners are required by law to offer aid to anyone in distress on the water. It is a law that is universally accepted. At sea everyone is at risk at any given time; we simply take turns being on the receiving end of trouble and hope that others will be available to help. This law is only binding to the point that you, your vessel and crew are put in danger. That's where the obligation ends. Given the conditions tonight, no one would fault us for passing by.

Looking at the radar screen I see sea clutter all around the ship, which indicates the tops of big waves tall enough to register on radar—not something you see in a flat sea. I grip the handles on the side of the radar tighter as the ship rolls to port and let out a sigh.

"What the fuck do they expect us to do?" I ask, and then, articulating the obvious, "We're a 688-foot loaded oil tanker drawing 35 feet, and there's a tropical storm crawling up our ass."

Jim stays quiet, which is his way, knowing that I do not expect an answer.

"Did they tell you anything else about the condition of the tug and its crew?"

"Not really. They just said they had a barge in tow and that they are having engine trouble. It wasn't a Mayday call, just a Pan-Pan. They said they weren't in immediate danger. They just wanted us to proceed to their location and stand by."

"Did you speak with the tug crew?"

"No. They're still out of range."

I move away from the radar and walk to the door of the chartroom, sweeping aside the curtain that keeps light from spilling out into the bridge, and step toward the chart table. Leaning over the table, I check our latest position. I notice that Jim has also drawn a mark showing the tug, a position east of Bethel Shoal. I look up at the GPS, 14.1 knots over the bottom, and then check the distance between the two points with a set of dividers. Fewer than 40 miles. We could be up to them by 0400. I'm not checking up on Jim; I know his calculations are correct. I'm just going through the motions, clearing my head and thinking about "what if."

I straighten up and walk out of the chartroom onto the port bridge wing. Outside it is warm and humid, the wind thick with salt spray, a smell that always excites. Turning aft, I walk behind the superstructure of the bridge to where I can see the stack deck. Taking the ladder down, I walk back to the edge of the stack deck and look down, first at the waves rolling up and onto the stern and then at two old mooring lines coiled up on the inert gas house.

Looking down at the lines, I think of the tug crew again. If they don't get themselves fixed up in the next few hours, these lines might find some use even though they're at the end of their service life. I know I can't get at my new mooring lines, stacked as they are next to the steering gear motors in the lazarette. In these seas I can't risk opening the hatch to the weather. One solid wave and—*bzzzt!*—no more steering, and then we're more a hazard than help.

I scramble back up the stairs and rejoin Jim and Frank on the bridge. "Listen, I'm going to go try and get some sleep since it might be a long night." Jim and Frank both glance toward me in the dark. My hand is on the door that leads back to the inside companionway. "Let me know if anything changes. I don't know what's going on with those guys. Maybe they'll figure out what their problems are. If not, maybe there's something we can do. Keep her running the way she is. Give me a call again at 0300 unless you need me earlier."

Back in my stateroom I kick off my Tevas and lie back on the bed. I shut the light off and close my eyes. I open them again and look at the clock: 0145. That means I have about an hour to get some rest before Jim calls.

I think fleetingly of the *Cherry Valley*'s hull, which is single-skinned—there is only three-quarters of an inch of steel separating the oil inside from the seawater moving by outside. This design would not be allowed to be built today in an age conscious of the threat of oil spill; if built today my ship would be double-hulled—an extra measure of protection to contain oil in the event of a grounding or collision that might rip open the steel.

I feel the steady roll again and listen to the sounds of the ship as I lay on my back in the darkness, staring up at the ceiling of my stateroom. When I first sailed on tankers as third mate all I heard aboard ship was noise, nothing distinct, just white noise that filled my ears. Nine years later, that noise has become an orchestra. I hear the sounds distinct from one another, the rushing of the wind outside—I can even tell from which direction it is blowing by the sound—the exhaust fans in the engineroom, the generator in use, the pitch of the steam turbine's whistle, and the slight waver in engine rpm as the top of the propeller occasionally clears the surface of the sea. Every sound is part of the rhythm of the ship. I had developed what veteran captain and author Jan de Hartog described as the "most ancient and mystical relationship between man and matter: the comradeship between a sailor and his ship."

Six months earlier a friend gave me copy of Farley Mowat's *The Grey Seas Under,* a classic tale of survival and endurance on the high seas that details the heroic exploits of the crew of a North Atlantic salvage tug, the *Foundation Franklin* of Halifax, Nova Scotia. Battling winter gales for weeks on end, the crew of Newfoundlanders and Novis responded to distress calls of stricken ships that needed to be towed to port. The book details one unbelievable exploit after another, feats of seamanship and bravery that are hard to imagine in this day of better-built ships, good communications, and more accurate weather forecasts. The men were true seamen and heroes for their selfless service in exchange for limited pay. Today's salvors, companies like the Netherlands-based Smit, and the Florida-based Titan and Resolve and a handful of others, still salvage ships in trying conditions, sometimes at sea and other times from the rocks, yet they have the advantage of modern equipment and communication that the crew of the *Foundation Franklin* could scarcely imagine.

We have come out of the lee of Little Bahama Bank, 40 miles off our starboard side, and are moving along at a respectable 14 knots—not bad for a fully loaded tanker. In my mind's eye, I picture the *Cherry Valley*'s propeller churning through the water deep beneath the stern of the ship. It's turning 70 times every minute. It is pushing my ship across a giant chart in my mind, a chart that includes the entire peninsula of Florida, the Gulf of Mexico and its western shores. The chart I see includes the string of islands that band the northern edge of the Caribbean Sea: Cuba, Haiti and the Dominican Republic, and Puerto Rico. Between them and the Yucatan Peninsula I see the start of the Gulf Stream, rushing between this narrow strait and then flowing eastward, sweeping along Cuba's northern coast before curling sharply north around Florida's southern tip. It sweeps along at a speed of more than three knots to where it meets us just a few miles east of Jupiter Inlet off Florida's Atlantic coast, about 70 miles north of Miami. The Stream is giving the *Cherry Valley* an extra burst of speed on our northward voyage.

I also see the storm over Key West—stationary for the moment with no clear sense of what its next move will be—picture the winds swirling from all points of the compass being drawn into the system. These northeast winds are doing double duty, feeding the tropical storm and being further powered by a massive high pressure system squatting over the Carolinas and Georgia. What I do not know is that where we are headed will be the exact point where these two weather systems will catch us in a vise, making conditions off Bethel Shoal much worse than in surrounding areas.

I think again about the fine line between foolishness and skill, how so often luck is more of a deciding factor than you might like to think. I think about some of the captains I have known and wonder what they would be considering were they in my position now, what they would be deciding. I think that whatever happens in the coming hours that I will always keep a margin of safety between myself, meaning my crew and my ship, and danger. After many years' experience, I know that if we are called on to help this tug we will need more than a simple Plan A; in fact, I expect we may get quite far down the alphabet when it comes to plans.

I open my eyes and look up again at the dark ceiling and realize that I will not be getting back to sleep. I look at the clock. It is 10 minutes after two. We will be in the vicinity of Bethel Shoal in about an hour and a half. I want to see the chart again. I want to talk to Jim. I want a news update from the Coast Guard or the tug crew. But I don't want to go back up to the bridge and pace and show the nervousness that I feel.

For the second time that night I swing my legs out of bed, pull on my Tevas, and leave my stateroom. I take the twelve stairs to the bridge two at a time.

CHAPTER 12

THE SEA CLAIMS TWO

November 14, 1994

Late Monday night, NASA transportation director Ernie Graham was at his home near New Orleans watching Monday Night Football; the Steelers' defense was crushing the Buffalo Bills' quarterback Jim Kelly with repeated blitzes and interceptions—when the phone rang. Bill Knodle, who had just returned to his room at the Radisson hotel in Port Canaveral to a message describing the tug's worsening condition, did not apologize for the late hour.

"Ernie, we've got some problems," Knodle clipped.

"What's going on?"

"The tug's lost one engine and two cylinders are down on the other," Knodle reported. "They're about 18 miles offshore, off Vero Beach, and drifting toward shore at a rate of half a knot."

After hanging up the phone, Graham looked at the clock, almost 9:30 Central Time. He turned his attention back to the game and hoped that Captain Wiles would solve his mechanical trouble. There was little Graham could do at this point but wait for Knodle's calls. Maybe the next would bring good news.

As the *J. A. Orgeron* struggled to stay off of Bethel Shoal, the abandoned and listing freighter *Jeano Express,* its house lights long since extinguished, was approaching the shoals of Tennessee Reef. The Coast Guard commanding officer in Miami had ordered the captain of the cutter *Decisive* to monitor the drift of the vessel and to sink it—with high-powered cannon fire—if the vessel approached the 50-fathom curve off the coral reefs of the

Florida Marine Sanctuary. The *Decisive,* a 210-foot medium-endurance cutter, had sailed from Key West just after 1700 and, once on scene several hours later, stood by the derelict, monitoring its drift by radar. Just before sunset, as the *Decisive* was getting underway, the crew of a Coast Guard helo had hovered briefly over the wreck, and dropped two strobes onto the wreck. This would allow the *Decisive* crew to also keep sight of the ship.

An hour after midnight on the 15th, the dark hulk of the *Jeano Express,* its two marker strobes flashing, appeared in the gloom to the crew of the *Decisive* who were standing watch on the bridge. The cutter hove-to 500 yards from the wreck, its engines at idle speed to keep its bow to windward to allow the crew the most comfortable motion, such as it was, in the unpleasant conditions. Permission had been granted from the Coast Guard Commandant in Washington, D.C., to "intervene on the high seas"—in other words, sink the freighter with its cannon before it would enter the marine sanctuary. The cannon, mounted on the bow, was capable of firing 170 rounds per minute when operated in automatic mode. But the gunnery crew—four men including a supervising mount captain, a gunner strapped into the cannon's shoulder harness, and two loaders—had all met in the ship's mess for a "pre-fire briefing" some hours before. Because of the rough conditions, they had agreed to use the gun's single-shot setting—at least until they were sure they could fire accurately. If all went well, the gun crew had permission to switch to automatic and deliver short bursts of fire, three to four rounds at a time. They anticipated using 175 rounds to sink the vessel on the first attempt. The gunnery crew, accustomed to endless hours of training in which they were only allowed to use the lesser-caliber TP-T—target practice with tracer rounds, were unabashedly thrilled to use their gun with high-incendiary rounds to sink the *Jeano Express.* Yet they stood by for the captain's order as the cutter closed on the wreck's position. As they approached, the captain ordered the bridge crew to maintain a safe distance of 500 yards from the *Jeano Express,* close enough for the gunner to make out the ship but far enough away that they would not be endangered by fire or explosions from the doomed ship.

At 0130 the order came—the ship was approaching the 50-fathom curve and still had not sunk. The gunnery crew donned their life jackets and emerged from the sheltered house, moving forward, hands on the grabrails, along the lee deck to the open bow. Clipping in their harnesses, the four men worked swiftly, arranging the 100-pound ammo boxes in their chute so they would not slide down the rolling and pitching deck. The gunnery officer removed the gun cover as the loaders opened four boxes of ammunition and began feeding the belt of rounds into the gun's feeder tray, being careful to align the belt's "nipples" so they would not jam. After loading one belt, which held 55 rounds of ammunition, the loaders mated the end of the belt with the beginning of the next.

The mount captain, his radio crackling with the voice of the captain on the bridge, noted the range and bearing of the target delivered by the bridge crew from the cutter's radar and relayed it to the gunner, who could then fine-tune his sight. He then shouted back, "Manned and ready!"

The gunner sighted through the laser-point sight, the red dot sweeping wildly on the loom of the hull until he could stabilize the swivel, and shouted to the mount captain, "On target!" The mount captain pressed his transmitter and reported to the bridge, "On target and tracking."

"Okay, commence fire," the captain responded.

The feeling of firing a 25-mm cannon with high-incendiary ammunition at an abandoned ship can only be described as "awesome," according to seasoned gunnery officers. The heavy *thump-thump-thump* of the powerful gun—and the rush of air venting from the barrel into the face of the gunner—was an unrivaled experience of power to the crew who were more accustomed to the light crackling sound produced by the training rounds.

In the darkness, the gunner kept the red dot stabilized on the doomed ship's starboard quarter and superstructure, the tracer fire confirming his repeated rounds. After firing a half dozen single shots into the bow, the gunner stopped, turned to his mount captain, and no doubt grinned: "Okay to switch to auto?"

The mount captain pressed his radio transmitter and hailed the bridge, "Captain, permission to switch to auto?"

"Okay, go ahead and switch to auto."

A cacophony of thumps rocked the cutter as the gunner unleashed bursts of four- and five-round volleys of automatic fire into the wreck. Several minutes later, the gunner elated by the steady pounding that he had ushered from the gun's smoking barrel, there was relative quiet on the bow. The only sound was the shriek of the wind and the pounding of waves breaking against the hull. The crew squinted toward the wreck, the pilot-house of which was now ablaze, and awaited word from the bridge. They could clearly see the silhouette of the ship in the darkness, settling lower in the water, but still refusing to sink.

After a few minutes—it was now just after 0200—the captain ordered the helmsman to swing around to the port side of the *Jeano Express*. "Stand by," he said to the gunnery crew. Once repositioned, he called them back with a new range and bearing, and the gunnery crew repeated the process, unloading another 170 rounds into the port side. The list was increasing, but still she continued to float. They shifted back to the starboard quarter and opened fire again—letting loose another 170 rounds. The ship was settling slowly by the stern, its afterdeck awash, when puffs of steam began to appear above the ship as the blazing superstructure was doused by the waves.

The *Jeano Express* slid stern-first beneath the surface at 0314, the position logged by the crew of the *Decisive* as 24 degrees, 42.7 minutes north, 80 degrees, 42.5 minutes west. On the return voyage to Key West, they would relay the coordinates to NOAA so a wreck symbol could be placed on charts for the area, the only written record of the previous day's drama. Charts of the Florida Keys are littered with wreck symbols, each one an anonymous monument to tragedy and untold heroics.

"She's lost all power, Ernie." Knodle sounded edgy. It was 0130, and Graham's Monday-night football game was long since over. Knodle's previous call, just after the game, had provided a shred of good news: the tug was holding steady. But now Knodle was calling to relay that the tug had lost both engines. "We've got another tug on the way, but we're running out of time."

"Where are they now?" Graham asked.

"Drifting toward Bethel Shoal, off Fort Pierce. The towing contractor has gotten a hold of a tug in Port Canaveral that will try and get to them. They will be getting underway shortly, but I'm not sure they will make it in time. They're drifting quickly; they could be on the beach in eight or nine hours."

"Is everyone okay? Anyone hurt?"

"Not yet, as far as I know. But they've had plenty of problems, including a fire in the stack, and they can't keep either of the engines going for longer than a few minutes."

There would be no sleep for Graham this night.

At about the same time the crew of the *Decisive* was pounding the *Jeano Express* with cannonfire, another freighter, the Turkish-registered *Firat,* was at anchor outside the entrance to Port Everglades at Fort Lauderdale. Built in 1970, the 507-foot ship looked like she belonged to an earlier era. Her inefficient yard-and-stay rig, a system that dates back to the days of sailing ships when one block would be attached to a stay over the hold and the other block attached to the end of a yard arm over the wharf, was an indication that she was relegated to carrying bulky, low-value cargo. She had five cargo holds, four forward of the house and one aft.

Anchored just two miles off the beach, the *Firat* was partially loaded with steel rebar, which would be offloaded at the port when the weather improved. The vessel had arrived over the weekend, but the owners had not wanted to pay the premium to have longshoremen discharge cargo at weekend rates. It would be cheaper to have the vessel lose a day at anchor than to pay the overtime rate. Then the storm moved in, and the pilots suspended their operations just hours before the *Firat* was due to pick up a pilot at the sea buoy on Monday morning. Not surprisingly, by the early morning the anchorage area was empty. Other vessels that had been at anchor over the weekend had departed the exposed anchorage, which was two miles from a lee shore—the sandy beaches of Fort Lauderdale—when Gordon had changed course and started heading up the Old Bahama Channel. At that time there were no restrictions for vessels anchoring to await a berth, and Captain Zafar Ozgen anchored the *Firat* instead of heading for sea to ride out the storm. He had the bosun pay out two extra shots of chain so that a full eight shots, 720 feet, of anchor chain was on the sandy bottom.

The *Firat* rode well through the night even as the wind rose to 40 knots and the seas built 15 feet. Beginning at midnight on the 15th, the ship's second mate was standing watch on the bridge, taking careful notice of its distance off the beach by using the range on the radar. Two hours into his watch, he noticed that the *Firat* was dragging anchor. Almost imperceptibly at first, the distance to shore was diminishing. The ship, buffeted by the wind, was closing with the beach. He picked up the phone and called the master to the bridge. By this time the wind had reached speeds between 45 and 50 knots, and the ship was yawing violently, tugging at its chain. Once a ship of this size begins to weave in this manner, the chain is no longer lying flat on the bottom; it is sweeping across the bottom as much as 45 degrees in each direction. For an anchor to be secure, the chain needs to lie flat, which keeps the big flukes dug into the bottom. Each time the chain swings to one direction or another it starts to work the anchor free. Add the ship's pitching motion and the force of the wind on the ship's sides as it sailed back and forth, and the anchor has little chance of holding the ship in place. A ship dragging anchor in a tropical storm toward a lee shore just two miles away will cause any captain to leap to action. That the lee shore was one of Florida's most popular beaches, lined with hotels brimming with the first of the season's tourists, no doubt contributed to the captain's unease.

Captain Ozgen gave orders to heave the anchor, and at 0330 had the chief engineer start the main engine and prepare to answer bells. In 15 minutes the deck crew had managed to start the windlass and bring aboard two shots of chain. The strain on the chain soon overwhelmed the old windlass, however. It could not bring aboard another link. Hearing this, the captain ordered the engine to dead slow ahead to ease the strain on the anchor. He quickly went to full ahead and then back down to dead slow as the strain eased off the chain. But confusion soon followed. The noise of the wind on the bow prevented the chief mate from communicating with the captain by radio. By 0400 half the chain was back aboard, which left four shots still in the water—but the captain's engine maneuvering pushed the *Firat* past the anchor, wrapping the chain tightly around the bow.

The windlass, meanwhile, lost power entirely, stopping dead just as the ship was drifting back, which meant the anchor was still on the bottom and couldn't be raised. They could neither get underway, nor stay at anchor because they were already dragging toward the beach. The electric windlass was powered by a diesel generator in the engineroom equipped with an automatic kill switch that was released when the engine overheated. When the windlass was overwhelmed by the excessive load of raising the anchor against the storm-force winds and waves, the generator overheated and shut itself down.

When the shut-down alarm sounded, the engineers scrambled to bring another generator online, but not before the *Firat* was blown broadside to the seas, pushed directly toward the beach by the full force of the wind blasting against her 30 feet of exposed topsides.

Mariners use a common formula to determine the force of the wind on a given object. There is a rule of thumb: when the wind speed doubles, from 20 to 40 knots, say, the force of the wind is increased by a factor of four. Which means that when the *Firat* was at anchor on Sunday evening and the wind was 20 knots, there was approximately 11,000 pounds of pressure on the anchor chain from the force of the wind on the bow and superstructure. When the wind increased to 40 knots and the ship began to drag toward the beach, and the crew were attempting to haul in the anchor, there was approximately 44,000 pounds of pressure on the anchor chain. This is when the ship was oriented roughly head-to-wind. Once the ship was broadside, however, presenting some 15,000 square feet of her hull as "sail area," in 40 knots of wind there would be more than 122,000 pounds of pressure against her hull, and at 50 knots more than 240,000 pounds. The ship's anchor, with only four shots of chain deployed, was doing little to slow the drift. At 0417 the *Firat*'s keel slammed into Fort Lauderdale's coral reef.

Down in the engineroom the engineers could hear the grinding of the steel on the coral heads and feel the vibrations through the hull as she pounded on the reef with each passing sea. The *Firat* ground on the reef with such force that the crew grabbed tightly onto handrails to keep from being thrown to the deck. The engineer's problems quickly compounded when the cooling-water valve for the main engine broke and, immediately after, the sight glass for the No. 2 diesel generator was smashed, allowing coolant to leak out and causing the generator to overheat. The stuffing tube around the shaft where it passed through the hull, meanwhile, was knocked out of alignment and began to burn as the shaft rotated inside it. The chief desperately wanted to shut down the engine, but because of the ship's dire straits, Captain Ozgen refused. Within minutes Ozgen ordered full ahead to attempt to break the ship loose from the reef. As he shifted the rudder from port to starboard the ship yawed back and forth as though on a pivot, but did not make way.

At 0430, with the cooling water having run out of the No. 2 generator, the generator died, plunging the ship into darkness. The ship was all but dead. The emergency diesel generator kicked on to restore lights and emergency power, but the main engine was down for good. The captain then made his first call to the Coast Guard. At 0445 heavy swells lifted the *Firat*, washing it over the reef, and the ship drifted quickly toward the beach. In a last-ditch effort—no master should ever let his vessel go aground with an anchor still in the hawsepipe—the captain ordered the crew on the bow to release the starboard anchor. At 0455 the *Firat* ran hard aground on Fort Lauderdale beach, 100 yards from the beach and in full view of the Yankee Clipper hotel.

CHAPTER 13

BETHEL SHOAL

November 15, 1994

Back on the bridge I walk to the coffee machine and pour myself a cup, carefully adding a bit of milk and sugar as Jim fills me in on what he's heard in the last hour and a half about the tug's condition. We stand at the forward windows, the intermittent spatter of spray against the glass and the howl of the wind around the superstructure forcing us to speak louder than usual. They have not solved their engine problems, he says, and no one else has volunteered to come out into the storm and offer help. We remain the only ones in any position to render assistance. What that assistance will be is still unclear, of course, although I have begun to formulate a plan in my mind, considering the available equipment and personnel and the conditions of the sea off Bethel Shoal.

I pick up the VHF mike and call the Coast Guard at Fort Pierce on their designated channel.

"Coast Guard Station Fort Pierce, Coast Guard Station Fort Pierce, this is the tanker *Cherry Valley* on Channel 22."

A moment later a voice responds: "*Cherry Valley,* this is Coast Guard Station Fort Pierce, go ahead."

A dialogue with the Coast Guard can be time consuming. They invariably want to know all the details to fill out their boilerplate forms—in this case, despite the fact that they will not be offering assistance and are relying on us, they want to know how many of us there are on board, our position, and the cargo we're carrying. At this point they're more impressed than concerned when I explain that we are a 688-foot tanker with almost 10 million gallons of No. 6 oil on board.

We are also close enough now—about 25 miles—that I decide to place a VHF call to the tug itself. The captain, his voice a distinctive slow drawl, comes back over the radio and recaps for my benefit their difficulties, failed engines, their drift rate toward Florida 15 miles away, and the facts that they have had intermittent fires in the engine stack and are all wearing life jackets. Yet the tone of his voice is so calm that it seems as if he is describing a minor problem on his car that will eventually need to be fixed.

Holy shit, I think as I hang the mike back on its mounts. Despite his calm manner, I realize in a moment that they are in serious trouble. I look down at the chart spread before us on the chart table and see that they are 15 miles off the coast, and at their drift rate it will take between five and seven hours for them to reach the beach, a fair amount of time to get things sorted out. But as I look closer, moving my finger between the beach at Fort Pierce and their charted position, I see that they are drifting directly toward Bethel Shoal, the spur of shallow water that I had noticed earlier and hoped we wouldn't get anywhere near. Using a pair of dividers I walk off the distance and determine that the shoal is about 5 miles from their current position. If we are going to be of any help to them we have to reach them before they drift over the shallows at Bethel Shoal. They could be over the top of it in as little as two hours. At that point, they'll be on their own.

I chart our position for 0240 and draw an intercept line to the tug's position and see that we have safe water all the way.

"Jim," I call out from the chartroom, "let's bring her left to 340 degrees. That'll take us up to the tug."

I hear Jim relay the order to Frank Dover on the helm, and with a small counterclockwise turn of the heading knob on the autopilot our course slowly changes 20 degrees to the left, and the quiet routine of a ship at sea is broken. As if to punctuate my decision, the ship begins to roll a little more in the beam seas.

I call the Coast Guard and the tug to let them know I have changed course and will be on scene within an hour and a half, at about 0400. There is no need to wake any one else on the *Cherry Valley*. There is nothing to do but wait. I pace the bridge, crossing the 30 feet between the bridge wing doors, back and forth with the roll of the ship, and look out into the darkness. There is no rain outside, just the sound of the wind and spray, and I can see the lights of Florida flickering to the west. Before the next watch comes up, I want to have a clear plan. Carl will be coming on watch in another hour. But I will need Carl running the deck during any attempt at rescue. I debate about calling him early to talk this over but haven't come up with a firm enough plan in my own mind.

At 0300 the *Orgeron* is still 18 miles ahead of us, too far away to see and too small to pick up on radar. If their drift rate stays the same they could be over the top of the shoal before we get there, so I have Jim call down to the engineroom and have them increase the rpm to 75. I would like to come up some more—five rpm is not going to increase our speed a lot— but we are still pounding pretty hard and I don't want to damage the ship.

I learn that the tug captain's name is Lanny Wiles, and I introduce myself as Skip, and from now on we call each other by our given names. He is not excited about a tanker coming to help him. He would prefer another tug, of course, a tug being specifically suited to take a vessel in tow even in these conditions. But, despite the fact that a single-screw tanker is not known for its maneuverability, he is not turning us away; on the contrary, he is grateful for our effort and appreciates what we are risking to save his crew and, if possible, the tug and barge.

Lanny and I have come up with three scenarios: take the tug and barge in tow; drop the barge and take the tug only; or get the crew off the tug and let both the tug and barge go. All of these options depend on how much time we have, how close we are willing to get to Bethel Shoal, and how well I can handle the *Cherry Valley*. I tell Lanny that I have had experience as a pilot and am comfortable maneuvering the ship in tight quarters with another vessel close by. We don't talk much about the barge, other than for him to describe the fact that it is relatively light and has a lot of sail area, which is why he is drifting at such a rapid rate toward the coast of Florida.

Our first priority is keeping the crew safe. We'll worry about the barge after that, but Lanny will do everything he can to save the barge and its cargo, too. Although I haven't formulated a complete rescue plan—and I want to discuss it with Carl and the other mates before committing—I describe for him the type of lines we have aboard that can be used for towing, if needed. We will do everything in our power to bring him to safety, but I will keep us out of trouble; in other words, I will not allow the ship to get too close to the shallows of Bethel Shoal.

The lines I have in mind, the mooring lines coiled up on top of the inert gas house on the stern deck, are the ones we use to tie up the ship. They are nine-inch-circumference, eight-braid, polydacron construction; about 700 feet long; and, when new, had a breaking strength of 137,000 pounds. These are the only lines we have available. I don't perform any mental calculations about the potential load of a tug, its tow, and the dynamic energy that will be imposed on them. There's no point. These are anything but new; in fact, they are getting ready to be thrown out because we have received new lines aboard. Though they are shorter than a true towing hawser, they should do the job. They have a high stretch coefficient and will absorb the shock load of towing. The disadvantage of polydacron lines is that if they part under load, they will snap back like a rubber band, seriously hurting anyone in the way. There is a scene in Farley Mowat's *The Grey Seas Under* in which the crew of the tug *Foundation Franklin* were towing a freighter into Digby, Nova Scotia, the legendary Captain Brushett in command. The steel towing wire snapped, recoiling with a loud explosion and whirring through the air, slashing off a steel ventilator as though it were made of butter. "A loop of it hit her after ventilators and sliced them off as cleanly as a cutting torch could have done," Mowat wrote, "and it was only by the grace of God that the bulk of that flailing cable passed to starboard and smashed harmlessly into the sea. It could easily have taken *Franklin*'s funnels and perhaps her bridge as well." What happened next in the book is another worry of mine: "A piece of Manila spring [line] also came back on the end of that gigantic whip, and this was flicked in under *Franklin*'s stern, where it wound itself about the tug's propeller." If I end up taking the *J. A. Orgeron* in tow, I will need to be keenly aware of all the dangers, to the crew aboard the *Cherry Valley* and the *Orgeron,* and also to the ship itself.

At 0330 the 4-to-8 watch is called. Officers have phones in their cabins, but to call the deck crew there is a watch-call system, a button we push on the bridge console that rings an annoying alarm in each of their cabins. They acknowledge the call by pressing the button next to their bunks. Jim calls Carl on the ship's phone, and I can hear him describing what has been happening.

Paul Donnelly, the first assistant engineer, will be getting his usual wake-up call from the engineroom, but he will not be getting the unusual briefing, the one Jim's given to Carl, since we haven't let the engineers in on our developments. Once Paul's on watch I will call him myself. As the person with the hand on the engine controls, he will be a crucial link to the success of a maneuvering operation such as the one I am proposing to do, coming alongside the tugboat with the *Cherry Valley* and passing over our towing lines before we all drift onto Bethel Shoal.

A few minutes later I pick up a target on the radar, registering about 12 miles away, in roughly the spot the *Orgeron* should be. Using the radar's automatic plotter, I acquire the target to learn its course and speed. It takes a couple of minutes for the radar to process the information and spit out the results, but when it does it confirms our belief that it is the tug, or more probably, the barge because it is the larger target. The radar displays a speed of 2.5 knots and a direction of 290 degrees.

The cloud cover is very low, but, with no rain, the visibility is fairly good, though we can't see the tug yet. Dawn will break at about 0630—too late, unfortunately, for daylight maneuvering. By then the tug will have drifted over the shoal.

Between 0330 and 0345 I consider all the equipment we will need before calling out the crew: line-throwing guns, messenger lines, and mooring lines; the engineers have to get ready for maneuvering by replacing burner tips in the boilers to give me maximum control over the engine.

I know with certainty that if we snap a line or the ship goes aground and one of my crew gets hurt or we put oil in the water, my career is over. But, politics aside, I'd be unable to live with myself if I sailed by without at least trying to help.

I call the Coast Guard again and ask the petty officer on watch specifically what he and his superiors expect us to do. All Coast Guard officers seem to come from Kansas or other landlocked states, so it is no surprise when in a flat, Midwestern tone, he makes it clear in the vaguest of terms that any assistance possible is what is expected. I put the same question to Lanny, and his answer is the same: any assistance possible. But, since I asked, he said, he would like to try Plan A, putting lines up to the tug and towing them and the barge.

I don't ask these questions so I will have a "get out of jail free" card if something goes wrong—there is no such thing in the eyes of the Justice Department, of course. I know I can't claim, "They asked me to do it." I ask the questions to clarify how serious the situation is, and that we are the only people around to help.

I believe if I tell Lanny that I can take only the tug and not the barge he will immediately open the break on the towing winch and cast the barge adrift without so much as a second thought. I say that because no captain wants to lose the cargo he has been charged to deliver safely, but cargo and barges can be replaced and lives can't.

At 0345 the change of the watch is a little more animated than usual. The 12-to-4 ABs are passing on to their reliefs what has been going on; Jim is filling Carl in on the details up to this point, while I finish up on the radio with the Coast Guard and the *Orgeron*. As I hang up the mike and look out the forward window, straining to see the tug through the gloom, I decide to commit us to trying to rescue the *Orgeron*. The quiet talking among the ABs and mates dies down as I hang up the mike and say, "Let's go see what we can do.

"Frank and Alex, go down and get the rest of the deck gang up. Tell them I want them dressed and ready to go in 15 minutes." As I'm saying this I look at the radar screen and can see huge bands of rain moving toward our position. As they head off the bridge, I add, "Tell them to put on their raingear."

Jim finishes the changeover, going over our latest position information with Carl, then heads down to his cabin to put on a pair of coveralls and grab his radio and raingear. While he is below he wakes up Chris Sotirelis and sends him to the bridge for a briefing.

After Jim heads down I pick up the handset on the console and call the engineroom to talk with Paul.

"Engineroom, First," he answers.

"Paul, it's the Captain. I need you to get ready for some maneuvering in a hurry." I then give him the 30-second version of the story up to now, but halfway through Paul stops me.

"I'm way ahead of you, Cap!" Paul responds. "There aren't many se- crets on a boat, and I thought you might want to maneuver. We'll be ready to answer bells before you're ready to give them."

"Thanks, Paul," I say and place the phone back on its mounts. He prob- ably knows how far we are from the tug, and when we will get there too.

When Jim gets back to the bridge I call him and Carl over to a small desk on the port side of the bridge. I turn the dimmer up on the light so they can see the plan—based on my discussion with Lanny Wiles—I am about to sketch on a plain sheet of white paper. Plan A is to approach the *Orgeron* from the south and stop between 200 and 300 feet upwind and to the east of them with the *Cherry Valley* beam-to in the seas, our port side toward the tug. I want the ship to act as a breakwater so the crew on the tug will be able to get out on deck and pull in our mooring lines without being swept into the sea by waves breaking over their bow. From my talks with Lanny I know he still has a generator running, so he has power to the capstan on the bow to help pull in our lines. When we are beam-to it will also allow my crew to work on the port side of the after deck, and they will be protected from the seas by the house and the en- gine casing.

I tell Jim I want him to take part of the deck crew and start getting the line-throwing guns and messenger lines down from their storage locker on the flying bridge and flaked out—ready to use from the stack deck. Carl will take the rest of the crew, I say, the ones who are most physically fit, and get the two mooring lines down from the top of the inert gas house and ready to run out the centerline chock on the stern.

When we get in position to weather of the tug, Jim will fire the line-throwing gun over the tug. The bitter end of the shot line will be tied to one end of the messenger. The other end of the messenger will be fed down to the main deck and run from outside the railing through the centerline chock on the stern and tied onto the eyes of the two mooring lines. Carl understands to keep the eyes of the mooring lines about 20 feet apart so it will be easier for the tug crew to pull the lines over the bow.

Once the tug has the "shot" line, they will have to pull it and then the messenger line—one-inch manila, about 1,000 feet long—aboard the tug to get to our two mooring lines. Meanwhile, I will be attempting to keep the two vessels close enough together so that we will be able to run our lines over. I ask Carl and Jim for any thoughts or suggestions.

They can't think of any. This is Plan A.

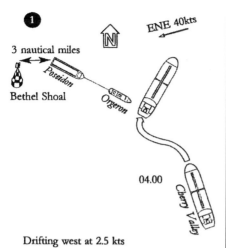

1

ENE 40kts

3 nautical miles

Poseidon

Orgeron

Bethel Shoal

04.00

Cherry Valley

Drifting west at 2.5 kts

The first planned approach–aborted
to make pass on starboard side.

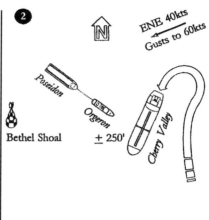

2

ENE 40kts
Gusts to 60kts

Poseidon

Orgeron

Bethel Shoal   ± 250'

Cherry Valley

15'-25' seas

Used line-throwing gun.
Lost line in the dark.
Ship's speed too great
for a second try.

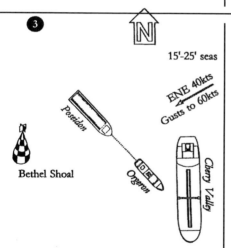

3

15'-25' seas

ENE 40kts
Gusts to 60kts

Poseidon

Bethel Shoal

Orgeron

Cherry Valley

The third pass had *Cherry Valley*
broadside to the sea with the tug
off to starboard
The AB on deck was able
to hand the heaving line across
to the bow of the tug.
The second and third (final) passes
were identical.

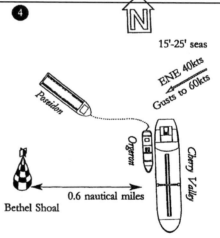

4

15'-25' seas

ENE 40kts
Gusts to 60kts

Poseidon

Orgeron

Cherry Valley

Bethel Shoal

0.6 nautical miles

Position of ship and tug
while passing the heaving
line and the messenger line.

Cherry Valley *as she looked when delivered from National Steel and Shipbuilding Company in 1974.*

Courtesy Keystone Shipping Co.

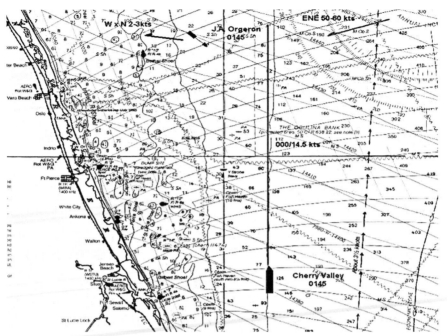

Chart 11460 showing the relative positions of the Cherry Valley *and* Orgeron *at 0145 on November 15, 1994.*

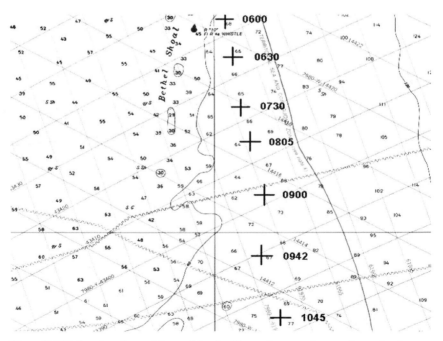

Chart 11474 showing the positions of the flotilla as they crawl away from shoal water waiting for the South Bend *to arrive. The vertical line is 80° 10′ west longitude.*

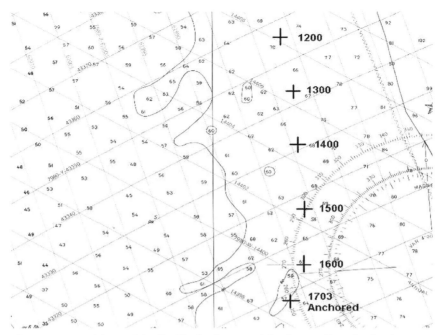

Chart 11474 positions of the flotilla for the rest of the day until anchoring just after 1700.

Me on the bridge of the Maersk Rochester while piloting in Penobscot Bay, Maine, Spring 2003.

The Cherry Valley *pounding through the Gulf Stream on the afternoon of November 14, 1994.*   Courtesy Frank Dover.

The deck crew of the Cherry Valley *working on running a new mooring line to the J. A. Orgeron. The mooring line is flaked out on the deck. The messenger line is being held by the crew and the shot line is piled at their feet. (l to r) Tommy Prevost, AB; Roberto Rodriguez, AB; Steve Ramos, GVA; Ancel Connor, bosn; and hidden, Carl Gabrielsson, chief mate.*

Morning of the 15th showing the two mooring lines leading to the Orgeron.

Courtesy Marcus Crumpton.

First photo of the J.A. Orgeron *and the* Poseidon *shortly after they are taken in tow on the 15th*

1400 on the 15th. The South Bend *getting into position to pass her line to the* Orgeron. *The photo is not out of focus, just taken during a torrential downpour.*

ABOVE: *Morning of the 17th as we get ready to release the* Orgeron *and* Poseidon. *The* Dorothy Moran *is alongside the* Orgeron *passing her tow wire over to be shackled to the pennant of the Poseidon.* Ocean Wind *is acting as a brake for the* Poseidon

RIGHT: *The* Firat *in the position no ship whishes to be in —hard aground off Fort Lauderdale.*
Courtesy U.S. Coast Guard

An external tank as viewed from the shuttle after being released into orbit.

PART III

"*Jadot's* crew worked against time to haul the bridle in so that a new section would bear on the chocks; but the big freighter was blowing fast to starboard and inexorably she began to drag the bight of the cable under *Franklin's* stern. There was nothing [Captain] Power could do about it. If he started his engines in order to escape the trap, he knew he would part the stranded wire at *Jadot's* bow. If he remained stopped, there was every likelihood that the bight would sweep under his counter and foul his propeller blades. He kept his engines stopped. The wire came under, and they could hear it all through the little vessel as it rasped against the blades."

from *The Grey Seas Under,* by Farley Mowat

CHAPTER 14

PLAN A

November 15, 1994

With the decision made, the *Cherry Valley* comes to life. The deck crew assembles on the stack deck just behind the house to wait for Jim and Carl. Jim is the first to arrive, as Carl stays on the bridge to brief Chris Sotirelis, the third mate, who will be on the bridge to assist with maneuvers.

On the stack deck, Jim takes the bosun and three ABs—Tommy Prevost, Alex Rivera, and Roberto Rodriguez—with him to the flying bridge to start breaking out the line-throwing guns and messenger line. The flying bridge is the highest deck on the ship. The lines are stored there because, theoretically at least, it is the last place the rising water will reach if you are sinking. In practice it is an awkward and dangerous place to work in bad weather, especially because the motion of the ship this high above the waterline is extreme. With the wind whipping over the flying bridge at 40 to 50 knots, it is all anyone can manage to just hang on and not be blown over the side. As they open the top of the storage box, the wind rips the 50-pound lid from their hands and two of the three hinges are torn loose. Luckily, the third hinge keeps the lid attached to the box, or we would have had a steel Frisbee skittering across the stack deck at 50 knots.

Jim and his crew start passing down the line-throwing guns and feeding out the messenger line to the port side of the stack deck, where it is flaked out so it can run clear. While not a true gun, that is what we call them. They are made by Pains-Wessex and called the Speedline 250. Each self-contained unit, in a tube seven inches in diameter and about 13 inches tall, with a handle and trigger attached, contains a weighted rocket attached to a light line and a primer charge to get the rocket clear of the tube before it ignites. When preparing to fire one, the operator pulls off the front cover, attaches a messenger line to the bitter end of the 4mm shot line, then points it over the target and pulls the trigger. This fires the small charge and launches the four-pound steel projectile clear of the tube. Once clear, the rocket ignites and hopefully flies rapidly toward the intended target. The shot line is 900 feet long, and the range is about two-thirds that distance.

Chris arrives on the bridge a little sleepy but ready for work. Carl quickly explains Plan A to him as they look at the radar to watch the movement of the tug. Fortunately the tug's generator is working, and we can see the running lights and deck lights. We can also see the barge's green side light, downwind of the tug. We are five miles away and we still lose sight of the tug's deck lights when she is in the trough. A few minutes later Carl leaves the bridge without a word and heads for the stack deck to get the rest of the lines ready.

Lanny Wiles and I have resumed our conversation, Lanny explaining more specific information about their heading, the position of the barge relative to the tug, and how much wire he has out. When he is able to run the starboard engine he can keep the tug heading south-southeast into the seas; when he has to shut the engine down, which he does every few minutes, the tug begins to wallow in the troughs. When I hear their heading, it solidifies my idea for the approach: to pick them up on our port side. I call Carl and Jim on the portable UHF radio and tell them to set up the gear for a port-side rescue attempt. With the wind whipping across the decks and the ship rolling, both groups have their work cut out for them. And it is completely dark outside. But Carl has even more to watch out for than the crew on the flying bridge. With only 12 feet of freeboard the seas are rolling across the deck in streams. Fortunately most of the work they have to do, setting up the lines through the chocks and around the bits, can be accomplished in the lee of the engine house. Getting hit by a wave is a constant threat for those working on deck, and from experience I know it can be terrifying.

Several years before, when I had been sailing as chief mate on the *Coronado*, we had been in rough weather on a trip from Venezuela to England. For several days running we had no chance of walking the deck for routine inspections without serious risk of being swept away. Finally, the weather moderated enough to allow us out on the starboard side as far as the midship house. I went out to inspect the ship and watch the pumpman as he took readings of the cargo temperatures from the tanks we could reach. The captain had told me not to go past the number three center tank and not to go on the port side. Standing in the lee of the midship house, I saw that the trough under the port cargo manifold was full of water because a drain cap had not been pulled when we sailed from the last port. I thought I would just zip across the deck, unscrew the plug, and be back safely in the lee of the house before the next wave broke. After a particularly large wave broke across the deck and the water cleared, I dashed across, only to find that the plug was frozen in place. As I bent down to put a little more torque on it, a small wave came up on the deck from abaft the beam and gave me a pretty good drenching. Instead of learning my lesson and getting the hell out of there, I was angry about getting soaked and even more determined to get the cap loose. The pumpman had seen what had happened and came over to give me a hand. Together we tried to loosen the cap.

The next thing I heard was a roaring coming from behind us before I was enveloped in white water. My eyes were open and all I could see was white and then some gray as I went tumbling down the deck and past pipelines. As I was moving with the water I had no idea which way was up or which way I was headed, just that I was moving fast. Fortunately I crashed into the pipelines, my arms and legs tangling in the piping, and not over the side. I had never felt so scared—and helpless—in my life. When the adrenaline stopped I also found that I was bruised from head to toe.

With this past experience in mind I'm acutely aware of the risk to my crew on deck, and I've impressed on Carl not to do anything too risky. I hope he's listened better than I had.

In the engineroom, first engineer Paul Donnelly and Ron Spencer, the second engineer who had been preparing to head off-watch prior to my call to prepare the engine for maneuvering, have replaced the top burner in each boiler so we can control the boilers' firing rate more easily. At sea speed the *Cherry Valley*'s steam plant operates with the largest burner tips, those that allow the most fuel to be burned. For maneuvers, I will have to go from full ahead, 75 rpm, to full astern, 50 rpm, and everything in between, and having a combination of burner tips in each boiler will let the engineers have better control over the boilers. While ordinarily the engineers will ask for a reduction in rpm before changing burners, I had told Paul that we needed full speed until the last minute, so he had asked Marcus Crumpton, the QMED, to change the top burner tips with the smaller-orifice style while we were at full ahead.

Paul has stationed himself at the engine-order telegraph and the throttle stick. When I ring for a specific rpm, Paul will answer the engine bell, then adjust the stick to the proper rpm. Meanwhile, Ron will operate the boiler controls. Ordinarily, the boiler's ratio of fuel, air, and feed water are adjusted automatically, but Paul has taken the automation system offline and stationed Ron at the controls. It takes time for the automated system to sense and then incorporate changes in the fuel-air-water ratio. If changes in the throttle controls are made too quickly, the automated system can become overwhelmed, shutting down the boilers, a delay that could result in grounding, collision with the tug, and quite possibly the loss of the tug and her crew if the boilers are not restarted quickly. With manual control Paul and Ron can precisely monitor the flow of fuel and steam to keep the engine operating smoothly—as long as I, on the bridge giving engine orders, respect their needs for a place to put the steam. The worst sequence I can give, I know, is to ask for "stop" after "full astern." The steam, which has been allowed to flow unimpeded through the low-pressure turbine for maximum rpm to the propeller, needs to go somewhere; when I order "stop" I have asked them to immediately cease delivery of 600 pounds of steam to the turbine for maximum shaft revolutions, and all this steam needs to be vented safely. Otherwise, the steam pressure can pop safeties, blow seals, explode valves—or worse.

Another problem that the engineroom crew is contending with is the roll and pitch of the ship in the heavy seas. When the water in the boilers' steam drums sloshes around, the system can report false water levels to the automated system. Although the automated system can compensate for this by reducing the speed of the propeller accordingly, I will be delivering engine-speed requests in rapid succession, which is why I will tell Paul not to let me break anything, to answer my orders quickly but at the same time keep me from damaging the ship's power plant.

At 0400, the chief engineer, Tim Croke, had been awakened and briefed. When Tim descends the catwalk into the engineroom, he nods at Paul and Ron, who are stationed at the console. While Paul and Ron respond to my commands, Tim will be scurrying all over the cavernous space, climbing several stories up, walking aft to the steering room to check that the steering motors do not overheat, and make sure that the entire plant is operating at acceptable levels of temperature and pressure.

Back on the bridge Chris and I plot our progress as the ship moves closer to the tug's position. There are three charts that cover the Bethel Shoal area. A small-scale one ("small scale, small detail" the saying goes) that covers from Key West to Cape Canaveral is good for offshore navigation, but not for working up close to the shoal. The other two charts are larger scale and provide more detail of the area. They're better for close-in navigation work. Unfortunately, the charts change at Bethel Shoal with only a mile or two of overlap. We have to go back and forth between them to keep everyone plotted and see where we are in relation to the shoal. A large buoy marks the shoal, but in the seas we have tonight we can't pick it up on radar. It would be very helpful to see it to have a reference point with the tug.

As I look at Bethel Shoal in the lower corner of chart 11476, I see that the 80 degree, 10 minutes west longitude line almost exactly matches the 60-foot depth curve which is four cables (a cable is one-tenth of a mile) east of the buoy on Bethel Shoal. That is our drop-dead point, I decide. With the seas we have running tonight and our 35-foot draft, I feel we can "safely" operate east of that line and not worry about touching the bottom.

"Chris," I yell out to the wheelhouse. "Come in here!" As he enters the chartroom I point to a line I've drawn on the chart. "This line is our drop-dead point. Or, as Muammar Qaddafi would say, 'the line of death.' Along with everything else I'm going to ask you to do this morning, you are going to expressly watch our longitude on the GPS, and under no circumstances are we going to cross over the 80-degree, 10-minute line. If we cross it, we run out of water. Do you understand?"

"Yes, Captain," comes his answer. It is the only one I expect. Chris is still new to the job, and this is way out of the ordinary, but he seems up to the task at hand. He is a few years older than the average new third mate, and a little more mature, having done two years of premed, planning on becoming a dentist before he realized his grades weren't quite up to med school standards. He changed course and followed his father's footsteps in the merchant marine by enrolling at Texas Maritime.

With a call to the engineroom, we start slowing down the ship at 0416 by dropping to half ahead and, true to his word, Paul is ready to maneuver before I am ready to give him bells.

We are only about two-and-a-half miles away from the tug, and we need to start slowing the ship early so we don't overshoot the position; we don't want to go barreling past the tug, especially not in such close quarters. When issuing the engine bell orders, I apply the standard rule of thumb for slowing a laden ship: you can expect to take off a knot of speed every tenth of a mile without working the ship too hard. If we're moving at 10 knots, we want to have at least a full mile to come to a complete stop. Since we're operating at almost 15 knots, I'll need at least a mile and a half.

At this point the repeated requests for information from the Coast Guard are interfering with my attempt to discuss the rescue with Lanny Wiles. Every few minutes the Coast Guard petty officer in Fort Pierce peppers me with questions so he can fill out his forms, including the nature of the weather, the color of our hull, and the status of our maneuvers. Finally, in frustration, I reach for the mike and ask the officer which channels he has access to. "Sir, do you have Channel 72?" I ask.

"Yes we do, captain."

"Okay, how about Channel 10?"

"No, captain, we do not have use of Channel 10," comes his reply.

When I heard this I switch back to the channel I have been using with Lanny Wiles and say, "Lanny, let's switch to Channel 10." We are now free to communicate without interference from a well-meaning, yet at this point powerless, Coast Guard. I will check in with them regularly, but I need to focus on the upcoming maneuvers.

One sure way to get people up on a ship at night is to slow the engine down. Breaking the rhythm at sea is a sure indication that something out of the ordinary is going on. Within a couple of minutes Steve Worden, the radio operator, comes to the bridge. He walks over to where I am standing at the forward windows and asks what is going on. I point out over the port bow at the lights of the tug, now a little over a mile away.

"They've lost their engines, and the barge is pulling them toward the beach. We're going to try and get a couple of lines to them and tow them clear," I say.

"What do you want me to do?" Steve asks.

I pause for a brief instant before responding: "Handle the radio with the Coast Guard. They mean well, but unless they can send a boat out here, they aren't much help. They are starting to get in the way of the captain of the tug and me being able to talk. We are going to go to Channel 10 to do our stuff. Keep the Coast Guard posted on the situation on 22."

With just about a mile to go to reach the tug, the rain hits. It is a torrential downpour that only tropical storms can produce. The deluge drops so fast and hard that the rain hits the deck and splashes back up in a pounding fury. Within a few minutes there is an inch of standing water on the bridge wings. Except it isn't standing still. With the ship rolling 20 to 30 degrees, the water surges back and forth across the wings, creating its own set of wave patterns. The wipers, even set on full speed, can't keep the windows clear, so I step out onto the port wing to see the tug better, propping the door open so I can issue engine orders to Chris and rudder orders to the helmsman, Smart Ebikeme, who is standing at the wheel. Through the sheets of rain and darkness, I can barely see the lights of the tug off our port bow. In less than a minute my shirt and shorts are soaked through. But at least it's warm.

I order five degrees of left rudder to turn the ship more to the west to close with the tug, planning to get in position to the south of them, then turn to the north to shape an approach that will keep them close to our port side. As I turn more to the west, and start heading the *Cherry Valley* almost directly at Bethel Shoal, the hairs on the back of my neck start to stand up. In most circumstances this is my subconscious mind telling me that something is not right, and I need to stop what I'm doing or I'm going to get into trouble. Tonight, though, I dismiss the feeling as a symptom of being wet and cold.

As the gyro clicks off the degrees as we continue to turn to port, the hairs on my neck are standing out straight and starting to vibrate. Even I can't miss this sign; over the years I've learned to trust my instincts, and it has saved my life on more than one occasion. To slow the ship I had ordered the engine stopped, yet we are still moving an estimated four knots and approaching the shoal with effortless inertia. This approach doesn't seem right and I quickly move to Plan B. Whenever I'm about ready to do something, and I get this feeling, I stop and do something else.

"Hard right," I yell to the helmsman. And then a second later, I yell to Chris, "Half ahead," as soon as I see the rudder has been put hard over. As soon as the engine is going ahead I order up full ahead to get us turned away from the shoal, and as soon as the bow starts to swing to the right the hairs on the back of my neck start to settle down.

"Carl, Jim," I call on the handheld UHF radio, "change of plans. I'm going to turn around and try to pick them up on our starboard side while we are heading south. You've got about 10 minutes to shift the gear to the other side." In my other hand I have a handheld VHF radio to talk to the tug and tell Lanny what we are going to do.

As soon as we are clear of the *Orgeron* I shift the rudder to hard left and start to swing to port, a course that will draw an arc through the water and allow us to come to rest with the tug on our starboard side. I drop the engine down to dead slow to keep us turning but hopefully not pick up too much headway.

As the ship passes through 180 degrees, Carl and his crew move back on the after deck to get the mooring lines set to run out the centerline, or Panama chock, on the stern and connect the messenger from the starboard side of the stack deck. The house is providing a lee for them from the seas that are now hitting us on the port side.

Jim reports that he is in position on the stack deck with the Speedline. All I have to do is get the *Cherry Valley* within range. I call Paul on the ship's phone: "I'm going to be asking you for some pretty hard bells, Paul, are you up for it?"

"Bring 'em on, Cap!" he answers without hesitation.

"I trust your judgment, Paul. If you can't give me what I want, get as close as you can, and then call to let me know what is happening down below. If you start to get concerned that I'm keeping a bell on too long, let me know—before you get into trouble."

"Don't worry, Cap. I won't let you break my engine."

With that important piece of business taken care of, all I can do is wait until we get into position. It only takes a couple of minutes to close with the tug, but it seems like hours.

At 0455 we are approaching the tug, which is oriented bow-to-the-seas, perpendicular to our now southeasterly course. The tug, while still out of range of the line-throwing gun, is drawing closer as the *Cherry Valley* slides ahead and, I estimate, will be about 300 feet off our starboard side as we come abreast. I'm standing outside on the starboard wing and can see that the ship's hull is beginning to act as a breakwater for the tug, and it is not bucking around quite as wildly.

I call Jim on the radio and tell him to take the shot when he is comfortable. Next, I call the tug and tell them that we are getting set to send the line over. A few seconds later, through the rain, I see the port side door to the tug's wheelhouse open and three men scramble down to the bow to wait for the line.

As we slide into position I call for half astern, and then, 30 seconds later, full astern to check the forward motion of the ship. I look down at Jim on the stack deck, one deck down, and nod, and he fires the Speedline toward the tug. It is a delicate balance in firing one of these: you want to get the line over the target, but you don't want to hit the target with the rocket, which could smash through a pilothouse window or seriously injure a crewmember on the bow. Jim takes all this into account, along with the 50 knots of wind at his back and the rolling of the ship. He pulls the trigger.

The initial charge launches the rocket out of the housing, and then a split-second later the rocket ignites in a flare of orange flame that streaks toward the tug. Above the wind I can hear the *whoosh* of the rocket as it takes off, trailing the shot line behind it. Instead of going down toward the tug the rocket inexplicably heads up into the clouds, which seem to be only a few feet above the bridge, and is lost from sight. We can't even see which way the shot line was leading.

We are still sliding past the tug when I yell to Chris to give a jingle on the telegraph, the signal for the engineers to give it everything they can on the indicated bell. He replies with a look that seems to say, "Huh?" and I realize that he has never had to give an emergency bell before. I run to the telegraph and with a couple of quick twists of the wrist give two jingles of the bell while keeping it on full astern. Paul duplicates the motion down in the engineroom and the bell rings reassuringly on our console as I watch the rpm surge to 50 astern and even a little beyond. "See, Chris, you're learning something new already today."

I dash back out to the wing to check our position. We are sliding past the tug but still in range of the Speedline. Jim is set up and ready to go with another Speedline after confirming with the tug that the first one did not reach them. He aims just over the tug, spreads open his feet, bracing himself, and then pulls the trigger. Nothing happens. I remember that the instructions say to hold onto it for a minute after pulling the trigger to make sure it doesn't fire late. I can see Jim give it a fast count—nothing—before tossing the whole thing over the rail and into the sea.

With the wind and seas pushing us along and pushing the tug away from us, we are quickly moving out of range for another attempt.

"Stop the engine," I yell to Chris, and I'm sure the engineers breathe a sigh of relief when they answer that bell. To give them a place for the steam to go, I ask for half ahead.

I call Carl, Jim, and Lanny and tell them I am going to come around and try again.

CHAPTER 15

THE UNMANNED BARGE

November 15, 1994

Back on the coast, Bill Knodle, NASA's resourceful harbormaster, and Bill Cantillon, the prime contractor for moving the barges between Michoud and Cape Canaveral, were exchanging progress reports and devising plans to keep the tug and barge off the beach and being beaten apart in the surf. Cantillon called several owners of tugs about helping the crew of the *Orgeron*. Each told Cantillon the same thing: it was too rough, too dangerous, and too dark. At daylight, or if Cantillon declared that the crew was in immediate danger of dying, the owners replied, they might reconsider. But, with the tug still 10 miles offshore and the information Knodle and Cantillon were receiving being delivered by a stoic captain who was engaged in trying to keep his vessel and crew safe, neither were prepared to judge the degree of peril with any certainty.

Cantillon eventually managed to reach Captain Bob Barr, owner and operator of the *South Bend* in Port Canaveral. Barr was sketchy about details of his tug's size and mechanical abilities, but he had listened to the weather reports—they were not bad as far north as Cape Canaveral—and agreed to get underway. Cantillon and Barr drafted a contract, which outlined the fact that Barr was being hired on an hourly basis. He would be given a bonus for offering to attempt the tow in such questionable conditions. At 0230 Cantillon called Knodle at the Radisson hotel saying the *South Bend* was underway. At 0300 Knodle shut off the light in his hotel room to get an hour or two of sleep.

≈

Two hours and twenty minutes later, the Coast Guard called Knodle to explain that a laden oil tanker, the *Cherry Valley*, was on the scene and was attempting to pass lines to the tug. Knodle immediately called Cantillon and passed on the news, adding, "I need to get to the barge. If I can get aboard, I can drop the anchors and keep the barge off the beach."

"How do you plan to do that?"

"I'll get someone to get me out from Fort Pierce," came the answer. "I'm leaving the hotel in a couple of minutes. I'll pick you up at home, and then we can get down to Fort Pierce."

As Knodle drove toward Melbourne to pick up Cantillon, the weather became progressively worse the farther south he got, the rain pelting his windshield blocking out all but 50 feet of the road in front of him. He had time to think on the 20-mile drive about how he actually would get aboard the barge if it came to that. The options were limited. He could likely get aboard in a small boat, probably one of the 41-foot utility boats the Coast Guard had in Fort Pierce, or he could see about catching a ride in a Coast Guard helo. Considering the conditions with the wind and seas, each had its drawbacks.

From a boat, he'd have to land on the barge's stern, which had a 12-foot-deep open deck running the width of the barge. Normally the deck rode about five feet above the water; with the barge bucking in the heavy seas, it would be surging from below the surface to eight to ten feet out of the water. Trying to match the barge's violent motion in the seas without the boat being caught underneath would itself be a daunting task. Then there would be the jump between the two vessels without being crushed or falling into the sea. There were also three entry ports on each side of the barge, set back into the hull, but the watertight doors that allowed access into the barge were secured from inside the hull. To make matters worse, a two-foot-wide sponson, a stabilizing projection, ran 200 feet along each side of the hull. If the barge rolled in the trough of a wave as a small boat came alongside, the boat could be seriously damaged, swamped, or even flipped.

As he drove toward Cantillon's home, Knodle could not help but recall his own days at sea. He had been through storms before; of course he was younger then, a naval officer. He remembered the late-September day his ship had recovered a pilot from stormy seas north of the Azores. Waves were 40 to 45 feet high, and the winds were gale force. Yet they had located the pilot bobbing in the waves, launched a rescue boat, and brought him safely aboard.

Knodle was also concerned about the *Cherry Valley;* he knew nothing of the ship or her crew. The captain's seamanship would be crucial to this endeavor, Knodle knew. And the ship? Tankers are not equipped for towing. They were the opposite of a tug, slow and ungainly. Could the *Cherry Valley* get a line over in time—before the vessels were too close to shoal water? These and other questions consumed his mind this stormy morning as his wipers slapped a frantic rhythm on the windshield of his rental car. He knew, too, that the *Cherry Valley*'s captain would not risk endangering his ship, especially given that the cargo was oil, so Knodle would continue his mission to attempt to board the barge.

And what about Captain Wiles on the *Orgeron*? Surely he was doing all he could to deal with a bad situation. Could he pay out more tow cable, let it drag the bottom to slow down the drift? It might, but the cable dragging the bottom could snag on an underwater obstruction. The *Orgeron* had an anchor but in these conditions it would be far too light to do any more than slow their inexorable drift. The anchors on the barge, now they just might do the job if they could be dropped—if someone could reach the barge. Above all, Knodle was compelled to do more than watch helplessly from the beach while there was still a chance to assist.

He was stopping to pick up Cantillon because, as the contractor's representative, Cantillon, too, felt responsible to do all that he could for the safety of the barge, its cargo, and the tug. As soon as Knodle told him of his intentions, Cantillon had asked to be included. It was not out of the way to pick him up, and Knodle knew he would be glad to have the help when he got to the barge. What he was contemplating was really not a one-man job, and, in the storm, it would be best to have someone else on board in case anything went awry.

Knodle knew the easiest way to get on the barge—such as it was—would be to find someone willing to fly a helo in these conditions, and the

Coast Guard has the best-trained pilots in the world for this kind of mission. Knodle had been lowered and picked up from helicopters many times during his career in the Navy. The flight time out to the barge would be minimal, and the idea of hanging 60 feet below the helo on a small wire didn't faze him. The trick for the pilot would be having the helo match the motion of the barge and get Knodle landed safely either on the afterdeck or on top of the pilothouse. It never occurred to Knodle, who was 61 years old at the time, to consider his age as an impediment. He would get the job done if he could reach the barge.

CHAPTER 16

THE LAST CHANCE

November 15, 1994

"Carl, get everyone off the deck. I'm going to come around and try again."
I'm standing on the starboard bridge wing, rainwater up to my ankles,
when I realize that the tug has slipped away. Our first attempt to get close
enough almost worked, but I hadn't judged the speed well enough. The
Cherry Valley had been moving too quickly, and the tug had passed astern.
Hopefully the next pass will bring success.

But the ship has slowed to the point that she is nearly dead in the water;
I will have to build speed and maneuver her through a 180-degree turn so
that we can try again. Turning a laden ship dead in the water and beam-to
in 20-foot seas—remaining close to an object adrift in these conditions—is
not an easy task. First of all, it requires hard work from the engineers. The
goal is to turn the ship without gathering too much headway, which I will
just have to take off again in a few moments once the ship has completed
the turn. The turn, if executed quickly, will likely shape a circle that is just
under a quarter of a mile in diameter. The engineers, responding to my
rapid-fire commands, will route steam from the boilers to the turbines, for
quick bursts of revolutions, or vent it to prevent damaging the seals. With
Paul Donnelly answering bells at the throttle and Ron Spencer manning the
controls of the fuel-air-steam system, I can confidently assume that the ship
will move in a graceful, however slow, arc through the breaking seas.

It is just after 0500 and still pitch black and raining hard as ever, as I
start the turn for a second pass.

"Hard left, full ahead," I say to Chris and the helmsman, hoping to
make as tight a turn as I can.

"Come on baby, start to turn," I mutter to myself. Glancing at the tachometer I see that the rpm have gone from 0 to 60 in what appears to be record time, and I can feel the wheel cavitate as it tries to bite into the water, but it takes what seems an eternity to hear the click of the gyro sounding off the turn. With no horizon to see—in the darkness and rain all I can see are the blinking lights of the tug a quarter mile away—I rely on the sound of the gyro and a look at the radar to see our heading. As she shoulders into the big seas on the port bow the click of the gyro almost stops, then picks up again as she slides down the back side. As she passes through the eye of the wind I bring her back to half ahead to keep the headway down and give her hard right rudder to steady her up on the new course as we reassess the situation.

"Chris, get a position. How far are we from the shoal?"

A minute later Chris calls back from the chartroom: "One mile, Captain."

Shit.

From the start of the first pass to now, a span of only 35 minutes, we have lost a mile to the west. If we keep this drift rate up, I'm going to be dangerously close to the shoal before I can get around again.

"Steve," I say to the radio officer, Steve Worden. "I have a new job for you. I want you to watch the GPS for me. All I care about is the longitude. Just keep reading it off to me." By stationing the radio officer on the GPS, I have gained two things, constant updates on our proximity to the shoal, and a stationary Chris, who will not have to keep moving from the console, where he is operating the engine order telegraph, to the chartroom.

We are pointed north again, halfway through the turn, and I think briefly about trying to pick the *Orgeron* up on the port side again, but decide against it when I realize I will have to put the ship in an awkward position, bow toward the shoal, while we are trying to make up with the tug. I tell Carl and Jim on the radio that we are going to try another attempt from the starboard side.

Carl's voice comes back over my handheld radio: "Captain, how close are you going to try and get to them this time?"

"As close as I can. Why?"

"If we can get close enough we might be able to use a heaving line."

A heaving line, a lightweight line with a weighted monkey's fist on the throwing end, with the bitter end tied to a messenger line, can be thrown close to 100 feet by a skilled crewmember, especially downwind. On the *Cherry Valley* most of the heaving lines are made out of ⅜-inch polypropylene (so it will float). Inside the monkey's fist is a bolt with a couple of nuts threaded on to give the weight of a softball. It takes practice to toss a heaving line. A beginner tends to get the line tangled, and the line more often than not ends up dropping into the water far short of the intended target. You often don't get a second chance because of the time it takes to gather the line back in, recoil it, and attempt a second throw. But I know that Carl wouldn't have asked if he didn't think one of the deck crew couldn't handle such a shot.

"That would mean real close, Carl. But yeah, that's a good idea. Get set with a couple of heaving lines down on the main deck after we get turned around again. Jim, you stay up on the stack deck in case we don't get that close and need to try another line-throwing gun."

I call Lanny on the other radio and tell him we are getting ready to come around again. This time, I add, I'm going to bring the ship even closer to them to try and land a heaving line on their deck.

As the stern passes through the seas, the bow approaching the intended heading for the next rescue attempt, Carl and his crew can now get back down on the main deck without fear of being swept away. As we head south I steer for the tug, now less than half a mile away, keeping them fine on our starboard bow, and start to slow the ship down.

The view of the tug through the streaming forward windows of the bridge presents an eerie picture. The rain has seriously reduced visibility and is making halos around the lights of the tug as she heaves up and over the seas. On the deck of the *Cherry Valley,* the same seas are breaking just aft of the beam and spilling across most of the deck.

"Make sure you guys keep one hand for yourself and one for the ship," I say into the radio. "Let's not do anything stupid out there."

As our bow starts to come in line with the *Orgeron,* their motion settles down; the *Cherry Valley*'s hull is forming a floating breakwater. Our speed is down to less than three knots, but I need to get it down to zero in less than 600 feet.

"Full astern," I yell to Chris from the starboard bridge wing. There is so much water on the bridge wings now that the scuppers can't keep up with it, and with the ship rolling 20-plus degrees, foot-high waves are washing into the open doors leading into the wheelhouse, making the waxed deck very slippery and allowing water to get into the base of the radars. To prevent waves from washing through the bridge, I have to shut the doors, which means I have to use the radio or yell my commands through a partially opened window.

"We are going to be close enough to use the heaving lines, Carl," I say through the radio. "You might have to go up forward on the main deck"— he and his crew are still positioned in the lee of the house—"to give yourself more time to pass them over. Jim, head on down with your guys to give Carl a hand."

I see Carl below me, venturing slowly onto the main deck with the bosun, Ancel Connors, and Steve Ramos, the GVA, general vessel assistant. Each has a heaving line clutched in his hands, and I can see Carl watching both the *Orgeron* and the port side of the ship for any seas that might be coming aboard so he can warn the other two.

As the tug passes by amidships, about 50 feet off our starboard side, Steve Ramos throws his heaving line to the bow of the tug where three of the *Orgeron*'s crew are waiting. I can see the three dark figures scurry for the line.

It's a strike.

Once they have the line, Carl, Ancel, and Steve move swiftly aft with their end of the line to make it fast to the messenger line. They had not tied the heaving line in advance because of the likelihood of missing the toss. The drawback to this plan was the need to tie the end off to the messenger—in a hurry.

From my stand on the starboard wing, high above the action on deck, I see that the tug is drifting slowly past us and realize we are still going too fast. I tell Chris to give a jingle on full astern. This time Chris doesn't hesitate; he gives the telegraph knob a quick twist. A moment later I see the gauge register a full 50 rpm astern. The crew below me are working frantically to get the heaving line tied to the messenger, but the streaming water on deck and extreme rolling of the ship have made a mess of the lines.

We are still not stopped. I can see the ship's prop wash working its way up the hull as the propeller works astern, but it is just now getting to the wing where I stand. For us to be dead in the water it needs to be another 75 feet ahead, and with the tug just clearing our stern I realize we're not going to make it.

Below me I see the heaving line has been attached to the messenger, and the crew are quickly streaming it over the rail. As it goes over the side, though, the messenger line becomes fouled on the railing. But before it can be cleared, the heaving line, which has been secured on the bow of the tug, comes up taut as the ship glides ahead, and suddenly snaps, severing the tenuous connection between us.

"Stop the engine!" I yell to Chris and cringe as soon as I say it, knowing what Paul must be saying about me as he tries to find a place to put all that steam.

"Steve, how far from the shoal?" I yell into the chartroom.

"Eight-tenths of a mile," comes the reply. We are running out of room. The *Cherry Valley* is just over a tenth of a mile long and we are only eight ship lengths from our drop-dead point. The good news is we didn't lose much ground on the last pass.

Keying the mikes on both radios, which broadcast to both the deck crew and the crew of the *J. A. Orgeron*, I say, "Practice is over, guys, it's game time. We have just enough room to try one more pass. If we don't get it, then we are going to have to call it quits because we will be too close to the shoal."

I'm planning to perform the same kind of racetrack turn that we did on the last pass—a circle to the left that would bring the tug back on our starboard side—and all is going according to plan until we start to turn to the left at the top of the turn. Looming in front of us, just coming out of the rain, are the sidelights of the barge. The tug is just forward of the port beam.

"We're not going to make this turn, Chris; we're too close." With no other option I order hard right and full ahead to bring her 270 degrees around the other way, which would shape a figure-eight in the water and position the ship a bit farther to the north, gaining more room to shape an approach. It's not what I had planned, but it's better than hitting the barge. As we get the bow through the seas I order up full astern to check the headway and help twist the ship the rest of the way around. Once it is safe to get my crew back on deck, Jim takes his crew down to the main deck ready to pass heaving lines and then the messenger to the *Orgeron.*

With the practice of the first two passes behind me, I anticipate the need for less engine speed so we won't overshoot the tug. Carl is standing by in the lee of the house with Frank Dover and Steve Ramos, who each have heaving lines waiting for the tug to get close enough so they can go forward on the deck. I hear that Frank has gotten "his" heaving line from the doghouse going down to the lazarette. This is the one he says he always uses, and he knows it will not kink when he throws it. We all understand that this is our last chance to get a hold of the tug and rescue the crew.

As the tug creeps ever so slowly down the side of the ship, Carl, Frank, and Steve move forward. Carl is watching their backs again as they get set to send a heaving line across. I have the helmsman keep steering the *Cherry Valley* closer to the tug, and as she goes by amidships, their bow pointed straight at us, Frank is able to reach out and simply hand the heaving line to one of the crew of the *Orgeron* as she passes down our starboard side, only one foot away.

With the extra crew down on deck we have one end of the messenger already attached to the end of the heaving line, and some of the crew are attaching the other end of the messenger to the mooring lines.

"Stop the engine," I call to Chris as the *Orgeron* moves down our side at an almost imperceptible rate. The crew on the *Orgeron* has the heaving line aboard and are now working frantically to gather in all 1,000 feet of the messenger line so they can get to the mooring lines. I've never watched three people work harder or faster to get a line aboard.

My goal had been to be stopped directly upwind from the tug, which I managed to do. Unfortunately, with us being beam-to-the-seas, and rolling pretty heavily, the ship comes down—sideways—onto the Orgeron, and soon we are banging into each other, our starboard side to the tug's port side, both headed in the same direction, as we each roll in the swells. They are still moving astern but painfully slowly, and I can hear steel hitting steel with each roll of the ship.

Below in the engineroom, Paul Donnelly, Ron Spencer, Marcus Crumpton, and Tim Croke can see nothing. But they can hear the tug sliding down the side of the ship making a thunderous racket as steel hits steel that makes them stare at the hull plating just 30 feet away. Holding their breath, they follow the noise down the hull with their eyes and, as it reaches the area of the boilers they say a silent prayer that the tug doesn't punch a hole and let seawater come pouring in onto the red-hot boilers.

Cold seawater hitting the boilers would cause them to explode. All the superheated steam in the boiler, compressed at 600 pounds, would be released and instantaneously fill the entire engineroom with steam and shrapnel. The only good thing about that is, with the maneuvering platform only 30 feet from the boilers, the end would be quick.

On the bridge, it is my turn to worry.

As I look down from the starboard bridge wing I can see three guys on the *Orgeron* pulling in the messenger line in water up to their knees, the line swirling around them. But when I shift my gaze back to the stern of the tug and see the tow wire I feel a sinking feeling in the pit of my stomach and say to myself, "Oh, fuck!"

I know that the barge *Poseidon* is downwind of the tug, and the tow wire should be going over their starboard quarter. It isn't. It is leading over the port quarter of the tug, which is now almost in line with my propeller and rudder. The consequences of getting a two-and-a-half-inch wire fouled in either the propeller or rudder of the *Cherry Valley* are just too scary to imagine. The wire drapes over the port side into the dark water, and I can't tell where it is going. It might be leading under the tug. Or it might be under my ship. I just don't know. For the first time in the whole operation I feel as if I have no control over what is going on.

"Chris, call the engineroom and tell them to stop the wheel. *Right now!*" I am screaming for the first time in my career as a seaman. "And do *not* move the rudder until I give the order."

And, of course, the *Orgeron* has stopped moving aft, pinned as she is along our starboard side, the force of the ship sliding sideways in the wind and seas having captured the relatively smaller vessel.

I call Lanny on the radio and say, "Lanny, if you have anything left on that starboard engine, you better use it now to get clear of us. I can't do anything until you are clear of our stern."

"Roger, Skip." Lanny responds instantly, and a few seconds later oily black exhaust comes pouring out of the starboard stack, and the *Orgeron* starts slowly sliding aft. Soon they are past our transom, and I breathe a huge sigh of relief as I tell Chris to call the engineroom and tell them they can roll the wheel over again.

Back on the stern Carl, Jim, and the deck crew are passing the two lines out through the Panama chock on the stern. They have staggered the eyes of the mooring lines on the messenger line so that when it comes time for the *Orgeron*'s crew to pull the lines over the bow they have to pull only one line at a time, hopefully making their job a little easier and minimizing the risk of parting the messenger.

A few minutes later both eyes have gone over the bow, and in the gray light of dawn I can see one of the crew give the universal sign—arms crossed in front of him—to signal that both lines are made fast. Simultaneously, I hear over the radio the same thing. It is 0620 on Tuesday, November 15th, 1994.

CHAPTER 17

CALLING THE OFFICE

November 15, 1994

"Dead slow ahead," I say softly to Chris, and a few moments later the ship begins to creep forward.

The *Cherry Valley,* the tug *J. A. Orgeron,* and the barge *Poseidon* may be joined together by a string of hawsers and wire, but we are still being driven onto a lee shore by the storm. Now I must get us all moving in the same direction, away from the shoal and without parting the lines. I've told Carl to slack out the lines together and try to keep an even strain on them as I start to get some headway on the *Cherry Valley.* As we pick up speed and the tension builds on the lines, Carl and Jim supervise, watching the tension and keeping track of how much remaining line they have flaked out on the deck. Carl keeps me posted on how they are doing and how much line is left. At 720 feet long, the lines are short for towing to begin with, and we want to keep some aboard to be able to pay out if the lines start chafing.

It is dawn. As the three of us start moving forward the sky has gone from black to light gray, and now—for the first time—I can see the two vessels strung along behind us. The tug is a familiar sight, just not in this position; but the barge is unlike anything I have seen before. Standing on the bridge wing and looking astern at the barge through the brightening dawn, I see what looks like a huge Quonset hut with a house on the forward end of it.

I call back to the tug and ask, "Now that we have things settled down a bit, what the hell do you have in there?"

"Well, I didn't want to tell you before," Lanny responds, his words coming slower than normal. "But it's the liquid fuel cell for the space shuttle."

Seeming to guess my next question, whether the tank is potentially explosive, he adds, "Don't worry, it's inerted." I clear with Lanny, and then hang the mike back on its mounts and look out at the storm.

It's not every day a loaded oil tanker picks up a tug and barge carrying a big piece of equipment for NASA. Steve Worden interrupts my thoughts by calling out the longitude from the GPS, and what I hear is not good. Our heading is about 150 degrees, which should take us clear of the shoal, but with the drag from the tug and barge, and the set from the wind and seas, our course over the ground is about 185 degrees. In other words, we are getting closer to the shoal and the coast of Florida, not moving away from it. I try to turn to the left, to get away from the shoal, but our speed diminishes, and we lose more ground to the west. I let her steady on 140 degrees, which seems to be the course where the speed is best, and give everything a few minutes to settle down. It takes time to get the 44,000 tons of the *Cherry Valley* moving using a dead-slow bell.

While everything is settling I run down to my cabin to get my cell phone and camera. I figure a picture would be worth having, and it's time to call Keystone and tell them what we are doing. I have relaxed considerably, and now, with the initial danger of the shoal sort of astern of us, I'm dumbfounded by what has taken place.

Back on the bridge 30 seconds later, everything is the same. Both mooring lines are out about 600 feet, Carl tells me, and have as even a strain as they can. Carl's crew is careful not to let too much of the load be transferred to one line, which might set off a chain reaction of snapping lines. Every time the tug heaves over a wave the lines seem to stretch a little more as they go bar-tight, the crew on deck wincing and preparing to duck for cover. Our course over the ground is still just west of south and Steve continues to call out the longitude to me. We are now just about a half mile from the 80 degree, 10 minutes west line and closing to it slowly as we crawl south. If I give it any more rpm I risk parting the lines, and if I turn more to the east I slow down and drift farther westward. It is a fine balancing act to get us away from the shoal, where the difference of a degree or two in heading, or a change of one or two rpm will determine success or failure.

Steve is now just reading out the fractions of a minute of longitude to me to monitor our painfully slow progress. We will eventually leave the shoal curving away toward the coast of Florida if we can continue to claw our way southeast. But we are running out of room. As with most GPS units, the readout goes down to thousandths of a minute, and it is the third number that I listen to most intently. If it increases, we are going to the west—toward the shoal. If it decreases we are going to the east, gaining sea room. The thousandth readout is roughly equivalent to six feet, realistically a meaningless number considering the accuracy of the GPS is no better than 300 feet, but psychologically it is very important for us.

I take a break from the drama of listening to the longitude to call my boss at home outside Philadelphia and let him know what's going on.

"Good morning, Art. It's Skip Strong," I say cheerfully as Art Bjorkner, Keystone's fleet manager, answers the phone. "I'm going to be a little late getting to Jacksonville."

"Is the weather giving you trouble?" he asks.

"Yeah, we're still feeling the effects of Tropical Storm Gordon, but it's really the tug and barge I'm towing astern of me that's slowing me down."

I can tell I now have his undivided attention. I give him a one-minute version of what has transpired over the last five hours and explain that we are still pretty busy with maneuvers. I will call him again at 0900 at the office.

"Okay, Skip. Keep the crew and ship safe."

CHAPTER 18

THE TUG THAT COULDN'T

November 15, 1994

Back on the bridge I manage to find the right balance between heading and speed, and we're slowly moving away from the shoal. We are making a course of 180 degrees and a speed of about a knot and a half by 0730 as the sun begins peeking out from behind the clouds between the squalls, blindingly bright after the gray of the rain. We can now see the wake of the ship trailing astern, which is brown with mud and sand, a reminder of how shallow the water is. The fathometer has been on since the rescue began, and at one point we note a scant, scary 10 feet between the keel and the bottom as we drop into the troughs, a reminder that we are not yet safe.

We learn from the Coast Guard that a tug named the *South Bend* is on its way from Cape Canaveral and should be on scene in a couple of hours. It appears that we will not have to tow this bizarre string of vessels indefinitely, and it will likely all be over by noon. I also get a call from NASA's Bill Knodle, a sober voice I instantly respect, relaying the same information the Coast Guard had.

At 0900 I place a call to Keystone's offices on the first floor of its office building in Philadelphia and greet the unflappable Louise Gilbert, who has served Keystone as secretary steadily for almost 40 years. "Good morning, Miss Gilbert," I say as cheerily as I can. "It's Captain Strong on the *Cherry Valley.*"

"Oh yes, Captain," she says. "They are expecting your call. Let me transfer you to the conference room." She's obviously been told something is up, and I wince when I hear the reference to the conference room; the entire Keystone operations department, it seems, is expecting my call.

George Clark, Keystone's VP for operations, picks up the phone on the first ring and places me on speaker phone so that everyone can hear my report. After I hit the high points he says he is relieved to hear that everyone is safe and that the *Cherry Valley* has not been damaged, aside from some scraped paint on the starboard quarter where the tug hit the hull plating. Keystone's business is the safe movement of oil, not towing, and he wants to make sure that, if necessary, we can quickly get the ship out into deep water. I can only imagine what Art Bjorkner has told them about what we have done, so I appreciate the opportunity to put their fears to rest.

I assure him that we have a freshly sharpened fire axe on the stern, and we can cut the tug loose at any time if we think we are standing into danger. We hope to hold on until the tug *South Bend* arrives to take over the tow, which will hopefully be within the next couple of hours.

The operations people have their say—their overriding concern is for the safety of the crew and the ship and the 10 million gallons of No. 6 oil in our tanks, after which I fill in the details of the last few hours. Then a voice I don't recognize, brusque and distant through the speaker phone, comes to my ear.

"Captain Strong, Ralph Hill, general counsel for Keystone. Congratulations on a terrific feat of seamanship," he says. "I want to let you know that you have done something pretty extraordinary and that you are probably entitled to salvage rights to the tug, barge, and fuel cell. You didn't happen to get the captain of the tug to agree to a Lloyd's Open Form, did you?"

"No. That never entered my mind. All we were trying to do was help the five guys on the tug," I reply. "I certainly wasn't thinking about trying to get salvage rights; I just wanted to help them." Tankers are generally the salvee, not the salvor, neither were we aware that there was anything of value aboard the barge until after we had the tug and barge in tow.

We don't talk much more because I am uncomfortable being away from the bridge and want to get back to keep track of the situation, but the word "salvage" certainly gets my attention.

I hang up the phone and head back to the bridge, trying to recall my Admiralty Law class at the Academy that covered salvage. The class was held on Tuesday and Thursday afternoons, right after lunch. Professor Wallace Reed was very knowledgeable about maritime law, but his presentation was a little dry. He had a tendency to speak in a monotone that earned him his nickname among the students, "The Sandman." During most classes I wound up getting in a pretty good nap but fell a bit short in absorbing the intricacies of admiralty law from The Sandman's lectures. I did read the textbook, though, and managed to do reasonably well in the class.

As I return to the bridge I try to remember the key factors for salvage to be claimed. The danger must be imminent, I recall, the service voluntary, and, above all, the salvage successful. The form that Ralph Hill referred to, Lloyd's Open Form, is the standard agreement between a ship in distress and a potential salvor. Its essence is the unambiguous phrase "no cure, no pay." The LOF, which was drafted by the Lloyd's Committee in London at the end of the 19th century, offers incentive for potential salvors to begin work without waiting for lengthy paperwork. A salvor who gets the stricken ship's master to sign an LOF has an understanding that, first, they will be paid for their work only if they succeed, and, second, they will be paid for their work at a reasonable rate that will be considered by an arbitrator after the fact. The amount of payment depends on the value of the ship, the value of the cargo, the danger involved, and the degree of skill required to effect salvage. If you don't sign a form and claim salvage rights, you can still file a claim with an admiralty court later, but your case is more difficult.

Most of us in the business of transporting cargo on the high seas don't think about Lloyd's Open Forms; they are part of the realm of professional salvors who don't want to leave their compensation to chance or the whims of the courts. So far it looks like we might have a claim for salvage, but—regardless—my first priority is to keep the crew of the *Cherry Valley* and the *Orgeron* safe.

Back on the bridge we are still making slight progress toward the east at what seems like a foot at a time, but it is better than going to the west. The rain is coming down just about as hard as I have ever seen it, and the northeasterly wind is driving it sideways. As I look forward I can just make out the midship house 300 feet in front of us. Behind us I can't even see the tug, just the two lines disappearing into the gloom.

The *South Bend* is still on the way, but when I talk with the captain he tells me he is hove-to waiting for this squall to pass. As I look at the radar screen, all I can see is solid rain clutter out to the edge of the 24-mile scale and think that it will be awhile before this one lets up. He is having a hard time making headway in the seas and the heavy rain is knocking out his radar picture, so he is proceeding with caution.

Bill Knodle had said the tug was 2,800 horsepower and assumed it was twin-screw. Unfortunately, as the tug gets closer to us it also gets smaller. The *South Bend* is, I learn, a 1,600-horsepower, single-screw tug with a soft hawser for towing instead of a wire. It is still a capable boat but not the powerhouse we had been expecting.

I can tell from the tone of Lanny's voice that the true size of the tug is far less than he had been hoping for, but having anyone come out in this weather is welcome news.

I call Carl on the radio to see where he is. Trying to stay dry in the lee of the engine casing, came the reply. I grab my still-dripping foulweather jacket and head down the ladders to meet him on the stern.

"How's it looking back here, Carl?" I ask as I meet him by the winches on the stern.

"So far, so good. Junior is setting up some chafing gear on the lines and keeping them greased. That's about all we can do."

"Do as good a job as you can. I just got off the phone with the office. It seems that we may have salvage rights to all the stuff back there," I say, nodding to the tug that is now just visible through the rain. "You might want to pass that on to the boys so they keep a close eye on the lines."

Carl and I walk back to the stern to look at the lines. They are led as fairly as possible out the centerline chock, and Junior is already getting some canvas to use as chafing gear. I am uncomfortable with crew standing by the lines for too long with the amount of strain on them. The lines, taut as steel, appear about half the diameter they usually are. If one of those lines were to part, the recoil could be deadly.

After a couple of more minutes I head back to the bridge to dry off and wait. As I step back into the wheelhouse I feel the chill of the air conditioning on my soaked skin. The foulweather jacket had helped, but not much.

All we have to do now is wait for the *South Bend* to show up, and keep people informed. The Coast Guard wants updates every 15 minutes, Bill Knodle and Keystone every hour.

At noon the "squall" that had started about 0900 is still over us. Rain is working itself into places I didn't know it could get into. It is overwhelming the drains on the bridge windows and running down the inside bulkheads and finding its way to the ceiling of my office. I am having my own little tropical rainstorm right over my desk. Georgina Young, one of the steward utilities, has found some plastic sheeting to cover the computer. And we've got a mop and bucket to keep it from getting too deep on the deck.

Just after noon, Captain Barr and the *South Bend* have finally gotten up to us, but we all agree that it will be best to wait until the squall passes before trying to transfer the tow. The plan calls for the *South Bend* to take the *Orgeron* and *Poseidon* in tow and take them in to Fort Pierce. Under normal circumstances it would be a difficult tow to complete, but in these conditions it seems like it would be impossible. But these are Captain Barr's home waters, and he thinks it can be done as long as we have daylight. A second small tug, the *Ocean Wind,* is waiting inside the inlet at Fort Pierce and will come out and assist them as they reach the jetties. Lanny isn't so sure about getting into the inlet—towing downwind through a narrow inlet is always challenging, and the lightweight, high-profile barge would be especially skittish—despite Captain Barr's insistence that he is "the only game in town."

By 1400 the squall has let up a bit, the rain reduced to the point that I can see the tug riding astern of the ship. We decide to attempt to transfer the tow. If the transfer goes swiftly, they should have enough time to reach the inlet 12 miles away before dark.

The *South Bend* gingerly approaches the *Orgeron,* staying about 200 feet upwind—off the port side—of the disabled tug. The single-screw boat is not as easy to maneuver as a twin-screw boat, and Captain Barr doesn't want to take any chances of getting fouled with the tug or our mooring lines. He matches the *Orgeron*'s heading and drifts back to close with the disabled tug. When they are close enough to the *Orgeron,* I see one of the crew from the *South Bend* throw a heaving line to the bow of the *Orgeron.* Three of the *Orgeron*'s crew are on the bow to catch the heaving line and run it through the staple on the bow, over the top of our mooring lines, and to the winch. Attached to the heaving line is a short length of messenger line made fast to a wire bridle attached to the end of the towing hawser, which is made from Spectra, an impressively strong synthetic fiber that is lightweight and easy to handle. The wire bridle will go from the bitts out over the bow, keeping the hawser from chafing, something that has been a big concern with our lines.

When Captain Barr sees the messenger go aboard the tug he orders his crew to pay out the hawser, and he gently works the *South Bend* away from the *Orgeron* as the hawser goes over the side. Spectra's big disadvantage is that it breaks easily if any kinks get in the line, as when it is made fast around a tug's bitt. The line sits in an enormous coil on the after deck, and the crew, not wanting to risk wrapping the line around the tug's H-bitt, attempt to gently pay out the line by hand. In the confusion and excitement— with Captain Barr maneuvering the *South Bend* to windward of the *J. A. Orgeron*—the crew loses control of the process and dumps the entire 1,800 feet of line overboard.

As the hawser is going out and Captain Barr is moving the *South Bend* upwind, the crew of the *Orgeron* winches aboard the messenger line. When the eye on the bridle comes up to the staple, it snags. Our two mooring lines are taking up too much room in the staple's hole. On the *Orgeron* they take another wrap on the winch to get more friction on the line, to force the eye through. The strain on the line proves too great, and the messenger parts with a sudden snap. The shaky connection between the two tugs has been broken.

I expect them to circle back in position and try again, but Captain Barr radios to say he will now have to pull in all 1,800 feet of the hawser before he can try again. And, since their capstan isn't working, they will have to gather the line by hand. It's going to take a couple of hours to get the hawser in, he estimates.

Lanny and I both know the consequences of this delay. They will not be able to get into Fort Pierce before sunset, and trying that approach in the dark is just not an option. After seeing the tug up close, Lanny has serious doubts about the *South Bend*'s capabilities and explains to me—as the *South Bend* disappears from sight—that he would rather stay with us for the time being.

We still hope that the *South Bend* will take the *Orgeron* in tow, but it looks like they might have to spend the night outside and try to make the inlet tomorrow morning. Lanny is growing more skeptical by the hour about the ability of the *South Bend* to get them in safely, but he is willing to see if the weather improves during the night.

The supposed lull that we had around 1400 is long since past, and the wind and rain have picked up again with renewed vengeance. It has veered from the east-northeast to east-by-south and has picked up significantly in strength. The Coast Guard, as well as asking us for updates, is giving us updates on the weather and has told us that there are waterspouts and tornadoes in the area.

Great.

Tropical Storm Gordon seems to be working its way over the Keys in a halting path, as though we are the intended recipients of the worst it can deliver.

In my call to Bill Knodle I tell him of our concerns about the *South Bend*. He is working closely with Bill Cantillon and Lee Orgeron to try and find a more suitable tug, but so far no one is willing to venture out into the storm. And I certainly don't blame them.

"I'm happy to pass the *Orgeron* and *Poseidon* over to the *South Bend*, Bill, but I'm not sure they are up to the task."

"How long can you hold onto them before you get into danger, that being, of course, a relative thing?" Knodle asks.

"Five to six hours, maybe. The coast of Florida is working out to the east all the time, and I'm just a mile outside of the 60-foot curve. There are also some fish havens on the chart that we are going to get close to, and if we catch the wire"—from the tug to the barge—"on something on the bottom, my lines won't hold. I'm surprised they have held this long. Let's hope the *South Bend* can get back here quickly and take them over before I run out of room."

Back on the bridge at about 1600 the *South Bend* calls to say they have their hawser aboard and are going to try again. I can't see them, but we only have about three-quarters of a mile visibility right now. "Where are you?" I ask.

"Five miles, downwind. It will take me a little over an hour to get back there."

Not good. From 1530 to 1600 we have lost ground to the west with the increase in wind, and our course over the ground is 195 degrees. Making this course, we are going to run out of room for the *Cherry Valley* in two hours.

I give Bill another call to update him, telling him I'm about out of ideas and options. We are going to have to cut the barge loose soon, I say, but we should be able to make better speed with just the tug on the end of our hawsers.

I have not underestimated the intelligence of the person whose voice, in that Texas twang, has been a calm presence in the last few hours. Knodle again impresses me with his next question, "What about anchoring the *Cherry Valley*?"

Having someone on the end of the line who knows the situation you are in, has had lots of experience at sea, *and* is removed from the scene is a captain's dream. As soon as he says it, it makes perfect sense. We are only in 65 to 70 feet of water with good bottom for holding the anchor, and I know if I put the anchor down with 10 shots—900 feet—of chain, the ship will stay put. The big question is what will happen to the tug and barge when we fetch up on the anchor. Will the hawsers snap or will they hold fast?

"I think it's our only option, Bill. Let me check with Lanny and call my office, and I'll get right back to you. We could have the *South Bend* stand by until after we anchor in case the lines part. They would at least be able to pick up the tug if not the barge also."

I call Lanny on the handheld VHF and outline the plan, asking if he wants to stay with us and try to anchor or go with the *South Bend*. It is, after all, his decision.

"Well," he comes back, "I'm pretty comfortable back here right now and I like the size of you better than the *South Bend*, so I guess I'll stay with you."

"Roger that."

The *South Bend*, overhearing our exchange, says they will start heading for Fort Pierce. I ask Captain Barr to hang around until we are anchored just in case the lines let go. Reluctantly, he agrees.

Once I have informed Keystone and Bill Knodle of our decision, I get Carl on the radio and tell him we are going to anchor the tanker. "Get the bosun and Steve, and get set to head for the bow." As I look out the forward porthole in my office, I see a big wave hit the port side of the ship, rise up, and send about 6 feet of water over the rail surging across the deck, all the way to the starboard side. "Hey, Carl?"

"Yeah?"

"Make sure all of you are in life jackets."

By 1630 the three of them are on the way to the bow. They take shelter behind the midship house and wait for a break in the seas before dashing to the raised foredeck. From the bridge I have a good perspective and call Carl when I see a break. The three of them make a mad dash to the bow—at one point with water up to their knees—but make it safely. Once on the fo'c's'le head, Junior and Steve get to work readying the anchor. With their heads down concentrating on the work, Carl watches over the bow for any particularly big seas. A couple of times a sea comes up to the chocks and washes down the sloping deck, but its force is dispersed by the hull. The cement that seals up the hole leading to the chain locker, to prevent water entering the chain locker at sea, has to be broken apart with sledgehammers, and the cover removed. The devil's claw and riding pawl have to be cleared away from the chain so that it will run free, and finally the windlass has to be disengaged. It takes 15 minutes before the anchor is clear and ready to drop. While they have been working, I have been slowly taking turns off the vessel to slow the ship.

The battery in Carl's radio dies just as he is getting ready to let the anchor go. Communication is vital, so Carl makes the dash back to the house, covering the 400 feet across the deck in a near sprint, gets a new battery, and a minute later is headed back to the bow.

As Carl is working his way back up to the fo'c's'le head, the VHF in the wheelhouse comes to life.

"Mayday, Mayday, Mayday. The tug *South Bend* is taking on water eight miles east of Fort Pierce Inlet," I can hear Captain Barr shouting into the radio. So much for our backup plan, I think. A split second later the voice of the Coast Guard officer with whom I had been speaking for the last several hours responds. Barr's voice is understandably tense as he describes how his tug has become overwhelmed by water in the engine-room. He is attempting to reach the beach, but he is racing the flood of water.

Carl breaks my concentration by calling on the UHF radio that he is ready to drop the anchor. We are down to 15 rpm and moving to the west at about a knot.

"Okay Carl, let go the port anchor," I say into the radio, logging the event at 1703. He relays the order to the bosun, who spins open the brake, and the anchor roars out of the hawsepipe. As three shots run out in a blur, Junior tightens the brake to slow the chain.

"Carl, let it out slowly until we get 10 shots on deck. Keep me posted on the lead and strain." As the chain gets out to 10 shots the bosun sets the brake, and a heavy load builds on the chain. Ever so slowly the bow starts to turn into the seas as the anchor sets firmly into the bottom, and the ship and the tow swing like a weathervane. I'm on the port wing watching the tug and barge behind us. This is going to be the moment of truth, I know. If the lines are going to part, this is when it is going to happen.

As the ship settles down with her head into the seas and the tension on the chain just heavy, not severe, I watch the tug and barge as they swing into position behind us like two little baby ducks behind their mama. At 1724 all three of us are safely at anchor in 63 feet of water.

CHAPTER 19

A MEASURE OF RELIEF

November 15, 1994

It feels like a huge weight has been lifted from my shoulders as we settle at anchor with the *Orgeron* and *Poseidon* securely behind us. The *Cherry Valley* is pitching heavily now that the bow is oriented directly into the waves, the decks lashed with spray breaking over the bow, and the mooring lines are still stretched out straight astern.

The storm, at 1730 on November 15th, has moved just north of Key West and is nearly stationary, waiting for another weather system to give it direction. I'm surprised the lines have held up this long given the condition they were in when we started. With the stern clear of water and no possibility of transferring the tow until another tug can get out here, not likely in this weather, it is time to see about getting some more mooring lines out to the *Orgeron*. We could use the extra protection against chafe and the violent motion of the vessels.

"Lanny," I say into the handheld VHF as I'm standing on the wing, "how do you feel about us putting up another couple of lines? I'm not sure how much longer these two will last."

"I'd feel a whole lot better with a couple more, Skip."

"It's been a long day," I say. "I'm going to send my guys in for a quick bite to eat and then pull up some more lines from the lazarette. We'll figure out a way to run them back to you. We should be ready to start in about 30 minutes."

Before heading down to the galley I stop in the office and make a round of calls to let everyone know what has happened and what we are going to do. We've updated the Coast Guard, so I just have to call Keystone and NASA's Bill Knodle.

I am looking forward to getting some dinner. The only thing I have consumed today was a cold grilled-cheese sandwich at noon and far too many cups of coffee. With all the added excitement of the day, my stomach is beginning to complain.

I plow through two platefuls of dinner in about five minutes before looking over at Carl, who is also just finishing. "I'm done, Carl. Let's get to work."

On the bridge I learn that the *South Bend* was able to reach the shelter of Fort Pierce Inlet, running aground just inside the breakwater to escape sinking. That he was able to reach the inlet—his tug wallowing in the waves because of the weight of water shipped through a loose hatch on the after deck—is a testament to Captain Barr's determination. Two Coast Guard 41-footers alongside the *South Bend* had transferred pumps aboard the vessel. At a few minutes after 1900 the tug is afloat again and has backed away from Dynamite Point under its own power. I can hear relief in Barr's voice as he thanks the Coast Guard crew and heads for the dock at Fort Pierce.

The rest of the *Cherry Valley*'s deck crew has also eaten quickly and are waiting in the passageway outside the mess hall. Outside it is getting dark and the sky is ominously black. The ship's house lights and deck lights are on, and we can see the faces of waves rolling down the side of the ship at just about eye level, 15 or 16 feet above the waterline. With the ship heading into the seas, most of the waves are running straight down the sides and not coming aboard.

Pulling the lines up on deck is routine for the deck crew; it is something they do every time we go into port. The bosun has set the crew to the task, and each man takes his customary position. Soon, one at a time, the lines come snaking up out of the lazarette and are flaked out on deck in giant loops.

Carl and I watch as the lines come up, checking for damage or splices that might cause the line to break. It takes about 10 minutes to get each of the 720-foot, eight-inch-circumference lines on deck. While the crew works, Carl and I discuss how to get them back to the tug. I wasn't impressed with the way the Speedline worked this morning trying to shoot downwind, and the tug is now well beyond the range of a heaving line.

The easiest way to get something to the *Orgeron* would be to float it back to them, but the trick will be to control the lines' direction. Between the corner of the engine casing and the inert gas house we store trash in round 55-gallon Rubbermaid drums. We could take one of the lids and cut out the center, making a doughnut. We will split the rim of the lid to get it over the mooring lines stretching between the ship and the tug and then lash the two edges together, securing the doughnut around the mooring lines. The doughnut will ride along the mooring lines, right to the bow of the tug, carrying a shot line tied to the doughnut. To provide the drag needed to pull the shot line downwind we can tie on a life jacket with about 20 to 30 feet of line to the doughnut. With any luck the wind, still blowing at a steady 45 knots, and the seas, running 15 to 20 feet, will work the life jacket to the bow of the tug for the *Orgeron*'s crew to grab with their boathook. They already have a one-and-a-half-inch messenger line that they will tie to the shot line and send back to us, and then we can send back the ship's new mooring lines, one at a time.

Carl and I immediately start cutting apart one of the lids and getting ready to try our idea. It doesn't take long before we are ready to set our contraption on its maiden voyage. Remarkably, it works great. The life jacket is floating along beneath our doughnut, on a straight course downwind to the tug…at least until the doughnut gets halfway down the lines. As it reaches the midpoint, the seas begin washing over the mooring lines as they race from the stern of the *Cherry Valley* to the bow of the *Orgeron* 600 feet astern of us. The motion of the lines going into the water soon causes them to spread apart—not much, but more than the diameter of the doughnut—and it blows the doughnut apart. The shot line is still attached to the life jacket and Carl tries briefly to manipulate the drift, but the jacket drifts wide of the tug.

"Bring it back Carl, we'll try again." We're hoping this time the mooring lines won't spread apart too far.

As Carl is pulling the shot line back aboard, one of the old mooring lines to the tug gives way, dropping slack into the water from the stern of the ship.

The constant pitching of the tug has chafed through the line where it goes over the bow of the tug. Thankfully, the water absorbs the recoil of the line, and no one is injured, but now we are left with only one line holding us together. If that line parts, the crew of the *Orgeron* will be on their own.

The meal I have just eaten seems to turn to stone in my stomach as I realize the implications of the parted line. I grab the VHF from the pocket of my shorts and call Lanny, shouting above the whistle of the wind. "If you have anything left on that starboard engine, now would be a good time to use it, and if you have any wire left on the drum, pay it out."

"I'm already doing it," comes the reply.

The *Cherry Valley* crew starts working at a feverish pace, getting the new mooring lines up on deck with one winch and using the other to pull in the broken line. Carl has gotten the shot line aboard, cut off the doughnut, and tied a large loop of the shot line over the remaining mooring line with the life jacket 20 feet beyond the loop, and sent it on its second voyage. It seems to take forever for the life jacket to work its way to the tug, but soon I can see one of the crew reach over the bow with the boat hook and, after two misses, come up with the shot line and life jacket. They had their messenger line rigged and ready, and it isn't long before four of us are pulling the shot line and messenger back to the *Cherry Valley*.

Two of our best lines are laid out on the deck by the Panama chock waiting to be bent on to the messenger. We have spaced the eyes about 30 feet apart on the messenger to make it easier for the crew to get the lines over the tug's bow. I call Lanny when we are ready, and they immediately start pulling the messenger line, now made far heavier by the weight of the two new mooring lines, back to the tug. Everyone on the *Cherry Valley* is watching as the lines slowly come over the bow of the tug and the eyes are dropped over the bitts.

My radio crackles, "All set, Skip. Lines are fast." We quickly put the lines on our winches and take a strain to match that on the existing line before stopping them off and putting them on the bitts.

With three lines made fast, we all breathe a collective sigh of relief. Something drastic will have to happen to part all three lines, we tell each other. Yet Lanny calls, explaining there is space in the tug's bow staple for one more line, and since this has already been a day of drastic things happening, we happily send him a fourth line.

By 2045 we have four lines made fast to the *Orgeron,* all taking an equal strain. For the first time I feel we have a good chance to keep the crew, tug, and barge safe until the storm passes. For the first time since the previous day I also start feeling the effects of fatigue, but there is still work to be done—notifying the company and starting the mountains of paperwork.

I can also sense a subtle shift in the events. Until now everything has been centered around the guys in boiler suits, those of us doing the actual work on the boats.

I sense the lawyers in business suits are becoming actively involved, all on account of one word—salvage.

CHAPTER 20

WAITING FOR
GORDON TO PASS

November 15, 1994

With the lines secure to the *Orgeron* we have done all we can do to keep the crew of the tug safe. The adrenaline is still flowing hard after watching the line part, but I'm starting to feel the effects of a very long day and not much sleep. But, as the saying goes, the job isn't over until the paperwork is done, and I head to my office to give everyone a status report—and give my wife a call to let her know what I've gotten myself into.

Just after 2300 I'm finished with the phone and the messages. Bill Knodle has told me they are still working hard on getting a bigger tug to come out, but no one is interested until the storm lets up. We have the situation stabilized and there is no longer a physical risk to the crew, so no one wants to risk coming out in the storm.

Before leaving the bridge I write the night orders in the log:

"Sorry, but no standing orders cover this adventure. Watch our position to make sure we do not drag, and have the ABs check the lines every 15 minutes; the mate on watch shall inspect the lines once an hour. Check with the tug periodically and give the Coast Guard hourly updates. Watch for waterspouts/tornadoes. Call me if you need me."

Down in my stateroom I feel fatigue tugging at me. I didn't do much physical work today, but the stress has sapped the energy out of me, and I'm exhausted. I look out over the deck from the porthole in my cabin. The glass is streaming with water from the torrential rain, and I can barely see the midship house 300 feet in front of me. The rain is still being driven by

40 knots of wind, and it sounds like thousands of tiny hammers tapping on the bulkhead.

I turn off the light, and as my head hits the pillow I fall asleep thinking about the events of the day. I sleep fitfully, waking with each passing squall as it pounds on the bulkhead, and I get up every hour or so to peer out an aft porthole and check on the boats behind us.

I am up by 0530, not feeling particularly rested. I check in with Carl on the bridge and check our position, knowing that if we had started dragging I would have been called. I call the tug, but the mate tells me that Lanny is sleeping, and I am happy to let him catch up on sleep. Everything looks good, though, the mate says, and they have had a well-deserved quiet night—lumpy, but quiet. The weather is still bad, maybe even a little worse than the day before, but the anchor is holding and we are riding well. Carl puts on a fresh pot of coffee on the bridge while I shower and try to steam out some of the knots in my back.

By 0645 the phones start ringing. Everyone wants updates about how the night has gone. All is secure, I assure them; we are just waiting for the weather to break and for a tug to get out here. Can they provide me with an update on when the tug might arrive? No one can say for sure.

Tropical Storm Gordon is still drifting around north of Key West, apparently waiting for another weather system to steer it one way or another. That the storm has stabilized is bad news for us—conditions will stay much the same until the storm moves along.

The day's big task is taking place far from the *Cherry Valley*. After hearing about the disabling and near-sinking of the tug *South Bend*, Bill Cantillon at Yowell, NASA's transportation subcontractor, is trying to find another tug to get the *Orgeron* and *Poseidon* safely into port. The crew of the *Robert J* in Cape Canaveral don't want to come out, unless NASA will assume all responsibility for life and liability if something goes wrong. NASA eventually agrees, but the *Robert J* will still not go out because of the conditions. So the search for another tug resumes until they locate the large and powerful *Dorothy Moran*, a 3,300-horsepower tug out of Jacksonville. The tug, which is equipped with a towing winch, had already departed, hoping to be alongside of us at about 2100 this evening.

Keystone has contacted Bob Parrish, an attorney in Jacksonville, to look after the interests of the ship. He has been hard at work finding out what he can about the fuel cell and the barge and starting the process of negotiating a salvage claim. His manner when I speak to him by phone is straightforward, but I have begun to hear from people ashore that he is confrontational and threatening legal action, before the two vessels are safe in port, and that is the last thing Keystone or I want. We have engaged in this rescue to help five guys on a tug, and have wound up—through very hard work from both crews and a lot of luck—involved in unusual, perhaps extraordinary, circumstances. I hope that the events won't dissolve into a proverbial pissing contest, but there is little I can do aboard the ship except maintain an atmosphere of civility and professionalism.

The morning passes quietly as we ride out the storm. At one point one of the lines chafes through at the bow of the tug and has to be replaced, but with a messenger line already strung between us it is a simple process of hauling in the old line and running out a new one. With three other lines holding us together we don't have the urgency of the previous evening.

As the *Dorothy Moran* works her way toward us, we learn that she will stop in Port Canaveral to pick up Ernie Graham and two crewmembers from the Solid Rocket Booster recovery vessels, who have ridden the barge before. These three will go aboard the barge and ride it to Port Canaveral. They are due to be picked up between 1700 and 1800 and then head out to us. Their revised ETA is now midnight.

The phone calls start at a faster pace as the afternoon turns into evening. There is concern over the type of contract the *Dorothy Moran* is operating under. I couldn't care less; I just want the tug to get here and finish the job, since I certainly am not going to tow them into port. But the lawyers have other concerns. They want to make sure that the *Dorothy Moran* cannot claim salvage, something that might be considered superior to what we have done. The hard, dangerous work is over, but we need this tug to finish the job. We secured lines to the tug and barge before they were swept ashore and have the tug and barge safely astern. Keystone's lawyers know we need the *Dorothy Moran,* or another tug like her, to finish the job, but if there is going to be an award for salvage they want to be sure that it is the *Cherry Valley* that has the claim and that the *Dorothy Moran* is just getting paid for towing. How do the lawyers expect me to know such a thing?

The storm picks up speed in the afternoon, moving along an upper-level trough toward the northeast. "This fucking thing is making a beeline for us," I think to myself as I watch the weather updates on TV. "It's going to steamroll over the top of us."

But as the hours pass the storm tracks to the north, and at 1800 its center passes northwest of us, about 17 miles away, hopefully the last we'll see of each other. The wind had been slowly veering to the right all afternoon as the storm approached, but the change as it goes past is dramatic. The wind shifts to the northwest and drops to 20 knots—like someone has flipped a switch. The three vessels swing with the wind and soon we are all pointing to the northwest, watching the storm clear.

To sailors in the Northern Hemisphere there is a great feeling of relief when the northwest wind picks up. It is a clearing breeze. The storm has passed and the weather will improve. Our spirits and the barometer rise together, and we know that this adventure will soon be over.

Over the course of the evening Ralph Hill, Keystone's in-house counsel, and I have several conversations, the gist of which is that I am not to let the tug and barge go until either he or George Clark, Keystone's operations manager, gives me permission. This doesn't sit well with me. As captain of the ship I like to think that I know what is best for the circumstances at hand and don't like to be ordered about by a Philadelphia lawyer who has never been to sea. But, despite my frustration I understand his position and agree to have the contract clarified before turning over the tow.

I head to my stateroom to grab a short nap. The *Dorothy Moran* is to arrive at about 2300. Although the storm has passed, the seas are still big and steep, and the northwest wind is kicking up a cross chop that is slowing down the *Dorothy Moran* on her trip down to us. She doesn't arrive until 0050.

As she comes on station I can see her searchlight slanting in the darkness astern of the ship, and I know that NASA's Ernie Graham is sweeping it over the barge trying to see if there is any exterior damage. They maneuver to the stern—trying to see past the spray curtain to look at the external tank—but the curtain is doing its job and they can't see the tank, I hear on the radio. The seas are still running high, eight to 10 feet, even though the wind has dropped further. The lines to the *Orgeron* now have a good belly in them, with nowhere near the strain they had earlier in the day. After the *Dorothy Moran*'s crew has completed a quick survey, the three captains get together on the radio to talk about the transfer, quickly deciding that it doesn't make much sense to try the transfer now. It is dark and the seas are still dangerously high.

"So far we have done this with no injuries and very little damage," I offer. "I don't think it is worth the risk to try this now when we can wait six hours and have daylight. And the seas will have laid down even more."

There are murmurs of agreement, and a minute later the *Dorothy Moran* turns away and heads west for Fort Pierce to spend the rest of the night. They have had a rough trip and are likely looking forward to getting a few hours' sleep tied up to a dock. The plan is for them to start out at daylight, take the barge into Fort Pierce, and then come back for the *Orgeron*. After the *Dorothy Moran* departs, her white sternlight disappearing in the darkness, I head below for the first real sleep in almost three days.

The crew of the *Dorothy Moran* depart Fort Pierce about 0800 along with the *Ocean Wind,* a tug based in Fort Pierce and contracted by Yowell, the towing contractor, to tow the *J. A. Orgeron* to port. It has been decided that the *Dorothy Moran* will take the *Poseidon* in tow and deliver her to Port Canaveral, and the *Ocean Wind* will take the *Orgeron* and bring her into Fort Pierce for repairs. The weather on the trip out is much better than the night before, the two capable tugs making easy progress through the low swells. The seas are down to three feet and the wind is a mere to 10 to 15 knots, a much nicer day than we have had for a while. They cross the eight miles to where we are anchored and are slowing their engines for their approach to us at 0900.

From the bridge wing I see the *Dorothy Moran* sidle close to the stern of the *Poseidon* and see three men leap aboard—a much easier task now than it would have been the night before.

Ernie Graham quickly checks the tank, finding it secure and with no apparent damage. He calls the captain of the *Dorothy Moran* and asks him to call "Red" Bird at NASA and tell Red "the tank looks in good shape." He also mentions that the *Poseidon*'s generators will not start, which means there is no way to release the barge's anchors. If Bill Knodle or anyone else had tried to get aboard the *Poseidon* during the storm, they wouldn't have been able to anchor the barge.

While Ernie Graham and his crew are checking the tank and barge, we are preparing to let everyone go. There is excitement on the vessel, anticipating the successful completion of this adventure, but ashore, in Keystone's home office, the excitement is of a different nature.

Keystone has not yet learned the details of the contract with the *Dorothy Moran*'s owner, Moran Towing Co.

I call Ralph at 0920 and say that we are ready to transfer the vessels.

"Do not do it until you hear from me or George Clark," comes the reply.

"Ralph, we have done all we can do here," I respond, attempting to conceal my annoyance. "There is no way I can finish this up and get them safely into port; we have to use these two tugs. So far we have been the white knight in this whole affair; if we start slowing things down to wait for paperwork, it is not going to go over well."

"By law, you control the vessels behind you," Ralph responds. "You can keep them as long as you want."

"How long before you get the paperwork sorted out?"

"Soon. I don't know exactly."

I look at the clock on the wall of my office, 0930. I think for a few seconds, take a deep breath, and say, "I'll give you 30 minutes. At 1000 I'm turning them loose."

"You know I can fire you, don't you?"

"Yup."

Ralph was not happy with a junior captain questioning his authority, but he can't replace me in the next 30 minutes, either. I like sailing as captain, but sometimes making the right decision is better than keeping a job, and I am giving him a half hour more. After all, he has had since midday yesterday to get this sorted out.

I climb the 12 steps to the bridge, muttering unpleasant things about lawyers, and walk out on the wing with the handheld VHF.

"On the *Orgeron, Dorothy,* and *Ocean Wind:* I'm going to have to ask you guys to stand down for a few minutes. The fucking lawyers are starting to get in the way. I do not know all the details, but there is a question about the paperwork. I've given them 30 minutes to get it straightened out. At 1000 I'm going to start the transfer whether they have the paperwork straightened out or not. Everyone grab a cup of coffee."

I am so frustrated with the situation that I can't stay on the bridge, so I head down to my office. Muttering and pacing, I watch the clock, feeling hog-tied by a lawyer in a suit 1,000 miles away from me.

Steve Worden hears me from the radio shack, comes across the hall and taps on the door. He has been my right-hand man during this whole thing, helping with phone calls, telexes, and generally keeping people informed when I wasn't able to. And he has acted as my sounding board as I would think out loud, helping me organize my thoughts and keeping me from getting too wound up.

"Shakespeare was right, Steve; the first thing we should do is kill all the lawyers. It would make things a lot simpler."

"One way or another it will be over soon, Skip. And I know, from watching you for the last two days, that there isn't anything more, or better, that you could have done. You've kept the crew of the tug safe and saved the tug and barge, no one could have done better than that."

"Thanks Steve, I appreciate that."

My anxiety stems from the fact that until now we have acted swiftly and selflessly, seeing an opportunity to assist and acting immediately. Until now I have largely controlled the situation, within the limits of my abilities. To have a team of lawyers step in and pull rank is degrading, especially in front of my peers on the ship and on the tugs. Yet the lawyers, unlike me at this moment, also seem to understand the context of what we've done, perhaps seeing a larger picture that may have historical and legal implications. Which is why I have agreed to stall, at least until 1000.

Steve goes back to the radio shack and I continue to pace and watch the minutes tick by. When the clock reaches 1000 I walk out of the office and head for the stairway leading to the bridge. As I push open the door, the cell phone in my office starts ringing. I smile a little as I turn to answer it, thinking that at least they believed me when I said I was letting it go at 1000. As I answer the cell phone, the sat phone starts ringing also. Ralph Hill is on the cell, and Steve Worden talks with George Clark on the sat phone. They say the same thing: the paperwork is done; release the vessels.

I dash to the bridge and key the mike: "Okay, guys, let's get on with it."

The *Ocean Wind* moves in to the stern of the *Poseidon* and puts up a line. They will act as a brake while the *Orgeron* pulls in the tow wire so the barge will not run over the *Orgeron*. While Lanny is in the doghouse running the winch, the strain comes up on our lines and one more of them parts under the heavy strain. Lanny slows the winch down, and I, standing on the port bridge wing, report to him the tension on the lines. As they come up tight, I call Lanny and have him slow the winch further. They soon have the pennant on the stern of the *Orgeron*, and the *Dorothy Moran* moves in alongside the *Orgeron*. The *Dorothy* passes the end of her tow wire to the *Orgeron*, and the crew on the *Orgeron* shackles the *Dorothy's* wire into the pennant of the barge. With the tow wire made up, the *Dorothy* takes a strain and starts to pull the *Poseidon* away as the *Ocean Wind* takes in her line.

With the *Poseidon* clear, the *Ocean Wind* gets in position downwind of the *Orgeron* and passes a line up to the bow. The *Orgeron* crew throws off two more of our lines to make room for the *Ocean Wind's* towline. Once the *Ocean Wind's* line is secure they cut our last line. It is 1102 on the 17th of November, 1994.

As the *Ocean Wind* takes a strain on their line, Lanny calls over the radio, "Skip, I want to pass on our heartfelt thanks to you and the crew from all of us."

"Thanks, Lanny. Who knows, maybe next time it will be you helping me. Good luck, and sometime I'd like to buy you a beer."

"You're on."

Back inside the wheelhouse I pick up the phone to the engineroom. "Paul, let's test gear and get the hell out of here."

Paul's voice booms from the ship phone, "Roger that, Cap!"

CHAPTER 21

A RACE AGAINST THE SANDS

November 15, 1994

Each morning of the year, the paved walkway snaking along the beach in Fort Lauderdale teems with activity—joggers, skaters, bicyclists, and walkers, whose brisk energy creates something akin to a human-powered rush hour. On the windswept morning of Tuesday, November 15, 1994, the spectacle of the grounded Turkish freighter *Firat* greeted this healthy bunch, its dark hull, battered by the breaking surf, looming in silhouette against the lightening eastern horizon.

When a ship ends up on a beach, a dizzying chain reaction—an instant flurry of phone calls between ship owner, government officials, insurance companies, ship agents, and salvors—is set in motion. From the time that the master of the *Firat* had reached for his VHF mike and issued his Mayday call to the breaking dawn just after 0700, the ship's agent had contacted the owners, the Coast Guard, the company's team of lawyers, and a man named Joe Farrell, president of Resolve Marine Group, which had been hired to extract the ship from the beach.

A mélange of trucks and four-by-fours were parked on the sand, and Farrell was among the cluster of assorted spectators, which also included a handful of local TV and newspaper reporters. His pant legs whipping in the wind and his graying hair blowing sideways from his head, Farrell was speaking quickly and into his cell phone, covering his mouth and the phone against the onshore wind.

"She's pounding like a bastard!" Farrell shouted, his coarse Boston accent sounding rougher from lack of sleep. "The Coast Guard's going to want us to get the oil off right away. I've got a barge coming from the

Bahamas, but it won't get here until tonight. Meanwhile, we'll get our beach gear set up and try and stabilize her." After clearing with the ship's agent, Farrell stalked down the beach to greet his crew, who were already unloading the contents of their trucks: lengths of chain with links more than an inch thick; coils of steel wire; numerous sheaves and heavy industrial machinery; and a pair of Navy anchors that weighed 8,000 pounds each. Resolve had been hired on a cost-plus basis, meaning that he would work with the owners to remove the ship as soon as possible, but Farrell would be paid for his time regardless of what happened to the ship.

His home phone in Fort Lauderdale rang at 0500 November 15, 1994. "Farrell," he rasped, impervious to the early hour. He was out of bed, into his car, and on the beach and looking at the beached ship less than 10 minutes later.

On the beach, Farrell was concerned about getting the 700 tons of bunker fuel off the *Firat*. Since the *Valdez* incident in 1989 and the enactment of the Oil Pollution Act a year later, the Coast Guard had been making it clear to the maritime community that spilling oil could be punishable, at the very least, by heavy fines, and possibly imprisonment if it could be proved by the Coast Guard and Justice Department that a crew or a vessel's owners acted negligently. Coast Guard port captains themselves are terrified of oil spills in their harbors, knowing that a catastrophic spill on their watch would likely end an otherwise clean career. Salvors understand this impetus, and plan first to remove oil from a ship in danger of breaking up. Earlier Farrell had called his crew in the Bahamas, who were using the company's open barge to transport gravel between Freeport and Nassau for the construction of the Atlantis Hotel, and told them to fuel up the tug and divert immediately for Fort Lauderdale. Farrell knew that offloading the oil would be best done with a tank barge, but he also knew that time was precious and that the sooner he could get the oil off, the sooner he could begin refloating the ship. Once he secured arrangements to get the barge over to Fort Lauderdale, he called the Coast Guard Captain of the Port.

"In salvage jobs you have to use the resources available to you," Farrell recalled later. "I knew there wasn't a tank barge available in the area. Unfortunately, the Captain of the Port did not agree with the plan. He didn't want me to use a barge that was not specifically built to handle fuel. But he was still demanding that we take the fuel off before we tried to refloat the vessel."

The only other barge in the area belonged to an oil consortium, but it was not available for charter to a non-member. Farrell maintained that he could get the oil off quickly with his barge, but the port captain refused, insisting instead on negotiating to use the consortium barge—negotiations that could take several days. Meanwhile the *Firat* was being pounded by the surf and digging itself deeper into the sand. A tense standoff ensued, but Farrell continued his plans to stabilize the ship and later in the morning joined the Coast Guard aboard a helicopter for an inspection of the vessel, since he and his crew could not board the ship through the surf.

"We went aboard the ship and saw that there were two cargo holds that were internally ruptured. You could see between the rebar that the tank tops were blown open by the pounding. The cargo was so heavy that it had broken through to the bunker tanks. The rebar was now covered in thick fuel oil," Farrell said later. "We would have to get the rebar out of the cargo hold as well—just to access the fuel tanks to pump them out. We were in a hell of a predicament with these 12- to 15-foot swells. Every time you get a ship grounded on a sandy beach, you've got a race against the sand." With every wave, the *Firat* was working its way deeper into the sands, digging itself a trench that was creating a suction-like hold on the hull.

CHAPTER 22

THE *FIRAT* FLOATS FREE

Ships are floating disasters—and disasters are Resolve Marine Group's specialty.

As Resolve's bombastic president, Joe Farrell has cheated death numerous times, surviving shipwrecks and explosions and rescuing hundreds of trapped crewmembers over the course of a 30-year career. ("I have been killed a lot of times, but it just doesn't take," he's said.) Now in his 50s, and with a reputation as one of the most indomitable figures in the U.S. maritime industry, Farrell runs Resolve Marine Group with a fierce determination. As a maritime salvage and emergency-response company based in Fort Lauderdale, Resolve sends crews of highly skilled, loyal workers—a ragtag, international group of divers, metalworkers, merchant seamen, explosives experts, and naval architects—all over the Western Hemisphere to recover ships in distress. Navigational errors or mechanical failures send ships aground on ledges; they catch fire and explode when a welding job goes wrong and sparks ignite a fuel tank; they collide with each other, tearing open their hull plating and allowing water to rush in so fast that no amount of pumping can keep them afloat.

Resolve has a file of more than 3,000 ships that—as required by the International Maritime Organization and the U.S. Coast Guard—have contracted with Resolve to formulate incident response plans in the event of an emergency. Resolve has in its files each of the ship's plans and loading and stability calculations. If something goes awry, the response team is equipped with knowledge of the ship's construction. And when this happens, Joe Farrell's phone rings.

"I'm a salvor; I save things," Farrell explains. He chafes at being considered a mere wreck removal specialist. "Salvage is saving something, rescuing people or ships or cargo; wreck removal is like feeding on carrion. I employ the best salvors in the business, and we can have our gear and crew anywhere it needs to be—North and South America, the Caribbean— within 24 hours," Farrell says. Like all salvors, Farrell thrives on the chaos of emergency situations, striving to bring order to the confusion with limited resources as quickly and safely as possible. Salvage situations are often so fluid that no salvage plan can be completely prepared in advance; they are refined and improvised on the spot.

The salvage of the freighter *Firat* would continue for several weeks. Joe Farrell went nearly mad with frustration as delay after delay—each of which he considered avoidable and costly to the owners of the ship—added to the complexity of the job. His direct manner and seemingly limitless energy and ability was at complete odds with the cautious, bureaucratic pace of the Coast Guard captain of the port, who, like it or not, was calling the shots. Farrell's ability to master complex situations had been tried in the past.

Raised in working-class Roxbury, Massachusetts—"I was the last white kid in Roxbury"—Farrell has had an ability to work quickly and intelligently at dangerous tasks from the time he was young. As a teenager he worked on boats in Boston Harbor, ferries, water taxis, and eventually tugs. As soon as he turned 18, he went straight to a Navy recruiter's office in Boston, wanting to enlist in the SEAL program. "I had a screwed-up nose from some trouble I'd been in, so they didn't take me," Farrell recalls. "But I went over to the Coast Guard and asked, 'You got divers?' And they said yeah, so I signed up and ended up going to Navy dive school anyway to train as a diver for Coast Guard icebreakers." Farrell also enrolled in the Coast Guard's engineering school, becoming certified as a diesel engineer, and served in the Arctic on icebreakers for several years. His job was inspecting the hull by blowing holes in the ice and then dropping into the hole with his dive gear and circling the ship. "We had to blow a hole in the ice away from the ship with 300 pounds of explosives—you never go into the water between the ice and the ship unless you want to get yourself killed—and then we'd swim under the ship to see if the propellers had been damaged by the ice." The job provided Farrell with exposure to several aspects of a life at sea that would remain passions for his entire career: diving, the use of explosives, and a yearning for adventure and the thrill that it provided.

He volunteered for service in Vietnam, recognized as the youngest E6—the highest enlisted rank in the Coast Guard's engineering program—and completed ammunition school, becoming an advisor in handling explosives in the world's hot spots. "I was trained to load and offload explosives in war zones without blowing up the neighborhood," Farrell says. After two years in Qui Nhon and Cat Lai, Vietnam, he finished his service at a lifeboat station in Scituate, Massachusetts. Intent on escaping the miserable New England weather of his youth, in 1972, at the age of 22, Farrell bought a 38-foot sailboat, a book on how to sail, and headed south in a blinding December snow squall. "I loaded aboard my two dive tanks, my seabag, and with $400 in my pocket sailed the hell out of Massachusetts. I didn't know anyone in Florida but I knew it was warm." He soon found work with RCA, which had a contract with the U.S. Navy recovering training torpedoes in shallow waters off the Bahama Islands. Farrell and his crew would drop from helicopters in full dive gear, recover the torpedoes, and then strap them beneath the helicopters for delivery to shore. He did this eight to 10 times a day for four years until he heard about a job on an ocean salvage tug departing for Europe.

When the *Tasman Zee* was launched in Holland in 1958 she was the largest and most powerful tug in existence. She was one of the finest examples of Dutch shipbuilding—at a time when the Dutch were known to be the best in the world in offshore towing and salvage. She had a draft of 18 feet and a pair of engines that delivered 30,000 horsepower, and, although almost 20 years old when Farrell joined the crew, was still a potent vessel capable of towing any ship afloat on extended ocean voyages. Farrell, wooed by the romance of sailing deep-sea tugs, was hired as engineer and, after learning enough Dutch to run the engineroom, sailed numerous runs between Europe, the U.S., and the Caribbean over the next several years. When the tug was put up for sale in 1978, Farrell heard about a ship aground in Saint Barts and—while the tug's owners sought a new owner for the vessel—contracted the *Tasman Zee* to perform the salvage himself.

Three salvage jobs later, he was owner of the *Tasman Zee*. "I used the boat to buy the boat," he says. "And then bought myself a sextant, a book about celestial navigation, and a captain's hat. I was captain and chief engineer of my first tug." Farrell rented office space on Pier 6 in San Juan, Puerto Rico, outfitted it with a desk, a couch, and a telex machine, and docked the tug out front. He was 28 years old.

These days when on vacation in Nantucket or Bimini, Farrell writes stories about his adventures in a notebook, his scrawl legible only to himself. "Maybe the kids can read it someday," he says.

There was his attempted rescue of the crew of a tanker that had blown up off the Dominican Republican after a welding job went wrong. The tug Farrell had chartered to rescue the crew and salvage the wreck sank on the voyage out, and he and the crew were adrift for hours in the storm-tossed seas, vomiting from seasickness, clinging to makeshift rafts, and reciting Our Fathers in Spanish and English until a helicopter came to the rescue. He eventually made it to the wreck, which had been blown in two, only to discover that its crew were dead and all he could do was open the seacocks and sink the vessel before it drifted ashore and fouled the south coast of the Dominican Republic.

He's written about the time he was hired to refloat a tanker on the San Juan River in Venezuela. The fully loaded ship, which had been topped off a little too heavily and was therefore running deeper than normal, had gone aground at a bend in the river, its 34-foot draft plowing a furrow into the muddy bottom until it was stuck fast in the middle of the channel. On scene the following day, Farrell contracted with the tanker's owners to divert another of its ships, then in the Caribbean, to offload a portion of the oil.

"When the second tanker arrived I got on board with the pilot—and the captain of the grounded ship also came along—and we had to go about eight miles upriver to turn the ship around before we could come alongside," Farrell says. "We were all on the bridge heading down toward the ship, all our hoses were ready to start pumping oil, we had the fenders all ready to come alongside, and the current was ripping like hell adding to our speed. I had contracted with a tug to help get us alongside, a big fucking tug with 3,000 horsepower, but the captain of the tug refused to tie alongside us because he was afraid he'd get dragged over because of the speed of the ship and the current. So how the fuck am I supposed to approach? 'I don't know,' they said, 'but we're not tying up to the ship.' So I put Garrido"—one of Resolve's engineers—"on board the tug and told him to push like hell when we got close. But as we approached, I realized we couldn't get close to the grounded ship. The captain of the grounded tanker had stirred up so much silt around the ship that he'd created a barrier of shallow water that we couldn't get through. Now the entire river was blocked at 22 feet of depth, meaning that now no ships could get in or out to get oil out of the port. Now we really had a problem. I was told that they were going to have to shut the wells down if they couldn't get ships in, and that it would take months to get the wells going again and cost the local economy millions.

"I told the captains and the pilot that we were fucked unless they wanted to do this one thing. I said we had to get through the silt; I knew it was only silt and that once we got through it we'd be able to get out the same way we got in. I recommended we go back upriver, pick up speed, and run through the bar of silt, and slide into position alongside the grounded ship. They said, we can't do that. I said, that's all I got; there are no dredges around and the oil's gotta flow and we're in the middle of the fucking jungle. 'You think you can do it?' they asked, and I said I didn't know but that's what I'd recommend. They said that I should talk to Norway—where the owners were—and explain it to them. So I said, fine, and got on the phone and they asked if I would drive the tanker myself, and I said, 'Well, your captains won't do it and the pilot won't do it, so, yeah.' They wanted to know the odds of success, and I said I didn't know but that if I failed the whole ship would blow up because, even though it was inerted, the tanks could blow open, which would introduce air and *boom!*

"They said okay.

"So I said, 'Here's the plan. Pull everything off the fantail of the grounded ship, the davits, the lifeboats, all the gear on the stern. I'm going to end up putting the flare of the bow right over the stern of the ship at a

30-degree angle as we come alongside. Garrido, when I come close to the turn before the ship I want you to nail me with full fucking power at 90 degrees to shape me up through the turn so I can come alongside. And I'll be at full fucking power too to get us through the silt. You clear?' All they said was, 'Holy shit.'

"So as I got the tanker back upriver and the crew of the grounded tanker were clearing the stern of the gear, I asked the captains again, 'You sure you don't want to drive this fucking thing?' 'No!' So I got the ship turned around and got going downriver at full power, and Garrido hit me with the tug straight on as we came through the turn, and we blasted through that fucking silt—sliced right through it—and came right against the grounded ship with all the fenders perfectly in place. On the bridge there was all this cheering and clapping, and the ship was lying perfectly, as though I'd done it in my sleep. They all wanted to know how long I'd been handling tankers because they'd never seen anyone handle a tanker like that before, and I said it was the first fucking time I'd ever driven a tanker."

Over the next three hours the crew offloaded 3,500 tons of oil, racing against the falling tide. The stranded ship was refloated, and both vessels headed safely downriver to sea.

The grounding of the *Firat* was not especially complex from an engineering standpoint. If Farrell had been allowed to do the job his way, the bunker oil (the fuel for the ship's engines) would have been taken off the ship two days after the grounding, when Tropical Storm Gordon had passed over Florida the first time and was off Cape Hatteras. In the days following the rescue of the crew of the *Orgeron,* conditions on Florida's east coast moderated significantly. It was during this brief weather window that Farrell would have mobilized his crew to pump the oil, offloaded enough cargo of rebar to lighten the ship. Then, the ship already stabilized with "beach gear," a set of monstrous Navy anchors weighing up to 20,000 pounds apiece deployed astern of the ship as well as a web of cable running through heavy sheaves, Farrell would have hauled the ship into deeper water with a couple of tugs. The operation should have taken a few days. It dragged on for two weeks as

Gordon built to hurricane strength and crossed back over Florida, batter-
ing the *Firat* again and causing extensive structural damage, costing the
company millions of dollars in extra repair costs.

In the pre-Thanksgiving bustle that marks the beginning of the tourist
season in South Florida, the ship's hulking shape remained an odd fixture
—its bow resting just 50 yards offshore. The longer it remained on the
beach, the more the Coast Guard worried that the hull would breach and
several hundred tons of heavy fuel oil would spew onto the carefully
groomed beaches. Resolve's salvors missed the initial opportunity to remove the wreck rapidly, yet, despite the extreme forces at work, the hull
was sound except for a hairline crack that allowed the slightest trickle of oil
to form a thin sheen on the water.

Farrell had been tracking the storm's progress by watching the buoy reports and speaking directly with forecasters at the National Hurricane Center
in Miami. His worst fears were confirmed—the storm was coming back, and
he and his crew were just getting their gear in place. Most importantly, the oil
barge, ordered by the Coast Guard after they had rejected Farrell's plan to use
Resolve's open hopper barge for lightering oil, had not yet arrived.

"The swells were eight feet when we started, and they built to 18 feet by
the time we got permission to use the barge. I had to get this 300-foot barge
alongside the *Firat* with a 20,000-pound anchor on its stern. Between the
ship and the barge I had a set of Yokohama fenders that are usually eight feet
in diameter, flattened out to 18 inches because of the pressure of the swells."

The timing of the operation to remove the bunker oil couldn't have
been worse. Resolve's crews successfully maneuvered the barge alongside
the ship in the breaking surf, securing the fenders and a series of heavy
mooring lines with a combined breaking strength of several hundred
thousand tons. But the success did not last. "We parted nine nine-inch
nylon lines. They went one after the other, *boom–boom–boom!* Like nine
fucking hand grenades. I said the hell with this, and pulled the barge out.
It was too damn dangerous."

Instead, Farrell devised a plan to pump the oil ashore by running a
six-inch-diameter hose to a bulldozer on the beach and securing it with a

nine-inch reinforced line. The oil would then be pumped into tank trucks parked in the sand. The sight of the hose and hawser being violently jerked in the surf, causing the bulldozer to be shaken like a toy, thrilled Farrell, despite the delays. Best of all, the operation was successful; the oil was removed.

Once the oil was off, the weather began to moderate, allowing the salvors to bring in barges and lighten the ship further by removing approximately 1,400 tons of rebar using the ship's cargo booms. At the same time, the ship was partially flooded to maintain contact with the bottom and prevent it from drifting farther ashore. Once several tugs were contracted and a web of heavy cable and polypropylene line was set up around the ship, the water was pumped from the holds and tension increased on all the lines. One tug, the 4,200-horsepower *Gulf Hawk,* was tied to the stern, along with two anchors, one 8,000 pounds and the other 20,000 pounds, that were run to the winches on the stern. The tug began pulling to the east, while another tug, the equally large *Gulf Eagle,* was secured to the bow, along with an 8,000-pound anchor, and began pulling to the northeast. Finally, the *Firat* began to move.

Farrell and the Resolve's crew finally floated the *Firat* free on November 27, 1994, 13 days after she went aground. After a brief layover at anchor off Fort Lauderdale for a hull survey, the ship was towed into Fort Lauderdale to discharge her cargo. Following the discharge she was towed across the Atlantic and Mediterranean and delivered to her owners in Turkey, a month later, for drydocking and repairs.

PART IV

"Salvage is the compensation allowed to persons by whose assistance a ship or her cargo has been saved, in whole or in part, from impending peril on the sea, or in recovering said property from actual loss as in cases of shipwreck, derelict, or recapture. Success is essential to the claim; as if the property is not saved, or if it perish, or in the case of capture if it is not retaken, no compensation can be allowed."

—Justice Nathan Clifford, from the Blackwall decision, 1869

CHAPTER 23

IN PERIL

Salvage law is one of the oldest codes in existence, predating the laws of the land, which depends on the existence of nations to be recognized. Long before there were sovereign states, though, there was trade at sea between ports throughout the known world by enterprising ship owners and their captains and crews, who plied the world's waters by sailing ship. A set of customs developed, probably well before 3000 B.C., when the Phoenicians began wandering the watery part of the globe in earnest. This set of codes could be easily understood by merchant seamen engaged in sea trade. Intended to protect property and the rights of ship owners and masters on the unforgiving, and unpredictable, high seas, Rhodian Law, as it came to be known, was codified by the Phoenicians around 1500 B.C. The code's namesake, the island of Rhodes, lies on the easternmost edge of Greece's ragged Aegean archipelago, making it uniquely suited to serve as a home base for merchant ships that connected Mediterranean ports, Asia Minor, and the Middle East. *Benedict on Admiralty,* a 10-volume set of cinderblock-size books that occupy shelves on every admiralty lawyer's library, credits the Rhodians with having the first disciplined navy and merchant marine and says they "were the first people to create, digest and promulgate a system of maritime law."

Lex Rhodia was a set of unwritten agreements between ship owners and mariners. In his 1950 book *The Law of the Sea,* William McFee makes it clear that the law was drawn from customs adapted by mariners themselves, not drawn up in court and distributed for compliance. Yet there remained a sense of mystery about the codes that required an understanding of the perils of the sea and an appreciation for the skills necessary to navigate the high seas.

Rhodian Law soon became accepted at Athens and at all the islands of the Aegean Sea. The Romans codified Rhodian Law after the Greeks, including in them a stipulation regarding how a salvage award is determined: "If a ship be surprised at sea with whirlwinds, or be shipwrecked, any person saving anything of the wreck, shall have one-fifth of what he saves." Another article, cited in *Benedict on Admiralty,* increases the incentive by adding a threat: "If the rope break, and the boat goes adrift from the ship with mariners in it, and they perish at sea, the masters shall pay their heirs one full year's wages. And if any person finds the boat, and preserves it safe, he shall restore everything as he found it, and receive one-fifth part as a reward."

Rhodian Law also sought to recognize the skill of the mariner involved in a salvage situation by considering the degree of danger involved. The reward could be increased or decreased depending on the level of peril. "If gold or silver, or any other thing be drawn up from the sea eight cubits [14 feet] deep, he that draws it up shall have one-third, and if fifteen cubits [25 feet], he shall have one-half, because of the depth. And if anything is cast upon the shore by the tide, and taken up only one cubit deep [20 inches], the finder shall have a tenth part."

The codes spread west, reaching Spain and the Atlantic coast of France where a similar set of laws were drafted at Oleron in the 13th century. This code ultimately served as the basis for English admiralty law.

The French codes articulated the need to guard against the possibility of human ill will, such as piracy or deliberately wrecking a vessel to recover property. Such ingrates would be "punished as robbers and thieves," and likely put to death. "All false and treacherous pilots shall be condemned to suffer a most rigorous and unmerciful death," the Oleron codes decreed, "and high gibbets [gallows] shall be erected for them in the same place, or as nigh as conveniently may be, where they so guided and brought any ship or vessel, to ruin as aforesaid, and thereon these accursed pilots are with ignominy and much shame to end their days." Strong incentive not to purposely wreck a vessel and claim salvage.

Although each set of laws had certain geographic variances, the core of the law was identical. In some of its basic tenets, *Lex Rhodia* remains unchanged and can still be considered, in the words of McFee, as "the foundation of modern maritime jurisprudence." One of the most significant aspects of maritime law—as distinct from the law of the land—encourages mariners to take risks to preserve property, risks that might otherwise be considered imprudent. The reward for such service—and it is considered a reward and not a wage—should be considerable, almost shockingly so, to ensure that mariners will always regard a ship in distress as a potential windfall and perform all acts within their power to prevent it from being lost. The stricken ship's underwriters will be spared the significant cost of a total loss, and the salvor will be rewarded a portion of the value of whatever it is he has saved. In other words: finders keepers, at least to a degree that will be determined by an admiralty court. Interestingly, rescuing people is never rewarded financially; such an act is considered voluntary.

There are two basic types of salvage: "contract salvage," the realm of professionals like the redoubtable Joe Farrell of Resolve Marine Group; and "pure salvage," when a captain performs a rescue without a formal agreement.

Traditionally, contract salvage had been done with the Lloyd's Open Form (LOF), with the premise that the salvor gets nothing unless the vessel is saved: no cure, no pay. In the last 30 years, however, salvors have been compensated for their time even if a full solution is not attained. Gone are the days when large salvage tugs wandered the world's oceans in search of quarry, as detailed in Farley Mowat's *The Grey Seas Under*. These salvors worked strictly under the "no cure, no pay" credo.

A 1967 incident led to an ecological disaster that changed the way salvors were compensated. The tanker *Torrey Canyon* went aground off the Scilly Isles, spilling millions of gallons of oil. In an exceptionally foolhardy attempt to burn away the oil spill, the ship was strafed by fighter jets, which set the *Torrey Canyon* ablaze. The resulting damage eventually led to an addendum to the existing Lloyd's Open Form that provided a safety net of sorts for salvors, allowing them to recover costs plus 15 percent. And while the addendum protects the salvors, to be sure, it is intended to protect the marine environment as well. Without it, salvors might be less inclined to

attempt a salvage job if the odds for success are less than favorable, the result being a potential oil spill on par with the *Torrey Canyon* or *Exxon
Valdez.* Lloyd's Open Form, revised to include the safety net, continues to
be the standard contract used by salvors and ship owners in contract salvage situations.

When a ship is in danger and is saved by another mariner and no prior
agreement is established—when the captain performs a successful salvage
yet knows little of Lloyd's Open Form—a court reverts to the foundations
of salvage law to determine a reward for salvage claims. This is pure salvage. The haunting tale of the *Mary Celeste* is perhaps the most famous example of pure salvage. On a bright November morning in 1872, Captain
Benjamin Spooner Briggs set out from New York across the Atlantic in
command of the 282-ton brig *Mary Celeste,* a wooden two-master with a
cargo of alcohol in wooden barrels bound for Genoa. Accompanying the
38-year-old captain were his wife and two-year-old daughter, and a capable crew of seven. After dropping off a pilot outside Ambrose Channel,
Briggs ordered the helmsman to steady up on a course just north of east
that would allow them to fetch the Straits of Gibraltar some three-and-a-
half weeks later. They were never seen again.

The *Mary Celeste,* however, her sails set and drawing, was found on December 4, by the crew of another sailing ship, the *Dei Gratia,* also bound for
the Mediterranean. The *Mary Celeste* was sailing under shortened canvas
and heading on an erratic westerly course, which caused the crew of the *Dei
Gratia* to draw close for an inspection. Seeing no one at the helm, the captain ordered the first mate, Oliver Deveau, to launch a rowboat and board
the mysterious vessel. He found not a soul aboard, and there was little trace
of the crew's fate. The cargo remained; the ship appeared tidy; and the personal effects of the crew appeared to have been left just minutes before, as
though they had all simply vanished at once. In his 1942 book *Mary Celeste:
The Odyssey of an Abandoned Ship,* Charles Edey Fay wrote that "something
of disturbing character happened. Whatever it may have been, it must have
been sufficiently serious to cause an experienced master-mariner with his
wife, child and crew, to abandon ship, and to do so in haste." The mate of

the *Dei Gratia* described the scene in his testimony afterward: "the men's clothing was left behind; their oilskins, boots, and even their pipes." The captain's bunk appeared to have an "impression as of a child having lain there." The galley was still stocked with fresh supplies; pots and pans were stacked clean in the drying rack. The only sign of disruption was the fact that the ship's boats were missing, the compass was smashed, the captain's sextant was missing, and there was a moderate amount of water in the bilge, although it was likely a result of rainwater and spray that had accumulated in the time since the ship had been abandoned. Judging from the logbook, which Deveau found in the captain's cabin, the vessel's last noted position was just a few miles off the Azorean island of Santa Maria on November 24. It had apparently sailed unattended for two weeks and covered more than 600 miles.

Deveau took command of the *Mary Celeste,* and with a crew of two seamen sailed the brig to Gibraltar and claimed salvage rights. In the months that followed, formal hearings in Gibraltar and Genoa found the cargo to be worth $36,943; the ship herself was insured for $14,000, but assessed by the court at $5,700. The master and crew of the *Dei Gratia* were awarded one-fifth the total value of the ship and cargo, $8,528.60.

How a salvage award is determined today stems from an incident in San Francisco harbor in 1867 involving the burning of the 1,200-ton British ship *Blackwall.* Shortly before 0300 on August 24, when the *Blackwall* was at anchor off San Francisco's docks, her cargo of 38,000 sacks of wheat suddenly caught fire. Flames leapt from the holds and an attempt by the crew to douse the blaze failed, and so a verbal alarm to shore was sounded, causing the San Francisco Fire Department to spring to action. The fire crew had no fireboat, so they coerced the crew of a steam tug, the *Goliah,* which was alongside at Broadway Wharf, out of their bunks to get steam in the boilers and get underway. The engineer agreed and sent for the captain, who, along with most of the crew, were home in bed. By 0600 the tug was fully manned and loaded with a pair of the city's horse-drawn fire engines—minus the horses—and had sufficient steam to draw away from the wharf and approach the burning ship. By this time the ship was almost totally ablaze, the flames reaching halfway to the mast tops. The *Blackwall's* crew had long since abandoned the vessel and departed with the personal effects in the ship's boats. The captain of the tug, though, came swiftly alongside, allowing the firemen to board over the rails and begin to douse the flames. Starting from the bow, the firemen trained their four hoses at the base of the deck fire, soon working their way to the holds, and within half an hour the fire was completely extinguished. The *Goliah's* captain ordered his crew to hoist the *Blackwall's* anchor, and he took the vessel in tow, bringing it to the anchoring flats near Vallejo Street wharf.

After the fire the ship and her cargo were valued at $100,000, and the owners of the tug filed a salvage claim. Both the lower court and the appeals courts ruled in favor of the *Goliah,* but the owners of the *Blackwall* appealed to the U.S. Supreme Court. Supreme Court Justice Nathan Clifford delivered the opinion of the court, finding that without the use of the tug, the vessel and cargo would have been completely destroyed by fire. He described the tug captain's skill in bringing his tug alongside a burning ship as considerable, and praised his skill further by pointing out that he performed these maneuvers despite the risk to himself, his crew, and his tug. The crew of the *Goliah* were in constant danger of being seriously injured—or killed—by the potential collapse of the burning masts. They had responded instantly, skillfully, without obligation (the firemen were obliged to respond as it was their job), and saved a vessel and her cargo that would have been destroyed without their assistance.

"Salvage is the compensation allowed to persons by whose assistance a ship or her cargo has been saved, in whole or in part, from impending peril on the sea, or in recovering such property from actual loss, as in the case of shipwreck, derelict, or recapture," Justice Clifford wrote in his opinion regarding the award of the *Blackwall* salvage claim. "Success is essential to the claim, as if the property is not saved, or if it perish, or in case of capture if it is not retaken, no compensation can be allowed."

Salvage is not payment or compensation, Clifford wrote. "Compensation as salvage is not viewed by the admiralty courts merely as pay...but as a reward given for perilous services, voluntarily rendered, and as an inducement to seamen and others to embark in such undertakings to save life and property."

This case gave way to what is now considered the foundation for salvage claims in U.S. salvage law: the Blackwall Factors, as they are now called, which were penned by Justice Clifford in his opinion in August 1870:

1. The labor expended by the salvors in rendering the salvage service.
2. The promptitude, skill, and energy displayed in rendering the service and saving the property.
3. The value of the property employed by the salvors in rendering the service, and the danger to which such property was exposed.
4. The risk incurred by the salvors in securing the property from the impending peril.
5. The value of the property saved.
6. The degree of danger from which the property was rescued.

To accommodate the concern for the environment in the wake of the *Torrey Canyon* and *Valdez* spills, a seventh factor is now considered, even in pure salvage situations:

7. The skill and efforts of the salvors in preventing or minimizing damage to the environment.

"If there be any high romance left at sea it lies in the adventure of salvaging," William McFee, himself an accomplished seaman who turned to writing after retirement, wrote in *The Law of the Sea*. "The man who remains something of an enigma is the salvage expert. In a special sense he lives not only by his skill but by his wits." These lines were written in the days before the addendum to the Lloyd's Open Form safety net clause that serves to protect the environment and guarantee payment for the industrious salvor. The addition made things safer, but it also removed a good measure of the thrill of contract salvage, the chance at the big hit. A chance that still exists in pure salvage.

CHAPTER 24

ALONGSIDE AT FORT PIERCE

Jerry Danos, Montco's operations manager, watched from the Indian River dock at 1400 November 17, 1994, as the *Ocean Wind* towed the *J. A. Orgeron* in through the jetties at Fort Pierce. After the *Cherry Valley* had taken the *Orgeron* in tow on the 15th, Montco's president, Lee Orgeron, had Danos load up one of the company's trucks with spare parts for the main engine and head to Florida. Danos also brought along Dean Chapman, the tug's other engineer, who had been at home on his time off. That the *J. A. Orgeron* had suffered mechanical problems irked Danos, whose personal responsibility it was to be sure that each vessel was in good working condition. He was determined to solve the engines' problems, and equally determined to learn if it was due to operator error or mechanical breakdown.

"There might have been a little bit of an ego thing," Lee Orgeron recalled of Danos. "You tell a Coon Ass he can't do something"—in other words, get the tug's engines running again—"he's gonna do it. He was responsible for maintaining the engines, and here you have two of his engines…. Could have been that sort of thing."

Danos glared at the tug as it drew alongside the pier.

After the *Orgeron* was tied up Danos climbed down to the deck of the tug, tersely greeting the exhausted-looking Lanny Wiles, and ducked below to the engineroom, spreading his tools out carefully on the filthy, and slippery, oil-covered deck. The list of problems he was handed by Chris Gisclair, the engineer, was long:

1. Port main won't run, possible dropped valve in number five cylinder.
2. Port main: if it would start, it would only idle.

3. Port gearbox grinding noise; would stop engine.
4. Port main: exhaust leak at turbocharger.
5. Starboard main won't run.
6. Starboard main: possible dropped valve before it stopped.
7. Starboard main: exhaust pipe internal fire.
8. Jockey bar between rudders broken on starboard side.

After a quick survey, he added to the list of problems. The air compressor relief valve was stuck open, which resulted in low air pressure to the engine controls. The air tanks had not been drained and were partially full of water. The port propeller shaft was leaking water into the bilge, and some shaft packing appeared to have been crammed between the nut and shaft with a screwdriver in a futile attempt to stem the flow of water. Danos opened the decompression valves on the port engine and rotated the engine by hand with a turning tool. He found that all cylinders had sufficient compression. He removed the port gearbox inspection plate and found the bull gear and clutch pack housing had suffered no damage. He traced the fuel system from the tanks, and found that the lines were airbound—a result of dirty fuel filters. He drained and bled the filters and injector fuel pumps and finally prelubed the oil system and checked all fluids.

Danos then started the port engine—with not a little satisfaction. All cylinders were firing cleanly; there was no dropped valve—just air in the system. With the engine running, Danos and Chapman engaged the port clutch and could hear no noise or banging. They had found that the gearbox needed 12 gallons of oil to bring it up to the correct level. Danos surmised that when the tug had been bouncing around in the storm, the gears were likely banging together because of a lack of oil to keep them lubricated. One gallon low, Danos figured, is bordering on dangerous; 12 gallons down is a good way to burn up the reduction gear.

Danos found the problem with the air tank: mud and water in a check valve in the discharge line. That should never have happened, he muttered to Chapman. If the tank had been bled every day, this problem simply wouldn't have occurred.

At 0200, when he was satisfied that the port engine was running well, Danos rang Lee Orgeron at home and explained what he had found.

"Sometimes little things make big things go wrong," he added, without directly implicating the inexperienced engineer, Chris Gisclair, who was in charge of the engine room during the voyage. After clearing with his boss, Danos and Chapman, who had been going since 0600, fell into a pair of spare bunks for a few hours' sleep. Danos wanted to be up when the company's insurance surveyor arrived at 0900 to inspect the tug.

John Williams, a surveyor from The Salvage Association based in New Orleans, walked down the dock at 0900 and met with Lanny Wiles and Danos. Judging from Danos's report, the three of them were now convinced that the root of the problem was contaminated fuel. Whether the problem was actually bad fuel—purchased from a contaminated shoreside station in Louisiana—or sediment stirred up from the bottom of the tank, they didn't know.

Over the course of the day, the crew drained the diesel out of the day tank and scrubbed it clean. They scraped some 25 pounds of sludge and rust out of the bottom of the tank before washing down the sides and scouring out the corners. They bolted the manhole cover back in place and refilled the tank. With new filters installed between the main tanks and the day tank, they transferred 5,400 gallons to the day tank. With the day tank full of clean fuel they found they could run the generators and port engine without worry.

The next item on their list was the port engine's exhaust flex, the source of the engineroom smoke during the storm. They replaced the gasket with spares aboard the tug, sealing up the exhaust leak.

They then went back to the rudder room to work on the steering gear. The jockey arm had come off the rudder again, sometime during the maneuvers with the *Cherry Valley*, knocking the starboard rudder out of commission. With a cutting torch and welding rods Danos completed the repairs in a few hours. By 2200 they had had enough and called it a day. They were back at it by 0600 on Saturday, November 19th, this time to work on the starboard main engine. Danos repeated the compression check he had done for the port engine, and this time found three cylinders with no compression. The number one cylinder head was cracked, and had to be re-placed with the only spare they had aboard. They hoisted the 400-pound-plus damaged head with a set of chain falls mounted above the engine. The number two and five heads had valve problems, simple problems that could have been repaired onboard. While working on the number five cylinder Danos found that the rod in the injector pump that controls the flow of fuel to the cylinder would stick in the open position, which, combined with the leaking exhaust valve, led to the fire in the stack. They replaced the injector pump with the spare they had aboard.

With the repairs done, they bled down the engine and cranked it up. It started instantly, and they let it run for an hour and a half. It ran smoothly, which meant they were almost finished. They just had the stuffing tube on the port shaft to finish, but that could wait until the morning. Danos was look-ing forward to getting a good night's rest after the last two days of hard labor.

Danos was awakened at 0300 by a heated argument between Terry Perez and Chris Gisclair about some missing money. By the time Danos reached the galley, the argument had degenerated into a fight and fists were flying back and forth, both men tearing at each other until the police arrived. Citing the strain of the last few days, Perez admitted he had had enough and wanted off the boat. Danos drove him to the airport.

The following morning the shaft was repacked quickly. The engine-room was cleaned up and made ready for sea. Lee Orgeron was anxious for the boat to get back to Golden Meadow. Meanwhile, the *Ann T. Orgeron*, a sister to the *J. A. Orgeron*, had been brought around to tow the *Poseidon*, now free of its precious cargo, back to Michoud. The *J. A. Orgeron* would run along with them. At 2000 the *J. A. Orgeron*, all systems working, steamed through the jetties of Fort Pierce and turned south for the three-and-a-half-day voyage back to Louisiana.

As the *Orgeron* pulled away from the pier, Danos loaded his tools into the truck and called Lee Orgeron. In the last five days he and Dean Chapman had logged 174 hours of driving and work time, averaging 15-hour days at work on the tug. Yet the tug was back at sea, shouldering through the remains of the swell left behind by Tropical Storm Gordon—under her own power.

CHAPTER 25

THE CASE FOR SALVAGE

As we dock at the Stuart Petroleum facility in Jacksonville at 0918 November 17th, I sense a quiet before another type of storm. By 1100 the lawyers are streaming up the gangway of the *Cherry Valley,* and we begin a series of long sessions of recorded statements in various cabins throughout the ship.

My experience with maritime lawyers up to this point has not been pleasant. Most were personal injury lawyers—the proverbial ambulance chasers—seeking large sums of money for clients (crewmembers) who claimed to have been injured while working aboard a vessel I have been on. There are times when people are legitimately hurt, occasionally seriously, and they deserve compensation. Operating a ship at sea involves certain risks, and occasionally our safety checks break down and accidents happen.

But the bulk of my experience has been with someone claiming an injury that is hard to prove, or disprove, then seeking fast cash settlement using one of the bottom-feeding lawyers to help his case. One such memorable case involved an AB aboard a ship when I was chief mate. He was an older man, nearing retirement age. He'd not been to sea for many years but still had a valid Z card. He had owned a limousine company while he was ashore, but I had heard that the company had recently filed for bankruptcy, and he wanted to return to sea to earn a little money before retiring. When I heard his story, after we were at sea, I knew that somehow he was going to get "hurt" on board. I told the bosun, in no uncertain terms, that this AB was never to be left alone during working hours to minimize the chance of an "accident." A week had passed, and I was in my office catching up on cargo paperwork when the bosun knocked on my door and said, "Mate, I'm sorry. I left him alone for two minutes while I went to get some paint, and when I came back he was lying on the deck saying he slipped and hurt his back."

"Okay, Ted, let's go get him to the sickbay and check him out," I said shaking my head in wonderment. We moved him gently to the bed in the sickbay and stabilized him, putting ice on the area and giving him some anti-inflammatory medication. He claimed to be in a lot of pain and not able to move, but at night, he was able to roll around in bed when he was sleeping with no apparent discomfort. He was sent ashore for medical treatment at the next port and did not return to the ship. Several months later an attorney representing the AB showed up on the ship claiming the AB had been permanently injured when he slipped and fell, and he wanted our statements to corroborate his client's claim. He was disappointed when several of the crew said they had witnessed his seemingly pain-free movement at night. He did not get the large cash settlement he was hoping for.

So it is with some trepidation that I greet the first attorneys, Chris Dillon and Philip Buhler, hired by Keystone to take statements from the crew, in my office.

Earlier, most of the day had been a blur. I had been awake—or napping with one eye open—for most of the last three days, and all I wanted at that point was a chance to get off the ship and away from the ringing phone. I had called our Jacksonville agent to arrange for me to get a massage—a quiet place to relax and let someone work the tension out of my back. He had found a masseuse who had space available that day and quickly set up an appointment for me. After I briefly recounted the past few days, she had me lie face-down on the table and went to work on my back. As she started, she said, "I think what will do the most good is a technique called Rolfing. Are you familiar with that?"

"I am." And though I'm not really fond of it, I knew I would feel better—later. Rolfing involves pulling the skin away from the underlying muscle to stimulate blood flow and loosen up the muscles. It hurts, but when it's done, the feeling of relief and well-being is incredible. This woman tore into my back with abandon, and as I lay prone on her table, I could feel the previous days' anxiety leave my body. It was one the best things I had ever done for myself. As the taxi took me back to the ship an hour and a half later, I was feeling ready to do battle again.

Back at the ship I learn that Keystone is going forward with a salvage claim against Montco, the owners of the tug, and NASA as the owner of the barge and external tank. Ralph Hill, Keystone's in-house counsel, was unhappy with Bob Parrish's confrontational approach to handling the case, and quickly put the firm of Burke & Parsons in charge. Burke & Parsons, an established New York firm specializing in admiralty law, is handling a large arbitration case for Keystone and has been asked to handle this case as well.

Our stay in Jacksonville is over before all statements can be taken from the crew, so Dillon and Buhler stay aboard for the trip to Port Canaveral, where we will discharge the balance of the cargo. The six-mile channel leading to Port Canaveral is well marked, but I can imagine that the *Orgeron* would have had a tough time getting in during the storm. As we enter the mostly manmade harbor of Port Canaveral we pass the *Poseidon* and the *Ann T. Orgeron* tied up at a wharf, both vessels pointed toward the sea. The *Poseidon* had returned to Port Canaveral earlier in the day after delivering the external tank to the Kennedy Space Center. We take a close look at the *Poseidon* as the *Cherry Valley* glides slowly past her on the way to our berth. She shows no signs of the adventure we had been through. The *Ann T. Orgeron* will soon begin towing the barge back to Michoud once the remnants of Gordon, which had become a Hurricane off the Carolinas, pass by again.

Once alongside at Port Canaveral, I greet Bill Dougherty, yet another attorney from Burke & Parsons, who has come aboard to help take statements. Bill is tall and slender, his thick, dark hair trimmed much as it must have been in his Navy days. I'm not sure whether Bill drew the short or long straw, but he will get to make the trip back to New Orleans with us to continue to take statements from the crew. Bill had spent four years as an officer in the Navy and is enjoying the chance to be at sea again. With two young daughters at home who don't enjoy sleeping at night, he relishes the chance to be at sea yet not have to get called for watch in the middle of the night.

Tropical Storm Gordon continues to taunt us. While we were in Jacksonville, Gordon had built to a hurricane just south of Cape Hatteras and now, after making a figure eight, it's turning back toward the coast of Florida—as though trying to go over the top of us one more time. We scoot south just in time, however, and miss the last little bit of energy that Gordon has. If we had met, it would have been the third time that we came close to the center of the same storm.

We continue our runs between the Gulf Coast and the East Coast for the next several months. But just 10 days after our rescue of the *J. A. Orgeron*, I experience a reminder of the true order of things in the world of shipping.

We have once again loaded the *Cherry Valley* with almost 10 million gallons of No. 6 oil and are heading out the Mississippi River through Southwest Pass when I slow the ship to allow the pilot to disembark. The wind is out of the south-southeast at about 15 knots and the seas are running about three to four feet, not a bad night as far as the weather is concerned. Normally we turn to the left and make a lee on our port side to drop off the pilot, but tonight there is a lot of inbound traffic and we do not want to turn in front of the other vessels. We want to stay close to the outbound side of the traffic separation lanes.

The pilot and I agree that we will pass close aboard the sea buoy, but keep it on our port side, and we will have the pilot ladder deployed over our starboard side. As we are approaching the buoy at about 1830 the pilot calls the pilot boat, which has been following us about 50 yards off our starboard quarter out from the pass, and says he will be down on deck in just a minute.

The pilot heads down with the mate, and I go out on the starboard wing to watch the pilot leave. Although the pilot is responsible for his own safety, I like to be sure that pilots get safely aboard their boats and clear of the ship. My best view is from the wings. The pilot boat is matching our speed, about seven knots, 20 feet off the side of the ship, waiting for the pilot to get down to the ladder. I turn away for a minute to give the helmsman an order, and when I look forward again I see that the pilot boat has moved about 150 feet ahead of the pilot ladder and is *backing up* to get back to the ladder.

I do a few instant calculations in my mind: If the pilot boat is backing up…and we are both supposed to be doing seven knots…then I must have slowed down a lot. Like to zero.

Shit! I have just run aground.

I've grounded the *Cherry Valley*, fully laden, in an area where I should have plenty of water, at least according to the chart. But obviously I don't. The pilot comes back to the bridge, and the pilot boat circles around the ship taking soundings, and we find that we have come to rest on a hump of silt, apparently left from recent dredging in the Lower Mississippi River. Knowing that it is soft bottom, and that we haven't done any damage to the ship, we try first to push over the hump. No success.

We then try to back off and are starting to move when the chief calls up from the engineroom to say that we are stirring a lot of silt and it is getting into the saltwater intake for the condenser. We can only run the engine astern for a couple of minutes at a time, and it is not enough time to get us off the hump.

Now I have to call Keystone and order some tugs to pull us off the hump. It takes about six hours for two tugs to get down from New Orleans. I have ample time to consider the irony of my situation: two weeks ago I rescued a tug; and now, watching the tugs approach, I feel effectively put in my place. The tugs quickly put lines up to our stern and apply just enough tension to stabilize themselves. As we wait for inbound traffic to pass, the tugs just idling, we slide easily off the hump. After clearing with the tugs and getting permission from the Coast Guard, we are underway again.

It would be Burke & Parsons' job, in consultation with Ralph Hill, to settle the case and bring in additional firms with other strengths as needed. In early December, Montco filed for limitation of liability in Federal Court in New Orleans, which would protect them from paying more than the value of the tug and pending freight—the fee they were paid for towing the *Poseidon*. Consequently, local counsel in New Orleans had to be retained since Burke & Parsons was not admitted to the Louisiana Bar.

Ray Burke, the New York attorney heading the case, knew exactly who he wanted: Hugh Straub, a prominent attorney with the nearly century-old firm of Terriberry, Carroll & Yancey. Burke and Straub had worked together on a complex shipping case that had lasted more than 10 years, the collision between the tanker *Dauntless Colocotronis* and a barge that had sunk in the Mississippi River. The *Dauntless* had run over the barge, torn open its bottom, and caught on fire—a series of events that almost resulted in what could have been one of the worst oil spills in U.S. history. Burke, who had hired Straub as local counsel on the *Dauntless* litigation, prefers to use local counsel because they know the local courts, but his fondness for, and confidence in, Straub was an added benefit. If the case couldn't be settled, Ray Burke wanted Hugh Straub to lead the New Orleans trial.

The complexity of determining the value of the external tank meant that we would need a firm with strong accounting skills and experience with "government-speak." Ross Dembling in the Washington, D.C., office of Holland & Knight has a strong background in Federal contract cases and is hired to handle the valuation portion of the case. Dembling is a perfect candidate for this daunting task. Dembling's father, Paul G. Dembling, was one of the founders of NASA in the late 1950s. During the race to catch up with Russia following the launch of *Sputnik*, the senior Dembling was hired to draft the law creating what would eventually become NASA. He went on to serve as NASA's general counsel, eventually being hired by the General Accounting Office to acquire facilities such as Michoud and the Marshall Space Flight Center.

In December 1994, each member of the *Cherry Valley*'s crew had signed a representation agreement with Keystone to let the company, and its attorneys, Burke & Parsons, handle the negotiations with the Federal Government and Montco to get a fair salvage award. With the crew and company united we are now in a strong position to negotiate. Keystone has agreed to pay all costs associated with obtaining an award. If anyone in the crew wants to pursue a claim individually they are welcome, but the individual will have to pay his own attorney. It could get ugly if there were 25 lawyers fighting for "their" fair share of the award.

Keystone's interest and the crew's interest are the same as far as obtaining an award, and it makes sense to join together, although our interests will diverge if there is a reward to split between the company and the crew. For that the crew will need its own lawyer, someone with a strong background in admiralty law and experience at sea.

The important legal issue regarding our salvage claim is focused on the value of the external tank. The tug and barge are relatively easy to figure out; they can be appraised and compared to other similar vessels. Unlike something that has value on the open market, though, the external tanks are unique and built expressly for, and used only by NASA; they exist nowhere else in the world. I learn from Keystone that the invoice for ET-70 is a staggering, "estimated" $51,900,000. The invoice, called the "material inspection and receiving report" (known by most of the people at NASA by its form number DD-250), is what Martin Marietta estimates each tank costs to build, as part of its 60-tank, $3.4 billion contract. This figure includes parts, labor, facility costs, research and development, everything that goes into the building of the tank at the Michoud Assembly Facility over the course of four years. This is the figure that Ross Dembling from Holland & Knight will try to prove is the value of the external tank. If ET-70 had been lost, that is the amount of money that NASA would have lost.

As might be imagined, the Justice Department's position is somewhat different. It will argue that the ET-70's value is immaterial. NASA has recently asked Martin Marietta, with the $3.4 billion contract in place and running, how much it would cost to add or drop four tanks. Using only the labor and material costs since all other expenses were blended into the larger contract, Martin Marietta came up with an estimate of $19 million per tank. This, asserts the Justice Department, is the actual value of the ET-70.

If we were to have a case at all, it would rely heavily on historical precedence in salvage cases. Admiralty courts typically look at fair market value when determining a salvage award, such as how to value the more than 37,000 sacks of wheat saved in the fire aboard the ship *Blackwall,* or the hundreds of barrels of alcohol recovered from the *Mary Celeste*. But the ET is a unique piece of hardware. It has no market value whatsoever. In these special cases—and there have only been a few—the courts have used the replacement or reproduction value in determining an award.

While maintaining its asserted value of ET-70, the Justice Department also continues negotiating with Keystone toward a settlement.

More than a year passes and I continue to sail as captain of the *Cherry Valley*, running between the Gulf Coast, Caribbean, and East Coast, and spending my time ashore in Southwest Harbor, Maine. On February 1, 1996—more than 14 months after the rescue—Burke & Parsons notifies Keystone that Matt Connelly, the Justice Department's trial attorney, will recommend a settlement, with NASA's consent, of $5 million to his superiors. Five million dollars. Depending on which valuation of the external tank is used, this represents an award that is either 10 or 26 percent. Ray Burke thinks this is a fair and supportable offer—and a buzz of excitement passes quickly through the ship and to crewmembers now spending vacation time ashore.

There is one stipulation: the settlement figure must be approved by the Associate Attorney General, Frank Hunger. Hunger, whose brother-in-law is Vice President Al Gore, is no doubt a fine attorney—and I'm sure his relationship with the Vice President had nothing to do with how he got the job—but his background does not include much experience in admiralty law. This might be a problem, Ray Burke tells me.

When the $5 million recommendation reaches Hunger's desk he is reportedly appalled at the amount of money that his subordinates have offered, and he tells NASA, in no uncertain terms, to put away the Government's checkbook. The most he will offer is $1 million. His review of the case shows that the *Cherry Valley* had been delayed for about two-and-a-half days and announces that a million dollars is more than adequate compensation. That may be true. But not if you have 5,000 years of salvage law backing up your case. It looks as though Hugh Straub will get the chance to try this case in court.

CHAPTER 26

TRIAL IN NEW ORLEANS

Hugh Straub, the lead attorney hired by Keystone to prepare for and manage the trial, was born and raised in New York, and attended Fort Schuyler (New York Maritime College), where he earned his undergraduate degree and a third mate's unlimited license. After graduation he served on break-bulk ships running between the U.S. Gulf Coast and the Far East. On those long trips he found that after two weeks at sea he had spoken to everyone on board. With nothing left to say and nothing left to ask, he found himself staring blankly at the horizon, wondering when he'd be back in port so he could escape the ship. He lasted less than three years as a seaman before enrolling in law school—Tulane University in New Orleans—where he focused on admiralty law.

A hard worker with a quick wit, he elected to stay in New Orleans after he graduated and was hired by one of the city's most respected firms, Terriberry, Carroll & Yancey, apprenticing with Alfred Farrell, an eccentric admiralty lawyer who'd been with the firm for decades. Farrell—a man Straub felt was both brilliant and honorable—handled much of the firm's "wet work," cases involving collisions and groundings. It wasn't long before his mentor retired and Straub himself was a full partner, specializing in shipping accidents.

Now in his late 40s, Straub has lost none of the energy and feistiness of his youth. His friends and acquaintances describe a skillful lawyer—he is rated as highly as possible by his peers—but they also mention his equally passionate interest in having a good time. Peering out from his round glasses with the demeanor of a tortoise who suspects the joke is on you, Straub appears well fed but is not overweight. He dresses in drag on his Krewe's Mardi Gras floats, tells bawdy Boudreaux jokes, and thrives on the

challenge of complex admiralty cases. When on vacation Straub looks for
excitement underwater, traveling the world with his wife on unusual dive
trips. On a recent foray in Southeast Asia, Straub approached a sleeping
shark that was slowly circling near the bottom and, hoping to get a free ride,
tugged sharply on its tail. "You know how when you grab a dog's tail, he
whips around with his snout?" Straub says. "That's what a shark does."
There was no free ride.

The Terriberry office is located on the 31st floor of a mirrored high-
rise, the Energy Center, on Poydras Street in downtown New Orleans, with
views of Lake Pontchartrain and the Mississippi River. ("The Father of the
Waters is rather serpentine," Straub says, "which is great for my business.")
The expanse of Lake Pontchartrain stretching endlessly to the north is visible from Straub's corner office. On Straub's office walls visitors will note a
framed picture of Fort Schuyler's training ship, the *Empire State IV;* an en-
graving of Henry VIII ("And people think *I'm* a smartass," he says); an aer-
ial photo of Pilottown, the water-bound headquarters for pilots at Southwest
Pass; a purple neon crescent moon that glows continuously next to his desk;
and a painting of St. Nicholas ("Patron saint of seamen, thieves, and fools—
I'm at least two of these"). His bookshelves are lined with a haphazard as-
sortment of arcane maritime and legal texts, including *Admiralty Law of the
Supreme Court,* the *American Merchant Seaman's Manual, Tug, Tow & Pi-
lotage,* and *Hydraulic Dredging.* A few recent novels by Nelson Demille,
James Patterson, and Stephen Coonts round out his library.

Accompanying Straub at the trial will be his cousin Mike Butterworth,
a towering, soft-spoken California Maritime graduate with shoulders like a
pair of cinderblocks. Before law school, Butterworth had sailed on tugboats
on the West Coast. In his spare time, Butterworth, now also a partner at
Terriberry, seeks the company of alligators, "fishing" for them from a canoe
with a chicken bone tied to a string. ("You don't want to hurt them, just
grab them out of the water for a photo.") Butterworth, tagged "Gator Mike"
around the office, also collects alligator roadkill, occasionally slinging fresh
animals into the back of his truck on his way to work. Because of his experience on tugs, he'll be managing the testimony of the *J. A. Orgeron* crew.

Straub knows that to win the case against the Government he must have sharp witnesses. Stanwood Duval, appointed to the Federal bench by President Clinton in July 1994, has a reputation as a diligent judge. He's grimly serious in the courtroom, but owns a track record that indicates he made every attempt to understand what witnesses have to say before ruling. A native of Houma, Louisiana, where his father was a prominent attorney, Duval is also known to enjoy spending free time on the water. He keeps a sportfishing boat at Grand Isle, and invites his colleagues on fishing adventures on the Gulf.

"He doesn't speak with a Cajun accent," Butterworth says. "He doesn't crack Boudreaux jokes, and he's a stickler for the rules."

The trial would be heard by Duval alone, a judge trial, as is customary in admiralty cases. "But judges are people too," Straub says. "While we knew we weren't going to have a jury trial, it's no less of a play. It's just less exaggerated. To say that you are putting on a show cheapens it, but there is drama too."

Straub was counting on the fact that his witnesses would provide that drama, without hyperbole.

"Everybody in this business knows that good lawyers don't win cases; good fact witnesses win cases. We wanted to put our witnesses on the stand and ask them to tell their story," Straub recalls. "We wanted the yo-ho-ho, the bucket of seawater."

To prepare us, Straub invited me and chief mate Carl Gabrielsson to Terriberry's office a few days before trial and began a grilling session, based primarily in his "torture chamber," a conference room he has fitted with a video camera for a trial's dress rehearsals.

"You stick a camera in front of someone's face and they get a little nervous, like how they'll be at trial," Straub says. "You also want to pick out any habits or mannerisms that might serve as a distraction, and work with the witnesses for their honest accounts to come across professionally."

With the prospect of a trial looming, it became essential to nail down the value of the ET, a task that proved far more difficult than anyone expected. Lead counsel Ray Burke, accompanied by our Federal contract expert Ross

Dembling, headed to the Marshall Space Flight Center in Huntsville, Alabama, to depose NASA's business experts.

Just before the deposition with Jody Adams, NASA's external tank budget manager, the pair agreed that Burke would lead the interview while Dembling would remain silent, passing along any questions he might have in writing. But the complexities of NASA's accounting methods quickly made Burke realize that his maritime expertise was not helping here and he was out of his depth.

Ten minutes into the deposition Burke asked for a short break, and he and Dembling stepped into the hall for a conference.

"You are passing me questions, and she is answering them," Burke said, "but I have no idea what either of you are talking about. Why don't you ask the questions, and if I think of anything, I'll pass them to you."

Burke and Dembling emerged from the Huntsville facility admittedly baffled by the Government's accounting procedures, but they were beginning to understand that the cost of the ET might actually be much more than the assumed sticker price of $51.9 million, perhaps as much as $90 million if one were to consider what it cost taxpayers to actually *build* the tank (not how much it would cost to *replace* ET-70, roughly $19 million, as the Government would argue).

On April 16, two weeks before our day in court, all parties met at a pre-trial conference in the hope of reaching a settlement. The day before, the Justice Department, following clear instructions from Assistant Attorney General Hunger, had sent out "offers of judgment" to Keystone and each of the crewmembers. The offers would allow the Government to pay everyone to settle the salvage claim without admitting liability. Under the Government's $1 million proposal, Keystone would get $401,000 and the crew would split $599,000. The entire crew would share in the award, with amounts ranging from $75,000 for me, as captain, on down to $10,000 for members of the steward's department. One attractive aspect of this settlement was the fact that the crew would be receiving a 60 percent share—opposite to most precedent in the last 100 years.

Continuing to believe that salvage law would support an award closer to $5 million, Ray Burke recommended that the company and crew reject the offers and go to trial. But he also made it clear to all of us that going to trial did have an element of risk. If the case went to trial and the award was less than the $1 million now on the table, the crew would be required to pay any court costs after the offer was made. After some initial jitters, in the end everyone agreed with the Burke & Parsons' recommendation. We would go to trial.

Despite progress on determining the value of the tank, the Government and Montco requested a postponement of the trial, since depositions (especially NASA witnesses) were taking more time than expected. A new trial date was set for July 8, 1996, 10 weeks later than we originally planned.

In the middle of June, Montco, the owner of the tug *J. A. Orgeron* and headed by the big Cajun Lee Orgeron, agreed to settle its portion of the salvage claim with Keystone for $220,000. Montco's attorneys argued that since the *Orgeron* might have been able to cast the *Poseidon* adrift and used the tug's anchor to keep from going aground, it was a reasonable amount to pay as far as salvage law is concerned. It was a solid contribution to the costs in diverting a laden oil tanker and endangering the lives of her crew. Montco was now removed from the pending trial.

At the same time, Keystone's lawyers, including in-house counsel Ralph Hill, Ross Dembling, and Ray Burke, met with Assistant Attorney General Frank Hunger, representing the Government, in Washington to discuss another settlement. Two hours had been set aside for the meeting, but Burke knew the meeting was over after two minutes.

At the Washington meeting both sides faced each other across the table, waiting for the other to blink. "They never intended to make a reasonable offer," Burke noted. "In fact, Hunger expected Keystone to make an offer substantially below $5 million before the Government would move past its $1 million offer. I did not consider the offers of judgment in the amount of $1 million to have constituted good-faith offers, and we would not make a counter-offer. I looked at Hunger and said, 'The ball is in your court.'"

Burke knew that Hunger had the authority to go up to $2 million and learned in the meeting that Hunger was willing to recommend a "reasonable" figure higher than that to his superiors.

"What is that figure?" Burke asked, but there was no response.

Hunger, whose gracious manner never faltered, had promised that a visit to his office in the Justice Department should include a tour of the agency's august library and imposing halls. Shortly after the meeting began, Hunger told Burke and Dembling that he was willing to go above $1 million but nowhere near $5 million.

Burke looked at Hunger, put his hands on the table, and took a deep breath. "How about that tour?" he asked. The meeting was over as quickly as it began.

Back on Pennsylvania Avenue outside the Justice Department's imposing headquarters, Dembling turned to Burke and said, "I've been to a lot of pre-trial settlement conferences that have been quick, but never to one that was over as quick as that!"

Ten days before the trial was to start, the two sides met before a magistrate in a last-ditch effort to settle. The meeting lasted all morning and the Government made a "final" offer of $3 million, which was eventually raised to a "final" offer of $3.3 million. The magistrate, eager to save the court the expense of proceeding with trial, urged Burke, Straub, and Hill to accept.

"Your honor," Straub had said in response, "you've got to see our witnesses."

"In any trial there's risk; it's a crap shoot," Burke recalls. "Keystone wanted their money—a bird in the hand and all that—but on the other hand we saved the Federal Government $50 million." Burke strongly recommended that Keystone refuse the offer, especially since he had Hugh Straub leading the case in the event of a trial, who was telling him he had prepared the strongest witnesses of his career for the trial.

"Lawyering is a lot like playing poker," Straub says. "When you've got bad cards, the conservative approach is to get out early, quick, and cheap. When you've got a strong hand, you stay in and try to get the pot up."

Keystone agreed.

≈

Two days before the trial, when the jungle-like heat of southern Louisiana had reached its apex, Carl and I met with Straub for our final preparation, working on our presentation.

During my deposition in March, I had been told I had an annoying habit of repeatedly using the word "again" when responding to a question, or in clarifying a point. It seemed that I would start with "Again, we did…" or "Again, I called…" Straub found this particularly annoying, and made it his personal mission to have me remove the word from my vocabulary.

Straub planned for me to lead off—"to throw a bucket of saltwater" on the judge—and to simply tell the story of the rescue. After the excitement of my retelling of the rescue, Straub figured, the judge would then be overwhelmed with facts and figures about how the Government handles its accounting. And just before he passed out from boredom, Straub would have Carl throw another bucket of saltwater on him to wake him up—and ultimately decide the case in Keystone's favor.

Late Sunday afternoon Straub declared the witnesses ready for trial, and it was time for a night out.

"You are not going anywhere near the Quarter tonight," he said. "We are going for a civilized meal at Café Degas, with the best crème brûlée for dessert in this city. You may have one drink—two if you behave—and I want you in bed by 2200. You have a very important date tomorrow morning."

CHAPTER 27

A BUCKET OF SEAWATER
AND A LOT OF FACTS

On the sultry July morning that the trial was to begin at the Federal Court-house on Poydras Street in New Orleans—after the men had been mugged by the heat on their walk from the Pavillon Hotel on the edge of the French Quarter—Judge Stanwood Duval opened the trial with a caution to the lawyers about their presentations. As in most admiralty cases, there would be no jury—and no need for theatrics.

"I am sure all of you remember this is a judge trial," Duval clipped. "Therefore, we don't need a lot of redundancy. I am sure there won't be undue histrionics. Let's not make the economic testimony"—the details of the value of the space shuttle's external tank—"more complex than the rocket itself.... Let's commence."

Matt Connelly, the Department of Justice's lead attorney, proposed in his pre-trial Proposed Findings of Fact that the *Cherry Valley* crew had per-formed admirably and deserved liberal compensation. But, he added, he would attempt to prove that the value of the fuel tank was far less than what Keystone attorneys claimed. His efforts in the trial would be directed at NASA's accounting procedures.

Hugh Straub, confident that his witnesses were fully prepared to detail the facts of the rescue and salvage in efficient and simple terms, opened his statement with a description of the Blackwall Factors, the governing prin-ciples behind salvage awards.

"The most important Blackwall Factor is the degree of risk to which the salved property was saved. The degree of risk," Straub said. "And I ask that the court consider the evidence that if *Cherry Valley* hadn't been there to help, [there was a question as to] whether that barge was going to be sacrificed to save the tug.

"When the court considers the second most important Blackwall Factor, that is the value of the property salved, I would ask the court to consider: if the value of the ET-70 is less than $20 million as the Government would tell you, why in the world does NASA pay $90 million for it?

"And I'd like for the court to think about the third factor of Blackwall: the risk the salvors took. I'd like for the court to be thinking, if the *Cherry Valley* and 9.9 million gallons of No. 6 oil ran aground on Bethel Shoal in that tropical storm, what would have been the consequence to Margate [a subsidiary of Keystone and the owner of the *Cherry Valley*]? What would have been the consequence to the reputation of Captain Strong? What would have been the consequence if the crewmembers who were working on deck in that storm with those lines had been maimed or killed by one of those lines parting?"

With that, Straub called me to the stand. Over the course of the next two hours, while I recounted the events of November 14 to 16, 1994, Straub interrupted only enough to keep the story moving, stopping me occasionally to ask, 'And what happened next, Captain?'

Judge Duval, a man with a reputation for listening intently to witnesses to be sure he understood their testimony, was clearly enthralled by the story being told to him that morning. At one point, roughly halfway through the testimony when I was describing the details of not allowing the *Cherry Valley* to pass the longitude line beyond which represented the shallows of Bethel Shoal, Duval broke in, "The 80 10 line?"

"The 80 10 line, yes, sir," I replied.

"That 80 10 line is approximately how far from Bethel Shoal?"

"Six ship lengths," I said.

"How close were you to the bottom, Captain?"

"We were very close ... less than 10 feet."

"Is that when you hit the trough [of a wave]?" Duval questioned. I explained that the ship's keel had at least once come within five feet of the bottom during the rescue and that the wake showed continuous traces of sand and mud being stirred up from the bottom. "This was not comfortable for us," I added.

After Straub released me from his questioning, David Howe, the Department of Justice attorney, began his cross-examination, and his questions allowed me further opportunity to elaborate on the complexity of the rescue. I was able, in Straub's plan, to throw another bucket of seawater in the judge's lap.

"Captain," Howe asked, "you said, and I'll try to quote you, 'If there had not been five guys on the tug, we would never have been in this area.' Did you believe it was necessary for your ship to save the crew of the *Orgeron*, that [it] was either you or they were going to die?"

"At this point in time," I began, "when we began the whole operation, no one else was coming out for them. The Coast Guard indicated they had no assistance in the area to come out and help these guys. No one else had spoken up on the radio. We had been on Channel 16, which is the international hailing and distress frequency, and Channel 22, the Coast Guard working frequency; no one else called in to offer any assistance at this time. We thought, if anything was going to happen, it was going to be because of what we did."

Howe quickly closed his questioning.

Don Kurz, president of Keystone, was called to the stand next and questioned by Ray Burke, who especially wanted Kurz to make clear to the judge exactly what was at stake for Keystone, and its subsidiary company Margate, if the *Cherry Valley* had gone aground. Kurz, whose pallid complexion and grave, doomsday manner pleased Straub, gave the impression that the world as Kurz knew it would come to an end in the event that the ship grounded. Margate and Keystone collectively operated some 33 ships, ranging in size from 38,000 deadweight tons to 400,000 tons, and employed more than 1,000 personnel around the world.

"Besides the *Cherry Valley*, [and] her crew, what else did Margate put at risk when the *Cherry Valley* went to the aid of the *J. A. Orgeron* flotilla off Bethel Shoal?" Burke prodded.

"We put at risk our vessel, our crew, our company, our company assets, our reputation—our very existence."

"I have no further questions of Mr. Kurz."

After Kurz stepped down, Mike Butterworth, the Terriberry attorney responsible for organizing depositions and testimony from the *J. A. Orgeron* crew, called Terry Perez, the *Orgeron*'s deckhand, to the stand. Butterworth had chosen Perez because he had admitted to being scared, and Perez made clear in no uncertain terms that he had believed his life was in danger and that he was thankful the *Cherry Valley* had happened along.

"When the vessel started losing power," Butterworth began, "what did you guys put on?"

"Life jackets," Perez responded.

One question after another—and Perez's harrowing testimony—painted a dire picture of the conditions aboard the tug that night. Where the other four crew were stoic about the peril of the situation, Perez was unabashedly terrified and had even sworn off going to sea following his hitch aboard the *Orgeron*. Perez described fighting the fire while wearing the bulky life jackets; the smoke-filled, slippery engineroom; the flames leaping from the red-hot stack; the difficulty breathing; the inability to make repairs because of the rough conditions ("You needed both hands to work with tools, and with the conditions being as rough as they was, you needed to hold onto something at all times"); and his fear of the flotilla being driven ashore.

"What did the captain tell you about going up on the beach?" Butterworth asked.

"If nothing happened soon we would let go of the barge, that way [we'd] save the vessel and crew from going on the beach with the barge," Perez said. That the *Orgeron* crew had made plans to ditch the barge was crucial to the Keystone case, which hinged upon the precious cargo being saved from certain destruction. Butterworth ended his questioning, and Howe declined his opportunity to cross-examine.

Keystone's witnesses included Norm Dufour, a surveyor who had been hired to evaluate the condition of the tug after being towed to Fort Pierce. Dufour had performed a complete survey of the *Orgeron*, and described for the court why the tug was incapable of keeping itself or the barge from being swept ashore. Dufour determined that the tug's engines had suffered the ill effects of dirty fuel. Since the *Orgeron*'s tanks had been scrubbed clean prior to his survey, Dufour couldn't say whether the tanks had been neglected, just that fuel problems were the ultimate cause of the engine failures.

"Either they had a dirty fuel tank to begin with or picked up some bad fuel, and the action of the vessel in these heavy seas was just agitating dirt, sediment, scale, whatever was in the fuel tanks. It became suspended in the fuel that was being pumped through the fuel system, some of it obviously being caught by the fuel filters," Dufour said. "The crew wasn't able, because of the conditions, to change the fuel filters as often as they could have, [and] all the contamination was getting to the engine and clogging up the fuel pumps, injectors. Eventually all the diesel engines on the vessel would have starved for fuel, wouldn't have been able to get any fuel. That is the best situation or the least dangerous situation for the crew. The immediate danger was the situation of the crew on board. In all probability, they would have had a recurrence of the stack fire that could [have led] to any number of things including engulfing the whole vessel in flames. If the stack gets so hot it starts igniting materials that are around it, if you lose the generators, you lose the fire pumps, you have no ability to fight the fire. It could have been a disaster."

"Why would they have lost the generators?" Butterworth questioned.

"Same fuel contamination problem," Dufour said. "You lose the generators, lose all power to the electric fire pumps, you are in big trouble."

"What action was taken by the tug crew to support your opinion, sir?"

"They had their life jackets on."

"What else, sir, what acts did the captain take after the *Cherry Valley* came on the scene, to support your opinion?"

"They shut the engine down as soon as they got the towlines aboard the vessel. Even though the *Cherry Valley* needed whatever assistance they could get, the only time [the tug crew] restarted the starboard engine [was] when they saw a severe squall coming to try to ease the strain on the hawsers from the *Cherry Valley*...."

Dufour also outlined the tug's steering problems, explaining that the tug had also lost steerage as a result of the damage to the jockey arm connecting the rudders.

Although the most damaging testimony—damaging, that is, to the Government's case—could likely have come from Chris Gisclair, the unlicensed engineer whose lack of training and failure to fully appreciate the fuel flow problems likely led to the deterioration of the mechanical problems, but the Government was spared his appearance. Despite a subpoena and a mid-trial warrant for his arrest by Federal Marshals issued by Judge Duval, Gisclair never arrived in the courthouse.

Hugh Straub then questioned a naval architect, John Leary, for his opinion on whether the tug-and-barge flotilla could have been effectively anchored prior to washing ashore and being pounded apart in the surf. Leary replied that the forces on the barge, with its 44-foot-tall hangar and minimal 10-foot draft, presented a large amount of sail area that would have overwhelmed any anchoring system and quickly dragged the barge ashore. The barge, being unmanned and its windlasses not functioning, could not have been anchored on its own, and the tug's ground tackle alone would have been insufficient. Leary calculated the size of the anchors and their theoretical holding power, combined it with the sail area and the force of the wind and seas, and decided that the forces far exceeded the potential holding power—by a great degree.

After a recess for lunch, Bill Knodle, Lockheed Martin's (in March of 1995 Martin Marietta and Lockheed merged to form Lockheed Martin) harbormaster, was called to the stand by Keystone. Knodle detailed the construction of the barge for the judge, described how the cargo was secured, and how, being unmanned, the barge could not have been anchored on its own; someone would have had to get aboard the barge, start the generator that powers the windlass, release the hydraulic brake, and let the anchors go. Knodle was asked about a note in the *J. A. Orgeron*'s logbook that described the crew asking for permission to put into Miami to avoid the storm and being told "by NASA" to continue their voyage. Knodle said he was unaware who had told the crew to continue on. It had not been him.

Knodle expressed his belief that without the *Cherry Valley*'s assistance, the barge *Poseidon* and the *Orgeron* would have ended up on the beach at approximately 0900 on the morning of November 15. The barge and its cargo, he said, would likely have been destroyed in the surf—not being built to withstand the dynamic pounding of the waves against the beach. Straub read from Knodle's report on the incident, which was used as evidence. Knodle's report concluded, "In spite of the salvage claim, the *Cherry Valley* performed a great service for us."

"I believe that is true," Knodle added.

"Where did you go to college?" Straub asked.

"The United States Naval Academy," Knodle replied.

"Thank you," Straub said. "I tender the witness."

Ross Dembling, Keystone's Washington, D.C. attorney who had been hired to lead the process of evaluating the cost of the external tank, took over the questioning, calling several NASA witnesses to the stand. Dembling knew that he had to keep the facts clear, yet the challenge he faced was enormous.

"We had the problem, with respect to the dollar amount of this tank, of having an enormous Government contract, a contract for 60 tanks to be delivered for $3.4 billion," Dembling recalls. "But it wasn't just a simple matter of dividing $3.4 billion by 60; that would be too simple. Lockheed Martin was using a Government facility; there were a lot of people employed at these facilities who were outside the contract. So there were a lot of hidden costs. Plus, you have all these program managers within NASA— and NASA is one of the most jargon-filled Government agencies—who speak this funny language. There's a whole vocabulary they use, a vocabulary that seems humorous when you're on the outside, but isn't funny to them because it's what they know."

Dembling's challenge was to bring these witnesses to the stand to support Keystone's position that the tanks were worth far more than $50 million apiece—because that is what the Government paid for them—yet translate their federal-bureaucracy-accounting-speak in a way that was salient.

To maintain focus, Dembling arranged to have two exhibits blown up and placed on display in the courtroom: a copy of the DD-250, the accounting report of the production cost of ET-70 that showed roughly $52 million, and a simple flow-chart that supported Keystone's claim that the true costs to the taxpayer were in excess of $90 million. These two exhibits were the backdrop to the testimony of several NASA account managers. NASA's external tank budget accountant at the Marshall Space Flight facility, Jody Adams, was brought to the stand first. Adams, whose resemblance to the country singer Reba McIntyre was disarming when she opened her mouth and began to speak in an obscure jargon-filled tongue, testified that the Government paid Lockheed Martin $51.9 million to construct ET-70; that claim was supported, she said, by the DD-250 form.

Fred Farkouh, a New York-based CPA with a background in maritime transport litigation, was called to testify about the Government's accounting procedures and how they specifically apply to the construction and billing procedure of the external tanks. In Keystone's pre-trial "Proposed Findings of Fact and Conclusions of Law," the attorneys pointed out that "[T]he true cost of ET-70 was significantly higher [than $50 million]. The DD-250 cost"—the invoice cost—"does not include a broad range of costs and expenses. Such as the fees paid to Lockheed Martin under the Assembly contract; NASA's cost to acquire the Michoud Assembly Facility; NASA's personnel and production supervision costs; NASA's cost to acquire the general-purpose plant equipment, special tooling, special test equipment and test tools, etc., used in the assembly process at Michoud; the cost of maintaining and operating the Michoud facility; the engineering and other developmental costs incurred in the design and development of the lightweight external tank; and the cost of the capital funds invested in an external tank during the construction and holding period. The sum of these expenses, both acknowledged and hidden, raised the true economic cost for the production of a single tank to more than $90 million." Farkouh was in court to explain these costs, to clarify the difference between "economic cost," the total cost of building an external tank, and the "marginal cost," which is the amount that it might take to build an additional tank that includes no overhead charges. Farkouh testified that the true cost of constructing the tank was closer to $93 million.

Dembling argued that if it cost the Government more than $90 million to build each tank, including ET-70, the salvage award should be a percentage of this figure. Matt Connelly, in his cross-examination of Farkouh, and in his later arguments, asked the court to consider not what the tank cost to build but how much NASA would have to pay to *replace* ET-70 in the event that it was lost in the storm. He was trying hard to convince Judge Duval that NASA could have bought an additional tank for $19 million. Farkouh explained "marginal cost" with this analogy: It cost Ford Motor Company $6 billion to develop the Ford Taurus, which meant that the first car off the assembly line cost $6 billion to produce.

"[Y]ou would say, I want the second one because the first one cost six billion [dollars]," Farkouh said; "the second one, the marginal cost [the cost of material and labor] is only six thousand dollars. I'll take the second one."

It would be this dispute, over the "true" cost of the tank, that would continue to haunt the case.

True to his word, Straub called Chief Mate Carl Gabrielsson to the stand after the dizzying accounts of NASA's finance records, his intention being to breathe life back into the trial. Throughout his hour-long delivery, Carl relayed the events in a measured tone, his large, tanned and calloused hands resting in his lap, offering the impression that the deck of the *Cherry Valley* could not have been managed by a more powerful and effective figure.

Carl described his involvement in the rescue, how he had navigated the *Cherry Valley* toward the *Orgeron* and fixed its position on radar at 0400 prior to me relieving him to take the deck and flake out the towlines on the stern. He then described how he managed the deck crew to pass the lines; monitored their strain; kept the lines greased to guard against chafe; how the tug *South Bend* had failed to secure a line to the *Orgeron* and been ultimately deterred—and nearly sunk—by the heavy seas; how the *Cherry Valley* crew scrambled to rearrange the lines after one of them parted due to the strain; and, after the flotilla was taken in tow, how he anchored the ship as instructed by me.

Duval was clearly impressed.

Late in the afternoon, Matt Connelly, the Justice Department's lead attorney, made his opening remarks, imploring the court to consider the fact that the Blackwall Factors were relevant to the case only in determining the salvage rights—but not in appraising the value of ET-70, a value he insisted should be the *replacement* cost of the tank, roughly $19 million. Connelly, who had no interest in rehashing the sea story that had so enchanted Judge Duval, called Jody Adams, the Marshall Space Flight facility accountant in charge of the external tank program, and began an exhausting examination of NASA's accounting procedures. Connelly's questions attempted to prove that adding another tank to the process would have cost NASA $19 million; it didn't matter what it had actually cost to produce ET-70. Despite the dizzying detail of business management at NASA and Martin Marietta, Duval remained attentive, frequently interrupting the questioning to have a point clarified.

When Ross Dembling cross-examined Adams, he asked whether the Government had ever paid $19 million for an external tank.

"We have not procured one tank for $19 million," she said.

"As a taxpayer, if you could, you would acquire a tank for $19 million?"

"Yes."

Dembling promptly closed his questioning.

Judge Duval had a few questions for the witness, however. He wanted to know what the invoice amount was for ET-71, the tank built immediately following ET-70. The answer, which Jody Adams read from an exhibit, was $51.4 million. For ET-72 the cost was $48 million. Each tank diminished in cost as more were built so that the last tank in a batch cost almost as low as $30 million—but no less.

By 1600 in the afternoon of July 8 Judge Duval announced an adjournment, adding that Chris Gisclair, the tug's engineer for whom a warrant had been issued, had been located by federal marshals—at least they located his mother, and she told them he was on a fishing trip and that he thought the matter had been settled out of court. He would come in for testimony the following day, she said.

The following morning Gisclair had still not arrived, so Straub presented his previously obtained deposition. Over the course of the day, Matt Connelly continued calling NASA and Martin Marietta budget managers. Connelly focused on a quote that Martin Marietta had written to NASA a year earlier that had outlined the cost of adding one tank. The cost was just over $19 million. Dembling pointed out, however, that the tank was never built and Lockheed Martin had withdrawn the quote, making it irrelevant, he said. After questioning Brent Clayburn, Lockheed Martin's Manager of Estimating and Cost Management, Duval admitted to being baffled.

"I am very confused. Let me tell you that," he said, adding a sardonic question: "Why are you getting $50 million [for one tank]; are you [really] making this kind of wretched profit?"

"You're not understanding me," Clayburn said.

"I want you to answer the question so I can," Duval said.

For several minutes, Clayburn attempted to explain the difference between unit value and contract value. "The unit value: the less you build, the higher the unit value," Clayburn concluded.

"Thank you. Anybody else have any questions?" Duval asked, clearly troubled by the unclear responses to his questions and annoyed that the witnesses were making the testimony "more complicated than the rocket itself."

"We wouldn't dare, Your Honor," Dembling said, not wanting to further irk the judge, and the witness was asked to stand down.

Geoffrey Brice, an English barrister (and Queen's Counsel, a higher rank) with extensive work in admiralty and one of the draftsmen of the International Salvage Convention of 1989, was called by the Government attorneys to provide his opinion, as an arbitrator for Lloyd's of London, on the amount he would award if the case came before Lloyd's. Brice was a visiting lecturer at Tulane on admiralty matters and was also author of *Maritime Salvage Law,* the definitive tome on international salvage law.

Ray Burke made it clear that Brice should be considered an expert on English salvage law and not on American law. Duval agreed.

Brice had reviewed my testimony. "He acted in a way which struck me, as a lawyer, in a manner that was particularly skillful. I thought that was something of considerable relevance to the assessment of an award," Brice said. Brice believed that the compensation should be liberal. He said he would award a total of $2.5 or $3.5 million, depending on which valuation ($19 or $50 million) of the external tank was used. When asked what would happen to the award if the salved value were $90 million, Brice responded, "The maximum I would award, or expect one to collect, is $4 million." Under English law, legal fees and interest would be added to the award, which could add another $1 million.

Craig Sumner was the last person to testify for the Government. As the NASA Deputy Project Manager on the external tank program, Sumner was responsible for production and operation of the tanks—getting them "ready to fly." Sumner was questioned only briefly, most saliently by Ross Dembling in the cross-examination, who asked, "Mr. Sumner, if the ET-70 had been lost, is it your understanding that the mission that had been scheduled for ET-70 would have utilized ET-71?"

"One of the tanks in flow at the Cape. It might have been ET-71. Or ET-69 was available," Sumner said.

"They had both been DD-250ed"—invoiced on the form labeled DD-250—"by that time?"

"Correct."

Dembling was showing that NASA would have used a tank they had available, not built another tank to replace ET-70, even if they could have added another tank to their production for as little as $19 million.

At the end of Sumner's questioning, Duval admitted to being amazed at how quickly the witnesses had been cycled through. "The court is a little caught by surprise by the speed with which you disposed of the case,"

Duval said. "Therefore, the court intends to rule today, [and] give you verbal reasons for that ruling, which will be transcribed by the court reporter. To make sure they are sufficiently cogent, let's come back at 2:00 and I will render our ruling."

After Duval announced the end of the trial, Hugh Straub requested the opportunity to provide closing remarks, an offer Duval accepted from both attorneys.

"There are several issues that I think are worthy of discussion, Your Honor," Straub began. "And I guess the first is the value of the ET-70. How do we value this tank? And I confess to the court that I have never heard more initials and acronyms than I have heard in the last day or so for things that were absolutely incomprehensible, and I am a little discouraged to see all the nouns that have been changed into verbs and all the verbs changed into nouns. I'm still trying to figure out how you DD-250 somebody."

Straub argued that to the DD-250 cost of more than $51 million, one had to add the costs incurred by NASA to get to the true economic cost of the external tank. To that number would be added the cost of the barge and transporter—agreed by both parties to be $2 million—to come up with a final cost of $95 million. "It is right and makes a lot more sense than some of the things we have heard," Straub said.

Straub continued with a discussion of the Blackwall Factors and how he thought they applied to the *Cherry Valley* case. A professional salvor, such as the Dutch-based salvage firm Smit, would operate under a Lloyds' Open Form and appear in front of an arbitrator like Geoffrey Brice. But the award in this case should be more liberal because the *Cherry Valley* was not in the business of salvage. It was in the business of transporting oil from one port to another.

He concluded his remarks with a final plea: "I think the court has to consider what the *Cherry Valley* and her captain and her crew had to lose. They had their health to lose. They had their reputation to lose. Their livelihood, their family enterprise. Think of the fortune that the *Cherry Valley* saved the United States. The government was about to lose $95 million. But ordinary people did extraordinary things. And those people [Keystone and the captain and crew of the *Cherry Valley*] are entitled to 30 percent of that which they saved, Your Honor. Thank you."

David Howe concluded the Government's case. "Your Honor, I agree with a few things that Mr. Straub has said, one of which is that in Mr. Brice's opinion, a professional salvor such as Smit should get $2.5 to $3.5 million, depending on where the court finds the salved value. Our law and the British law are both quite clear that professional salvors should get more than an amateur salvor, as Mr. Brice refers to someone not in the business.

"The purpose of salvage law," he continued, "is to encourage rescues in similar cases in the future. Encourage it generally. I think the court needs to be sensitive of encouraging loaded oil tankers to run this sort of risk. In the hands of someone less capable than Captain Strong, [this] could have been a disaster of the first magnitude. It wasn't. But the policy question I think has to be addressed by the court, in view of the fundamental purpose of salvage law, the bottom line on all this."

Regarding the value of the tank, Howe commented, "The legal standard, in the absence of market value, [is] what would the cost have been to replace that which was saved. What would it have cost to get another one if it had been lost? The law is very clear. The salved value is 19 plus 2, $21 million. The Government's whole point on crew expenses is to try to keep the award reasonable in light of all the circumstances. Plaintiff's Exhibit 42 shows that the crew of the *Cherry Valley*, licensed and unlicensed, together made a total of about $1.1 million a year.... If the court were to award $3 million in salvage—I'm not saying that that is a good number, it is in the middle of Mr. Brice's range—[then] if the court was going to split that one-third to the crew, two-thirds to the owners, that would be a million dollars to the crew, which is approximately one year's pay for two-and-a-half days' work. And that certainly has to be sufficient inducement to other mariners to go out and do likewise.

"The bottom line is two-and-a-half days of work. If we went with Mr. Brice's recommendation in the case, it would, as he said, set a record for amateur salvage. And we specifically asked Mr. Brice's opinion not to be partisan, but to ask what he would do as a neutral arbitrator in this sort of case. And I don't see how the court could err by taking his suggestion to heart. That's all I have, Your Honor."

"Thank you very much," Duval said. "If you will give me until two o'clock, we will render judgment."

CHAPTER 28

A SIGNIFICANT REWARD

1500, July 9, 1996

During the hours that Duval deliberated in his chambers, the Keystone team paced the pallid halls of the Federal Courthouse in New Orleans, eventually emerging outside to watch the deluge of rain that had finally broken the city's heat wave, unleashing torrents of water on the sweating city and flooding the streets. Ralph Hill, Keystone's jittery in-house counsel who had been anxious about going to trial in the first place, could hardly contain his nerves and appeared ready to explode with anxiety. Hill, fearing that the Department of Justice attorneys would corner him in a last-ditch attempt to settle while Duval was in chambers, and not wanting to be faced with that decision, eluded them by heading to the hotel for a long, hot shower.

While Hill went into seclusion, Hugh Straub led the rest of us to the cafeteria in the bottom of the courthouse for a lunch of Po'boy sandwiches, hoping that in hindsight this would not be seen as an ironic twist.

Two hours later Stanwood Duval briskly entered his courtroom through his chamber door and settled himself at the bench, a small stack of papers placed carefully on the desk in front of him.

Besides Carl and me, there were three other members of the crew who were there to hear the decision. Wilfred Luckie and Smart Ebikeme, the two ABs from the 4-to-8 watch, and Ron Spencer, the second engineer, had been watching the trial.

In a clear voice, Duval began: "Pursuant to federal rules, we are going to render our reasons for judgment in the form of Findings of Fact and Conclusions of Law."

Over the course of the next 10 minutes, Duval read his determinations, which included a description of the vessels involved, the storm's effect on the flotilla, the condition on the tug's engines, and the rescue and salvage effort. After detailing the chronology of the incident, Duval commented on aspects of the case needing clarification before a ruling could be made.

"The court finds that the salvage effort evidenced an outstanding effort on behalf of the *Cherry Valley*. Indeed, the master and crew of the *Cherry Valley* are not professional salvors, not trained in salvage operations, nor did the *Cherry Valley* have salvage equipment on board. Further, the *Cherry Valley* successfully completed this salvage in extremely rough winds and high seas," Duval said. "Captain Strong testified that green water continually beat the main deck where many men risked their lives in the salvage attempt. The *Cherry Valley* was forced to utilize certain of its equipment for unintended and potentially dangerous uses, including the hawsers."

He added: "Had the *Cherry Valley* gone aground, it risked environmental disasters of monumental proportion which would have been the responsibility of the interests of the *Cherry Valley* and its owner."

Duval's final point reflected his amazement with the case and would presage his ruling on the award itself. "The actions of the *Cherry Valley* through its captain, crew, and owner were far above and beyond the call of duty. They all showed great courage, skill, and more importantly were a paradigm of the most noble instinct of humankind, to risk your person and property for another."

He then began reading his Conclusions of Law, first describing the context of the case in general salvage law, which, he said, rests on three basic elements: "One: the existence of marine peril; Two: the voluntary rendering of salvage service; and Three: success." As the tension built, Duval then referenced the 1989 case involving the sunken barge that had been hit by the *Dauntless Colocotronis,* on the Mississippi River, an incident that precipitated a 10-year litigation that, ultimately, was successfully handled by a team of attorneys led by Hugh Straub and Ray Burke.

The court views the award of salvage compensation, Duval said, not as payment for time expended, but "as a reward for perilous service and inducement to seamen to save imperiled life and property." Listing the six Blackwall Factors as the foundation for his ruling, Duval then pointed to a seventh factor, the clause that awards salvors for their effort to minimize damage to the marine environment. Duval pointed to the desperate condition of the tug prior to the arrival of the *Cherry Valley,* its "overdue" need for a major engine overhaul (several surveys concluded that the tug's injector pumps should have been rebuilt long before November 1994) its steering damage, and the fire in the engineroom. He recalled Terry Perez's testimony describing that the tug crew had plans to release the barge, allowing it to drift onto the beach, to attempt to save themselves from the same fate. "Neither the Coast Guard nor anyone else had any capability of rescuing the flotilla," Duval said.

"Indeed, the tank manufacturer's marine transportation specialist, William Knodle, testified that had *Cherry Valley* not heard *Orgeron*'s radio calls to the Coast Guard and come to the scene, the *Poseidon* and the *Orgeron* would have [been] swept aground before the *South Bend* could arrive, and based on what we know about the *South Bend,* it is doubtful she would have been much help."

While Duval read his decision we all sat as still as possible and tried to take in all that he was saying. So far it sounded like things were going in our favor. Bill Dougherty, the other attorney for Burke & Parsons, was sitting next to me taking notes as the judge spoke and would nudge me every once in a while to look at a note he had written. Everything he was writing was positive.

Turning to the value of ET-70, Duval first announced that the court believed the tank, and barge, would have been destroyed after grounding on the beach. He ruled that the value of the barge and transporter equaled $2 million. The true value of ET-70 was based on the production cost, as detailed by the invoice report, DD-250, which equaled $53.8 million. (The original DD-250 valuation of $51.9 million was an "estimate"; after all costs were factored in the DD-250 valuation was revised to $53.8 million.) Citing a 1963 case involving the salvage of the Coast Guard Cutter *Invincible,* a vessel that had no market value because of its specialized design, Duval ruled that replacement value was an appropriate "yardstick" for such a ruling. While the Government had argued that the replacement value was roughly $19 million, Duval pointed to testimony from NASA's Craig Sumner and Jody Adams that even if a new tank could have been built for $19 million, NASA would have used ET-71 (or ET-69) as a replacement tank. Therefore, the replacement value of ET-70 was just under $51.4 million, which was the DD-250 cost of ET-71.

He had picked what we called the "middle" number. It would have been great if he had used the economic cost of the ET, but using the cost of ET-71 as the replacement value was a whole lot better for us than $19 million. The big question still looming was what percentage he would award.

Regarding the risk to the salvors, Duval allowed that the *Cherry Valley* faced the highest possible risk by "leaving their safe course to rescue the flotilla." He added, "To save the crew of the endangered tug and her tow, *Cherry Valley* and the crew voluntarily put themselves in a position where slight miscalculation could have led to *Cherry Valley* crewmembers' serious injury or to the *Cherry Valley*'s destruction and catastrophic pollution of the Florida coastline."

The success of the operation, the judge added, was "the most telling testimony of the skill and seamanship exhibited by the *Cherry Valley* under the most unforgiving circumstances. Even the Government's expert witness, Geoffrey Brice, testified Captain Strong and his crew performed an extraordinary salvage deserving of substantial remuneration."

Duval then outlined the value and risk to the salvors' property, namely the *Cherry Valley* herself and the cargo she was carrying, nearly 10 million gallons of No. 6 oil. The *Cherry Valley* was worth $7.5 million, and she was maneuvered within one mile of Bethel Shoal, he said. "The consequences of millions of gallons of this noxious cargo blackening the Florida beaches would have been disastrous. Thus the risk to the *Cherry Valley* was staggering," and her owners and operators would have borne a tremendous expense.

Finally, Duval said that after considering all the relevant factors, the crew of the *Cherry Valley* displayed "heroism of the highest magnitude" and deserved ample compensation.

"Accordingly, the appropriate salvage award to the *Cherry Valley* and her crew is 12.5 percent of the replacement value of ET-70, which this court finds to be $51,387,000 plus the $2,000,000 which is the stipulated value of the *Poseidon*."

We were looking at $6,406,440.

"Indeed, it is hard to conceive of a case presenting more compelling evidence in support of the two most important Blackwall Factors, the degree of danger from which the property was rescued and the value of the property saved. This is, indeed, an extraordinary case. Therefore, even if this court were to evaluate the replacement value of ET-70 at $19 million, as urged by the United States, the Court would increase the percentage of the award to adequately reward the *Cherry Valley* and the crew for their valiant, successful effort so that the ultimate award would not vary dramatically."

"With that, court is adjourned."

The trial had gone very quickly, and Duval's reading the decision from the bench had caught everyone by surprise. His decision had indeed set a record award for non-professional salvors, and one not likely to be surpassed anytime soon.

Everyone was pleased with the decision, even, I suspect, the attorneys for the Justice Department. Matt Connelly was the one who had recommended the $5 million settlement. Amidst all the congratulations, Craig Sumner, NASA's deputy project manager for the external tank program, came up and greeted me with a warm smile and a firm handshake. We had met a little over a year before, in June of 1995, for the launch of the shuttle *Atlantis*, which used ET-70. Holding my arm with one hand and reaching into his pocket with the other, he pulled out a lapel pin of the shuttle with the external tank and solid rocket boosters attached, and clipped it on the lapel of my jacket. "Next time this [rescue] happens, you and I will go out and settle the thing over a beer," he said.

"I'm really hoping there won't be a next time," I said, "but if it does happen I'll take you up on that offer." I introduced Sumner to the other crewmembers who were there and reminded him that it had been a group effort to perform the rescue.

We made our way out of the courtroom and down to the lobby where we could see that the skies had opened up again. We were elated by the decision and even the torrential downpour that waited for us outside couldn't dampen our spirits. We had won and won big. Hugh always says it is a gamble to go into court, but we had felt the odds were in our favor going into the trial—and we were proven right.

CHAPTER 29

BARBECUED SHRIMP
AND AN APPEAL

We celebrated that night at Hugh Straub's favorite uptown restaurant, a retro hole-in-the-wall with the curious name of Pascal's Manale—a place Straub reserves for celebration of victory in court. Known for its barbecued shrimp the size of lobster tails served in a searing Cajun sauce, the place appeared to have remained unchanged in some 50 years—dark walnut cabinets and white marble counters attended by an officious barkeep—as we burst through its doors on that rainy July evening, boisterous with good cheer. ("You're not taking me to someplace where they serve them with heads, are you?" Ralph Hill, notoriously picky about his food, had asked Straub prior to our arrival. "There are other things on the menu," Straub had answered, "but we will be eating shrimp, and you will enjoy it.") There were the six attorneys, Straub and Mike Butterworth representing the New Orleans team; Ray Burke and Bill Dougherty of the New York office; Ross Dembling from Washington—and the edgy Ralph Hill, who had visibly relaxed following the judge's ultimate decision and was almost enjoying himself. Of the *Cherry Valley* crew, I was accompanied by Carl Gabrielsson. Don Kurz, President of Keystone, was not among us; he had left New Orleans as soon as his testimony was over.

After a fine dinner of oysters and Cajun shrimp, we went out for some more drinks in the Quarter. Ralph Hill and I moved to a quiet spot in the bar for a little chat. Now that there was some money to split up, we, the crew and Keystone, would have to divide it among ourselves. One of the last things Duval did before adjourning the trial was to set a three-month limit, from the end of the trial, for splitting the money between the company and the crew.

"So how are we going to do this?" Ralph asked.

"I think we will need to get our own attorney now to negotiate with Keystone. Unless, of course, you would agree to the percentage split that the Justice Department put forth in their offer of judgment." I paused to see if he remembered. "Sixty percent for us and 40 percent for Keystone."

After he finished choking on his drink, he said the board would probably be looking more at 75/25—in favor of Keystone. "After all," he said, "we have paid for all the legal costs, not an inconsiderable sum, to get the settlement."

We talked awhile longer and knew that we would probably settle somewhere in the middle, but I had no authority to speak for the crew. We would need to get our own counsel to negotiate for us. I assured him that it would be someone that he could work with. With that, we stopped talking business and returned to the celebration and drank more than was good for us.

By deciding to award Keystone more than $6.4 million, Judge Duval had awarded the largest salvage award in U.S. maritime history—possibly the largest award in world history, according to Geoffrey Brice, who had remained in New Orleans an extra day to hear the judge's ruling. The award would likely be appealed, that much we suspected, but Duval's lavish praise and precise reasoning in his ruling allowed us to believe that a large salvage award was forthcoming.

Over the course of the evening, Straub admitted he was worried about the appeal. The one possible soft spot in Duval's rendering was his assertion that even if one accepted the Justice Department's reasoning that the external tank could be replaced for $19 (or $21) million, he would increase the percentage of the award so that the award would remain a similar figure. This could be seen by the appellate judges, Straub said, as capricious or arbitrary. The appellate judges had jurisdiction to reduce the award by a significant amount, but the attorneys had agreed on an appeal strategy that could lessen this possibility. In their proposal to the appeals court, they would ask for interest payments to be added to the award, an option Duval had chosen not to apply. By continuing to maintain that if the external tanks each cost taxpayers more than $90 million to produce—and the case fit the Blackwall Factors so perfectly—Dembling believed that there was clear evidence to support a large award in the neighborhood of Duval's.

Over the coming months, after the Government filed its notice of appeal in September, both sides filed appeal briefs, which were filed under seal because Martin Marietta had requested that certain facts related to production costs not be released in public, specifically what their internal costs were in manu-facturing the ETs. The Justice Department continued to focus on their view that the true replacement value was $19 million—and they continued to agree that our efforts merited a significant salvage award under the Blackwall Factors—but they urged the appellate judges to consider the purpose of sal-vage law: to encourage mariners to take risks in an effort to preserve property in peril on the high seas. The DOJ appeal pointed out that the Keystone legal team was promoting the significant risk to the salvors (the potential environ-mental disaster of spilling nearly 10 million gallons of thick, black oil onto Florida's white sandy beaches in the height of tourist season) as a reason for deserving a generous salvage claim. This was faulty reasoning, they wrote.

"After underscoring the risk [the salvage] created (and in the process confirming that the district court considered the risk to be a 'plus factor' in determining the award and further urging this court to do likewise), [Keystone] attempts to capitalize upon the 'breath-taking' environmental risk its vessel engendered," the appeal stated. "[Keystone] argues that its ex-traordinary award is justified because only the exceptional skill of the *Cherry Valley*'s crew averted the disaster they created.... Little response to this argument is necessary except to point out that the next oil tanker skip-per who risks blackening the American coastline with heavy fuel oil in search of a salvage bounty might not be as skillful as Captain Strong was here. By considering the environmental risk created (and averted) by the *Cherry Valley* to be a plus factor in determining the award, the district court erred as a matter of law and public policy."

As an oil tanker captain, someone who is immersed in the business of avoiding risk, especially considering the civil and criminal charges possi-ble as a result of spilling oil, I find it inconceivable that anyone would deliberately seek such risk in an attempt to gain salvage awards. An appropriate lesson from this event might be an examination of how it is that the U.S. Government spends almost $100 million on a tank that is towed on an unmanned barge built in the 1940s and towed more than 1,000 ocean miles by tugs that are the lowest bidder for the contract.

The appeal languished at the Fifth Circuit Court of Appeals for more than six months. Hugh Straub, calling periodically to check on its status, was told repeatedly by a clerk that it had not moved. One day in December 1996, however, the clerk called Straub with an apology: because it had been filed under seal, he said, it had been put away and forgotten. It had recently been discovered, however, and was being considered. The date for the hearing was set for the first week of February 1998.

Following the award by Judge Duval, and my brief bar-side chat with Ralph Hill, the crew set out to find an attorney to represent us. We ultimately decided upon an attorney in Portland, Maine, to assist in dividing the award between Keystone and the crew. Mike Savasuk, a Maine Maritime graduate who had sailed for Exxon as a deck officer for five years before going to law school and becoming a maritime lawyer, was recommended to me, and we met several times in Portland over the summer. I felt that Mike had an appreciation for what it was to be a mariner, he had been well recommended as someone who engaged in cautious negotiation rather than confrontation, and he had had experience in negotiating similar cases. With Mike as our counsel, he researched the case and started negotiations with Keystone. He was confident that he could negotiate a settlement for the crew of between 35 and 40 percent, leaving Keystone with 60 to 65 percent if they paid all the costs associated with obtaining the salvage award.

As far as the crew was concerned, one attractive feature of the one of the Governments' early offers had been the proportion of the split between the company and crew: 40 percent for the company and 60 percent for the crew. (Although this offer was eventually scrapped, it was helpful for the crew to know that there was opinion that favored awarding a generous share to the crew.) Traditionally, Mike told me, British Admiralty courts, following

Oleron law, allowed no award to the owner of the vessel, giving the entire award to the crew, the reasoning being that the owner had not personally participated in a given salvage event. "During the 19th century," Mike Savasuk wrote in a letter of proposal to Ralph Hill, "as ships' values increased, the courts began to recognize that ship owners had a great deal to lose when their valuable ships were employed in dangerous salvage operations. Consequently, the law adapted so that owners were allowed to share in the award. The courts continued to reserve the major portion of the award to the crew, allowing the owner one-quarter to one-third of the award." But in the last 100 years in British and American courts, the majority of cases have resulted in the award of two-thirds to the owner and one-third to the crew.

The court in which the *Cherry Valley* appeal would be heard, the Fifth Circuit Court of Appeals, had upheld that decision on three prior occasions. However, it is generally agreed by all courts in admiralty, regarding salvage, that there is no fixed rule for proportioning the award between the owner and crew. In one landmark case, *Cape Fear Towing and Transportation Co. v. Pearsall*, which was tried in 1898 at the Fourth Circuit, the court unequivocally asserted that "most frequently, salvage services are rendered upon a voyage, in the absence of the owners, and when the salving vessel is under the charge of and is controlled by the master and crew. As salvage is awarded for the encouragement of promptness, energy, efficiency, and heroic endeavor saving life and property in peril, the claims of the master and crew who have exhibited these qualities must meet the most favorable considerations."

This was one of the first cases to give a clear explanation to the differences in the award between the owners and master and crew. The court in that case recognized the 60/40 split but did not uphold it in the *Cape Fear* case, instead awarding two-thirds to the owner and one-third to the crew, explaining that this was because when the owners direct the services of salvage, or when the peril encountered is primarily to the vessel and not the crew, the award to the owner is more liberal.

With the case law indicating splits between one-third and 40 percent for the crew, we were a little surprised when Keystone first offered only 25 percent for the crew. Ralph's argument was that if something had gone wrong and the *Cherry Valley* had wound up on Bethel Shoal and put oil in the water, Keystone would be out of business. The liabilities would have been staggering, and they might have had to file for bankruptcy. Mike's argument was that if it weren't for the skill and courage of the crew, Keystone would not be getting any salvage award and that they should be happy to get the 50 percent we were offering.

It didn't take too long for both sides to meet in the middle and come to an amicable resolution. The crew would get 37 percent of the award and Keystone would get 63 percent, but they would pay all the legal bills in arriving at a settlement. The direct costs of the salvage, estimated at $150,000 to $200,000, the cost to Keystone for delaying the voyage, paying extra fuel, and employing the crew, would be taken out before the split between the company and crew. So far the only cost to the crew was for Mike's services, and that was under $20,000.

What Mike could not do for us was help determine how the award would be split among the crew. Since he had represented the entire crew in obtaining the settlement with Keystone, he felt it would be a conflict to determine who got what among the crew. He did offer us several ways to go to try and resolve the issue. One was to ask the court, which would have to sign off on any agreement anyway. The other would be to get everyone in the crew to agree to binding arbitration and have someone independently review the case and make a decision about how the award should be split among the crew.

Ultimately the crew decided to go with binding arbitration, using Norm Sullivan, an attorney in New Orleans with the firm of Gelpi, Sullivan, & Carroll, who Mike Savasuk recommended. There is a fair amount of case law on the subject of apportioning salvage awards among the crew, and Mr. Sullivan used this material to justify his decision.

From his decision, Mr. Sullivan wrote: "The Blackwall decision by the Supreme Court in 1869 determined the six elements to be considered in fixing the amount of the salvage award. Three of those elements bear upon the issue of splitting the money among the crew: the labor expended; the skill and energy displayed; and the risk incurred. It has always been recognized that the lowest seaman on the vessel, even one who did not actively participate in the salvage operation, is still entitled to a share of the crew's award.... The theory is that each crewmember contributed by virtue of his own responsibilities to the mission of the ship."

He continued: "The more modern cases discussing the crew apportionment issue can be separated into three categories. The first divides the award based on the merits of individual services and the risk incurred.... The second makes a proportional distribution based on the wages of each crewmember.... The third combines the two. A basic award is given to each crewmember (either based on wages or just a specific amount), and then additional sums are awarded certain crewmembers who experienced risks and/or demonstrated particular skills in the operation." This was the method he chose to use.

Sullivan rendered his decision while the appeal was still being ignored by the court, but his decision laid the framework for a split, and we all agreed to accept his proposal. These were the percentages he established:

Strong (master): 16.42

Gabrielsson (chief mate): 9.55

Kuijper (second mate): 7.74

Sotirelis (third mate): 3.73

Worden (radio officer): 3.81

Conner (bosun): 5.02

Rivera (AB): 3.25

Dover (AB): 3.25

Ebikeme (AB): 3.25

Luckie (AB): 3.25

Prevost (AB): 3.25

Rodriguez (AB): 3.25

Ramos, S. (GVA): 3.72

Croke (chief engineer): 5.76

Donnelly (first assistant engineer): 4.15

Spencer, R. (second assistant engineer): 3.74

Campbell (third assistant engineer): 2.73

Noceda (pumpman): 2.83

Spencer, F. (QMED): 1.81

Evora (QMED): 1.81

Crumpton (QMED): 2.41

Ramos, A. (steward): 2.03

McCloud (cook): 1.74

Young (GSU): 1.25

daLuz (GSU): 1.25

CHAPTER 30

THE END OF MY
SALVAGE CAREER

On February 3, 1998, Hugh Straub, Mike Butterworth, Ray Burke, Bill Dougherty, Ross Dembling, and Ralph Hill gathered again in New Orleans for the appeal. They met on the steps of the Fifth Circuit Court of Appeals, next door to the District Court where the trial had been held two years before, and filed into the courtroom, taking their seats in the audience. The Keystone team was among several appeals to be heard that day, and as they sat in the packed benches of the courtroom awaiting their turn, half listening to the proceedings of other people's affairs being heard by the panel of judges, Ray Burke noticed a silver-haired gentleman in a light-colored suit seated a few rows ahead on the other side of the court room and nudged Dembling.

"Is that Hunger?" Burke whispered. Frank Hunger, who was still serving as U.S. Assistant Attorney General, had hosted the fruitless Keystone attorney's visit to the Justice Department in Washington in April 1996, but he had not been seen since. Although he had made his opinions known during the course of the attempted settlements and trial, he had allowed Matt Connelly and David Howe to argue the case before Duval. Dembling surreptitiously dropped his pen to the floor and, bending to retrieve it, looked forward beneath the benches. The silver-haired man was wearing a gleaming pair of cowboy boots.

"*It's him!*" Dembling hissed. No one else would have had the temerity to appear before the judges in a light suit and cowboy boots. It appeared that Hunger would be arguing on behalf of the Justice Department to the appellate judges.

Hunger, who as a young lawyer had served as a clerk for a judge in the Fifth Circuit from his native state of Mississippi, likely saw his appearance at the appeal as a sort of homecoming, a chance to connect with his roots and put an end to the madness—the extraordinarily, *reproachfully,* high salvage award—that had been allowed to run amok in his absence. In his light-colored suit, flowing silver hair that dropped well below his collar, and his boots, Hunger projected the manner of a drawling character in *Inherit the Wind.* "Where I come from," he intoned in his opening remarks, "one million dollars is *a lot* of money!"

His argument reflected an apparent lack of understanding for the facts of the case and seemed to rest squarely on the fact that—in his folksy, down-home worldview—being paid $1 million for two-and-a-half days' work was plenty. This delighted Straub, who plowed into a forceful declaration of the facts, using his 20 minutes to bolster the Keystone argument—and reinforce Duval's ruling—that the rescue and salvage of the *J.A. Orgeron,* the barge *Poseidon,* and ET-70 during Tropical Storm Gordon saved the U.S. Government more than $90 million, and salvage law supported a generous percentage award of this value. Although the judges asked a few questions regarding the valuation, the appeal hearing was over in less than an hour.

On June 29, 1998, three-and-a-half years after the rescue, the appellate judges issued their ruling. On item after item the judges agreed with Judge Duval's renderings, addressing each issue that the Government's team had appealed. The Government's appeal was based on three arguments:

1. Duval had given too much attention to the value of the external tank in his application of the Blackwall Factors and had further increased the award by considering that the environmental risk posed by the *Cherry Valley*'s cargo of No. 6 oil as a reason to boost the award.
2. Duval was wrong in his valuation of the tank.
3. And he had abused the discretion of the court by awarding a percentage that was too high.

The judges found each of the arguments presented by the Government attorneys to be "wholly without merit…. Salvage awards are not based on the

altruistic principle of Good Samaritanism—that virtue is its own inducement and its own reward," the judges wrote. "The very object of the law of
salvage is to provide an economic inducement to seamen and others to
save property for the good of society by bestowing a fitting reward for their
services in the courts of justice. It is profit, not principle, that is the driving
force behind the law of salvage, and the question for the court is simply
what amount of profit is fitting in the case before it."

But the judges did find the soft spot in Duval's reasoning, a point largely
ignored by the Government's appeal. As Hugh Straub had intuited on the
night following the trial, the appellate judges felt that Duval had undercut
the force of his own reasoning when he had said that even if one accepted
the Government's argument that the tank was worth just $19 million (and
not $51.9 million or $90 million), he would adjust the percentages to make
the actual award amount comparable to the $6.4 million he had ordered.
The 12.5 percentage was firmly supported by the Blackwall Factors, the appellate judges wrote; to consider a fixed amount for a salvage award was arbitrary. Whether the judges felt bound to split the difference between the
Government's $19 million and Judge Duval's $53.9 million, simply because
the salvage award was impressively high, is immaterial. In their ruling they
explained that the replacement *cost*—not the value of the replacement tank,
which, if ET-70 had been lost would have been ET-71—was $19 million as
detailed by the memo to NASA from Martin Marietta. The memo, written
two years before the rescue and salvage of ET-70, described in detail that it
would cost an additional $19 million per tank, the memo had noted. But
the judges did not stop there, adding their own spin to the dizzying process
of assigning a value to ET-70:

"In order to truly replace ET-70, Martin Marietta would have had to
provide NASA with a new tank that incorporated all of the material features of the old one, both physical and temporal. Although payment of the
option price would have been sufficient to obtain a new tank with all the
requisite physical characteristics, that tank would have been somewhat faulty
as a temporal matter in that it would only have become available for use
three years after ET-70's designated mission. In a very real sense, ET-70's

value to NASA was enhanced by the fact that it was a completed tank, available for immediate use. Although the record is clear that no mission need necessarily have been postponed by a delay in ET-70's replacement, it is also clear that for three years' time NASA would have had three usable tanks in circulation instead of its desired minimum of four. Because ET-70's existence avoided this three-year shortfall, any acceptable replacement plan would have had to address it as well.

"In setting a minimum circulation of four tanks, NASA determined that it was worthwhile to have four tanks in circulation at all times instead of three. The reasons for this judgment no doubt included a desire to allow for additional defects, a commitment to avoid all foreseeable delays, and a host of other factors irrelevant to the instant analysis. The important point is simply that to fulfill its goals NASA itself decided to immobilize approximately \$50 million in additional capital every year to ensure that there were four tanks in circulation instead of three. In more colloquial terms, by keeping four tanks in circulation at all times instead of three, NASA was making a conscious choice to take \$50 million from its budget and put it on a shelf instead of spending it on other things.

"Although the government is sometimes wont to think otherwise, money is now well known to have a time value. The three-year treasury bill rate on November 15, 1994, was 7.41 percent, and we are confident that the cost to the United States of immobilizing \$50 million over the three years in question was approximately $(1.0741^3 - 1)$ x \$50 million = \$12 million. Whatever risks and costs NASA would have incurred by having three tanks in circulation instead of four, NASA itself determined that these risks were worth about \$12 million to avoid. By rescuing ET-70, Captain Strong saved NASA from this \$12 million in additional risks and costs as well, and it must be counted towards a proper valuation of the tank.

"Combining this additional \$12 million with the \$19,014,479 figure from the option, we arrive at a total replacement cost for ET-70 of approximately \$31 million. We therefore hold that the district court was clearly in error in valuing ET-70 at \$51,387,000, and that the correct value was \$31 million. Adding the \$2 million stipulated value of *Poseidon*, this leaves a total value for the salved property of $33 million. Applying the district court's 12.5 percent salvage percentage, we are left with a new salvage award of $4.125 million."

This award remains, in 2003, the highest salvage award in U.S. maritime history—perhaps even in international law, according to Geoffrey Brice—even if all previous awards are adjusted to modern dollars.

I had stopped sailing for Keystone, having started work for my friend Dave Gelinas as a Penobscot Bay & River Pilot, and was at home that early-summer day when the phone rang. "It's over, Skip!" Ray Burke clipped—the judges had awarded us more than $4 million, and our payments would be forthcoming.

After hanging up the phone I watched the fax machine churn out a copy of the decision. Each member of the crew would also receive a copy of the decision. Although I was disappointed to have the award reduced, I felt euphoric to know the case was finally over—and grateful to the numerous people who had helped conclude the most exciting and satisfying two-and-a-half days of my seagoing career. My wife Annie and I could now start to look for a house in earnest.

By the time the Government actually paid out the award, the interest amounted to $391,872 and, combined with the settlement from the tug, it brought the total award to $4,736,872, spitting distance of the $5 million Matt Connelly had recommended as a settlement two-and-a-half years earlier—before Hunger told NASA to put away the Government's checkbook.

After deducting our attorneys' fees and apportioning the 63 percent to Keystone, the crew and I were awarded a total of $1,752,642 for the salvage of the *J. A. Orgeron,* barge *Poseidon,* and ET-70.

In June 1995, while Keystone and NASA were beginning negotiations for a settlement for the salvage of the *Poseidon* and ET-70, the space shuttle *Atlantis* was prepared for launch.

The three components—the shuttle, two solid rocket boosters, and the external tank—were mated together in NASA's Cape Canaveral Vertical Assembly Building, one of the largest buildings in the world, and placed upon the Mobile Launch Platform, which was driven by two 2,750-hp diesel engines producing enormous torque at low speed, taking some five hours to roll the shuttle the five miles from the Vertical Assembly Building to the launch pad.

Mechanical problems and bad weather postponed the launch of *Atlantis* and ET-70, several times. Because the *Atlantis* would be docking with the *Mir* space station, there was only a narrow launch window that would allow them to reach *Mir*. The launch was scheduled for June 27, 1995.

As the date approached, the 10-minute launch window was slated to open at 3:32 P.M. If the launch took place as the window opened, *Atlantis* would dock with *Mir* two days later; if they launched in the final three minutes of the window, it would take another day to reach *Mir*.

The weather remained fine, and at T minus 6.6 seconds the shuttle's three main engines were ignited, one after the other, at 120-millisecond intervals. The fuel mixture from ET-70, liquid oxygen in the nose and liquid hydrogen in the lower tank, rushed to the engines through 17-inch-diameter feed lines, and at T minus 0 the solid rocket boosters (SRBs) ignited—instantly delivering 3.3 million pounds of thrust each. The 4.4-million-pound *Atlantis* assembly rose from the pad at 3:32:19.044 P.M.

With the combined burning of the SRBs and the shuttle's three engines, the ride experienced by Commander Robert "Hoot" Gibson and his crew during the first few minutes of flight was particularly rough. Two minutes after launch the fuel in the SRBs was spent, and they were jettisoned automatically. *Atlantis* was now at an altitude of 28 miles and traveling at a speed of Mach 4.5, about 3,200 miles per hour. The SRBs, meanwhile, fell back to Earth, and after reaching a lower altitude their parachutes were deployed for the gentle descent into the Atlantic Ocean off Florida, where they would be recovered and towed back to Port Canaveral for refurbishment and service on another mission.

Six-and-a-half minutes into the flight, the shuttle astronauts were experiencing the greatest G force of the trip—three times that of Earth's gravity. They were now traveling at Mach 15—10,710 miles per hour, at an altitude of 80 miles, the shuttle's three engines continuing to be powered by the remaining fuel in the external tank. They would have two minutes until the hydrogen and oxygen in the external tank were depleted.

Eight-and-a-half minutes into flight, the shuttle was free of the atmosphere, and its engines shut down. The fuel in the external tank was gone. Eighteen seconds later, a command from the shuttle's main computer fired a charge driving a shearing pin at each of the three points where the shuttle was secured to the ET, and ET-70 was jettisoned. As the tank fell away, the shuttle continued to gain altitude, and powered by inertia, began to orbit the Earth. Just 1,500 pounds of hydrogen and 500 pounds of oxygen remained aboard the tank.

During the first orbit the trajectory of the ET was relatively flat, but as it met the Earth's atmosphere on the second orbit it started to tumble— and heat up. It entered the atmosphere south of Hawaii, just over an hour after it was jettisoned. Heat from friction ignited the insulation covering the aluminum tank body, carving a blazing 1,500-mile trail. Most of the tank burned up in the upper atmosphere, but some of the larger pieces may have made it back to the surface of the ocean.

Atlantis, meanwhile, would be docking with *Mir* for the first time, and NASA celebrated its 100th manned space mission.

NASA would like, in the future, to have a space tug retrieve the ET after separation from the shuttle and pull it into a higher orbit with the international space station. The hydrogen and oxygen left on board could be used for fuel or combined to make water, both of which now have to be carried to the space station by the shuttle. But that is in the future. For now, the external tank that, in 1994–1997, took four years and $50-plus million to build, was used for a total of eight-and-a-half minutes before it was released to disintegrate in the Earth's atmosphere.

The last visible presence of ET-70 on Earth may have been seen by a second mate, on watch, his ship transiting a lonely expanse of the Pacific Ocean several hundred miles south of Hawaii.

Who's Where

Skip Strong

I continued to sail as captain of the *Cherry Valley* until the end of 1996. After leaving the *Cherry Valley* I started work as a full-time pilot on Penobscot Bay, Maine, moving ships in and out of Searsport and Bucksport. I used the settlement to pay off some student loans and put a big down payment on an old cape close to the water in Southwest Harbor, Maine. Today our two daughters, Emma and Maggie, can walk to the town dock and look at the boats with their dad—who doesn't spend six months at sea each year.

Carl Gabrielsson

Carl lives in upstate New York and still works for Keystone. He started sailing as relief captain in 1999. He sailed as captain aboard several ships, including the *Cherry Valley,* before being made permanent captain of the *Delaware Trader.*

Jim Kuijper

Jim lives in Vashon Island, Washington, where, with his share of the settlement, he has started a successful landscaping business. ("There was no opportunity to move up," he said after sailing another two years on Keystone's tankers.)

Chris Sotirelis
Chris continued to sail for Keystone, rising quickly to chief mate on the *Chilbar,* a chemical tanker. In 2000 when the opportunity arose he became a pilot in his home state of Texas with the Galveston/Texas City Pilots and has been a full-time pilot for the past two years. One of the vessels he has piloted is the *J. A. Orgeron.*

Tim Croke
Tim only sailed one trip as Chief aboard the *Cherry Valley* before going back to Mormac Marine. He and his family were the only ones who were able to get to Cape Canaveral to watch the launch of *Atlantis* with ET-70. Tim continued to sail as Chief for Mormac aboard Ready Reserve ships until the spring of 2003 when he died in a car accident returning home from work.

Paul Donnelly
Paul Donnelly continued to sail on the *Cherry Valley* until 1998 when he was offered the chief engineer's job aboard the *Denali,* a VLCC (Very Large Crude Carrier) almost five times the size of the *Cherry Valley.* He lives on Cape Cod, Massachusetts, with a very nice heated in-ground pool and a number of good investments, thanks in large part to his handling of the engine. He is still sailing as chief aboard the *Denali.*

Cherry Valley
She continued to trade along the Gulf Coast and East Coast of the U.S. until June 2002. Almost 30 years old, she was phased out under OPA 90 because her single-skin hull plating was no longer appropriate for carrying petroleum products. She made one last voyage starting in September 2002, loading grain in Washington State for delivery to Yemen and Pakistan before being delivered to the ship breaker's in India on November 21, 2002. The next day, at 1235 local time, she answered her last full-ahead bell as she was run up on the beach at the breaker's yard outside of Bombay.

Poseidon

She continued to carry NASA's external tanks until 1998 when she was replaced with a new barge purpose-built for transporting the ETs. The *Pegasus* is similar in size to the *Poseidon* and outfitted the same way, just newer. There is space for crew on the barge, but it is seldom manned. NASA did change their towing policy at the end of 1996, and the barges are now towed by the Solid Rocket Recovery Vessels.

J. A. Orgeron

The *Orgeron* went into the shipyard for an extensive overhaul in December 1994 and reentered service in April 1995. In 1999, Montco sold all three tugs to Crosby Marine Transportation. Montco now owns and operates some of the most sophisticated "lift boats" in the Gulf.

Lanny Wiles

Lanny still works for Montco as captain of the *M/V Myrtle*, one of the most sophisticated lift boats ever built, in service in the Gulf's Oil Patch.

Awards

Following the successful rescue and salvage of the *J. A. Orgeron*, *Poseidon*, and ET-70, the crew of the *Cherry Valley* and I received a number of awards.

The American Merchant Marine Seamanship Trophy

The award was established in 1962 by the Maritime Administration (Marad) to recognize outstanding feats of seamanship by U.S. mariners. Nominations for the Seamanship Trophy are solicited annually, but the trophy is only awarded if its selection committee determines that a nominee is worthy of special recognition. The trophy has not been awarded in some years.

The trophy, an ornate Sterling silver cup, is on permanent display at the American Merchant Marine Museum on the Academy's Kings Point, Long Island, New York, campus.

The trophy was presented to me and the crew of the *Cherry Valley* in 1995.

American Institute of Merchant Shipping—Citation of Merit
Issued jointly by AIMS and the National Safety Council, this citation was presented to the officers and crew of the *Cherry Valley* in 1995. We received one of 14 citations that year.

United Seamen's Service—AOTOS Mariner's Plaque
This award recognizes outstanding seamanship in rescue operations at sea. Given to officers and crews of American vessels, it was presented to the officers and crew of the *Cherry Valley* in 1995 and was one of six awards given that year.

Maine Maritime Academy—Outstanding Alumnus Award 1996
Each year my alma mater recognizes an alumnus who has performed a noteworthy feat of seamanship.

Maine Maritime Academy—Presidential Commendation 1996

End Note

I have often been asked if I would do this again. The answer is a qualified yes. I would certainly answer the call and look at the situation, but each set of circumstances is different. If my crew, or the crew of the *Orgeron*, had not been as good as they were, it would likely have been a very different outcome. But sometime, it might be me making the call for help, and I hope someone will be out there to answer it.

ACKNOWLEDGMENTS

Numerous people contributed to the creation of this book. The crew of the *Cherry Valley*, without whom there would have been no rescue and no salvage, deserve heartfelt thanks for their professionalism and skill and for their assistance in piecing together the events of November 14 to 16, 1994. The crew of the *J. A. Orgeron*, Captain Lanny Wiles, Bob Reahard, Pete Reahard, Chris Gisclair, and Terry Perez, showed unflappable courage during Tropical Storm Gordon. If it was the *Cherry Valley* in trouble that night off Bethel Shoal, I know they would have come to my assistance without hesitation.

Thanks to Bill Knodle for his assistance during the rescue and later for detailed explanations involving the complexities of transporting an External Tank and showing us the barge up close; Ernie Graham for a tour of the very impressive Michoud Assembly Facility; Ralph Hill for not firing an impetuous young whippersnapper of a captain; Ray Burke and Bill Dougherty at Burke & Parsons, and Hugh Straub and Mike Butterworth at Terriberry, Carroll & Yancey for orchestrating a great case, helping in immeasurable ways to bring this book to life, and most importantly, for exemplifying the best of mariners and lawyers; Ross Dembling at Holland & Knight for explaining the intricacies of federal contracts; Tom Fierke at Lockheed Martin for assisting in having the documents released to help write the book, and Craig Sumner at NASA (now at United Space Alliance) for answering numerous questions and checking facts. Thanks to Jim Brown at Legge, Farrow, Kimmitt, McGrath & Brown for seeing the merit of this story and hosting my visit to the International Towing & Salvage Conference to tell the story to the real salvage professionals. At Keystone, special thanks to Captain Tim

O'Connor, Captain Bill Moran, Jim Kraftheffer, and Tom Siwarsky. At Montco, thanks to Lee Orgeron and Jerry Danos for their gracious assistance. Thanks to Norm Dufour for explaining the intricacies of diesel engines. Thanks to Dr. Richard Pasch at the National Hurricane Center. Thanks to Dr. Wally Reed at Maine Maritime Academy for educating me in maritime law long after I should have learned it in school. Thanks to Joe Farrell at Resolve Marine Group for his countless stories and many hours of interviews. Thanks to the editors at *Professional Mariner* and *Ocean Navigator,* Tim Queeney, Evan True, and John Gormley for their repeated assistance.

Thanks to Annie Dundon, Leah Day and Toby and Gretchen Strong for being harsh but accurate critics. And thanks to our dynamic agent, Laureen Rowland, for her undying enthusiasm and leadership, and to our editor, Tom McCarthy, for his editorial skill and moral support.

Anyone interested in reading the full Appeals Court decision can find it online at the Fifth Circuit Court of Appeals website, www.ca5.uscourts.gov. On the opinions page enter the case name; Margate Shipping Co vs. JA Orgeron MV, or the docket number 96-30950 to view the opinion.